# HUNTERS IN A
# NARROW STREET

# HUNTERS IN A NARROW STREET

JABRA I. JABRA

INTRODUCTORY ESSAY BY
ROGER ALLEN

A THREE CONTINENTS BOOK
LYNNE RIENNER PUBLISHERS
BOULDER & LONDON

*A Three Continents Book*

Published in 1997 by
Lynne Rienner Publishers, Inc.
1800 30th Street, Boulder, Colorado 80301, U.S.A.

First published in the U.S.A. in 1990 by
Three Continents Press, Inc. © Jabra I. Jabra
Cover art © 1990 Max K. Winkler; © 1996 Lynne Rienner Publishers


ISBN 0-89410-585-X (pbk. : alk. paper)
Library of Congress number 86-51010


Printed and bound in the United States of America

The paper used in this publication meets the requirements
of the American National Standard for Permanence of
Paper for Printed Library Materials Z39.48-1984.

5 4 3 2 1

# Introduction
## Roger Allen

The creation of the modern state of Israel in 1948 and the
resulting war between Arabs and Israelis—which was neither
the first nor the last of such conflicts between these speakers
of sister languages—led to a Palestinian exodus which recent
research in Israeli archives shows to have been accelerated, if
not initiated, by acts of Jewish terrorism. That is the picture
drawn for us at the beginning of *Hunters in a Narrow Street*
when the narrator's beloved, Leila, is blown to pieces in her
house in Jerusalem, a harrowing vision which recurs throughout
the narrative. This exodus from the land of Palestine created
its own diaspora. Some Palestinians assumed that the absence
from their homes would be a short one, and fled to Lebanon
and the Gaza Strip; they are still there, housed in refugee
camps which have become the primary spawning ground for a
young and ruthless generation with no foreseeable future and
little to lose. Other Palestinians, particularly the more educated,
scattered to the four corners of the earth, to the Gulf, to
Europe, and to the United States.

Jameel Farran, who narrates our tale, travels to Baghdad
where he is to become a college English teacher. His degree in
English literature from Cambridge University certainly marks
him as one of the more educated of Palestinians. The Baghdad
to which he travels is the pre-revolutionary city. One character
in the novel has this to say about the city:

> It's all very well for foreigners, who live off the fat of our land
> unbothered by our problems, to say it's a wonderful place. A
> boom town—for them. But, for you and me, what good is it?

The Iraqi Revolution of 1958 that would sweep away the
monarchy in a bloody uprising has yet to happen, but the
enormous disparities in wealth and status and the tensions
caused by widely divergent political and social attitudes are
abundantly evident in the pages of this novel.

At the top of the social spectrum Jameel Farran introduces
us to the Nafawi and Rubeidi families. Imad Nafawi is a
thoroughly traditional figure who refuses to allow his highly
intelligent daughter, Sulafa, to go out of the house. Instead, he
hires Jameel to be her private tutor; even then their sessions
are chaperoned by one of the house servants. This does not
prevent the resourceful girl from showing her love for Jameel,
which he warmly returns whenever the constricting circumstances permit.

Ahmad Rubeidi is a senator and high-ranking government
figure who does not play a major role in the narrative until
towards the end when he threatens to use his influence to send
Jameel back to Palestine if Jameel does not stop seeing Sulafa,
who is Ahmad's niece. But if Ahmad does not play a major
role, the same cannot be said of his wife, Salma. American-
educated and a popular society hostess, she has a torrid and
bittersweet love affair with Jameel which for him is more a
matter of consolation and convenience than genuine love;
that belongs to his dead beloved, Leila, and to Sulafa.

The picture which Jameel provides for us of the higher
echelons of society comes then by way of the womenfolk, with
Salma and Sulafa representing the results of this male-dom-
inated society's attitudes. A related theme which runs through
this narrative is that of crimes of honor. Early in the novel,
Jameel is witness to the particularly brutal murder of a woman

whose brother stabs her to death for having a love affair, an echo of the cliché "to wipe away dishonor" evoked in a famous poem by the Iraqi poetess Nazik al-Mala'ika and in many works in modern Arabic fiction. The difference in attitudes is underlined by one of the characters who points out:

> There's honour for you . . . . Of course the honourable sheikh [who has just praised the brother's action] is going on a visit to a prostitute right now, but no matter.

The young men with whom Jameel comes into contact, for all their differences, are united not only by a restlessness perhaps typical of their age group, but also by a sense of bitterness and hardly contained fury at the things which they see going on around them. There is Towfiq al Khalaf, like Jameel a Palestinian and, unknown to Jameel until late in the novel, a suitor for the hand of Sulafa. Adnan Talib is related to the higher echelons which we have just described, but he is also a fervent if somewhat sentimental poet and Arab Nationalist who is arrested along with many others in the wake of a wave of student protests. It is clearly a highly significant event when late in the novel his visits Imad Nafawi's house and strangles him, saying these words:

> You're the evil one, the power that ever says No, the mud, the filth, the dung of the ages kept in silken clothes behind impregnable brick walls, amidst sickly roses. You are the darkness and the disease, the blight and the curse of our lives.

Husain Abu Amir shares with Adnan an interest in poetry and politics and a term in prison; the two of them undertake to commit suicide together by jumping into the Tigris, but their desire for life is too strong for such a negative act.

All these young men show a strong propensity for delivering disquisitions on a variety of topics: poetry, heritage, Palestine, women, East and West, and, of course, politics and society in Iraq. In much of this discussion they are joined by Brian Flint, an Englishman who is anxious to learn about Arabic culture and perhaps to serve as an antidote to the official British presence in the country. It is no doubt because of the political and social discussions and the activities which accompany them that, to quote the disarming final paragraph of the novel,

> In the long months that followed, while we waited, while the Adnans and the Husains and the Towfiqs impaled themselves on rows of political and social swords, the crows and the kites in squawking formations flew over the palm groves of a slowly refurbished land.

* * *

In addition to his novel-writing activity, Jabra Ibrahim Jabra is also a poet, a literary and art critic, and a major translator of English literature into Arabic; his translations include plays by Shakespeare and works of William Faulkner, and he has recently published a translation of Shakespeare's sonnets in Arabic, a truly virtuoso exercise in translation. I myself can also vouch for his intense interest in music.

Like the author, Jameel Farran, narrator of *Hunters in a Narrow Street*, is a poet who also possesses a knowledge of painting sophisticated enough to recognize the works of Chirico. However, as Jabra points out in a characteristic disclaimer at the beginning of the work, this novel is but a partial description of his own life. He admits only one similarity between himself and the narrator, and goes on to state that any likeness between them ends there. Such has been the claim of many Arab novelists, especially with regard to their earlier attempts in the genre; one thinks particularly of Ibrahim al-Mazini, who steadfastly maintained that in spite of all the similarities in his first novel between the protagonist and himself and the title of the novel, *Ibrahim the Author*, he was not the protagonist of the work.

Fortunately, modern literary criticism has afforded us a means of circumventing such largely fruitless quests. At issue here is the question of narrative distance between the character of Jameel Farran and Jabra, his creator. If there are elements of similarity between the two, that should hardly be surprising. It has often been wondered to what extent it is in fact possible or even desirable for novelists to exclude themselves from the characterization found in their own works. In the case of Jabra we are fortunate in having at our disposal a number of later novels, all of which contain characters who show traces of Jabra's life, career, interests and views. In *The Ship* (*Al-Safina*, 1969; English translation published 1985 by Three Continents Press), Wadi Assaf gives a detailed description of the fighting in Jerusalem and Bethlehem during the 1948 War, and both he and other characters indulge in prolonged discussions of philosophy, Italian art, and Russian novels. *In Search of Walid Mas'ud* (Al-Bahth 'an Walid Mas'ud, 1978) explores the intellectual life of both Baghdad and Beirut with great subtlety through the separate accounts of a whole series of narrators.

Jabra's novelistic technique has increasingly shown a tremendous concern with the use of different narrative voices and with the manipulation of time to create a spatial and temporal panorama that is more fractured and thus more authentic in a modern world "abandoned by God," to quote Lukacs. In one of his most recent endeavors, Jabra has taken this experimentation to interesting lengths by writing a joint novel, *World Without Maps* (*'Alam bi-la khara'it*, 1983) with his colleague and friend, 'Abd al-Rahman Munif.

In a word, *Hunters in a Narrow Street* is an early essay in fiction by one of the most important cultural figures in the Arab world today. Beyond one's admiration for a work created in a second language, there lie two other interesting issues.

This novel describes and analyses a particular period in modern Arab political and social life in English and presumably for an English-reading audience, although it has since been translated into Arabic. It thus emerges as an interesting example of an inter-cultural text, one which occupies a somewhat rarefied and largely unexplored middle ground between the established tradition of European fiction and the emerging tradition of the novel written in Arabic. The second question which might be posed is whether this narrative, originally published in 1960, is now somewhat dated. While it is reasonably obvious that the period of modern Iraqi history depicted here is now past, we have suggested above that Jameel Farran's narrative reveals to his readers far more than that. For while the issue of women's rights is broached here in shockingly stark terms, it remains a more extreme example of a larger phenomenon which is by no means outdated. Furthermore, the Arab World continues to be wracked by what Adballah Laroui called in his famous book title "the crisis of the Arab intellectual." Historical circumstances and geographical location can still be generalized to make this work of Jabra's a telling commentary on today's experience for many Arabs. As such, it is as relevant today as on the day of its first publication.

Roger Allen
June, 1986

# HUNTERS IN A NARROW STREET

# 1

I had exactly sixteen dinars when I arrived in Baghdad, and
it was to last for two weeks. This proved later to be an
optimistic estimate, for the first advance on my salary was
not paid until six weeks had passed. Even for two weeks
sixteen dinars was not a large sum for a stranger in a big
city, so I thought I should be careful with my funds and go
to a cheap hotel.

I told the taxi-driver to take me to a good hotel. He did.
He took me to the Shahrazad which had a pleasant front
with a garden. Leaving my things in the car I walked in to
the reception desk. It was very hot in the street. But as soon
as I entered the lobby a damp cool breeze blew on my face.
I immediately had misgivings about the rates, and the
receptionist confirmed them.

The driver was not surprised when I got into his car again.
I said: "Too expensive. Take me to a good hotel which is
cheaper." "Yes sir," said he and started. Some hundred
yards down he turned into a side-street and stopped. I got
out and saw a doorway that had not been swept for the last
twelve months. So I turned to the driver.

"This is dirty. Something better, please," I said and got
into the car.

As the car started he said, "This is a good hotel. I bring
many people here."

He drove for about three more minutes and landed me at
another entrance very much like the previous one.

"Listen to me, sir," he advised. "You either go to the
Shahrazad or to one of these hotels. There is nothing in

1

between. You will only pay 150 fils a night here, anyway."

With an air of finality he got out, put my luggage on the kerb, and walked with me up the steep stairs to the desk.

I was startled to be received by a bare-footed man who had not shaved for some days. He beamed at the driver then at me.

"I've brought you a friend, Shukri. Look after him," the driver said.

"Of course," said Shukri. "Where is the luggage?"

In a few minutes the luggage was up and the taxi-driver demanded one dinar. I gave him half a dinar and, though he complained, he was not dissatisfied. Probably a quarter would have been enough.

"And now my room, please," I said to Shukri. It had been a dusty night journey across the desert and I needed a wash and a good meal.

Shukri took me to a room with two beds, but assured me the other bed would be used by no other 'traveller' as long as I was there. Guests were called 'travellers'; in referring to the hotel Shukri called it a 'travellers' inn'.

"There are plenty of travellers' inns in this area," he said, "but very few of them provide you with the comfort that you will find here."

When I was left alone I discovered, to my horror, that the bed sheets had been used. Many forms of poverty I could tolerate, but to sleep in sheets used by some other 'traveller' was just beyond my powers of fortitude.

I went back hurriedly to barefoot Shukri and found him talking to a tall dark woman, whose eyes were black-rimmed with kohl. She was wearing a graceful black aba that rested on her head and came down to her toes.

"Shukri," I demanded, "will you change the bed sheets?"

"Sorry, sir," he said, "I can't today."

"But they have been used."

2

"Only once, last night. The new lot of sheets comes from the laundry tomorrow."

"Do you expect me to use those dirty ones?"

"They're not too dirty, sir."

The girl in the black aba told him to change them, but he swore by God he couldn't. A bell rang and he slithered away to one of the rooms.

"A stranger?" the girl asked.

"Yes."

"From Damascus?"

"No, Jerusalem."

"Don't worry, we look after strangers very well."

She had a gold upper tooth which glinted each time she opened her mouth.

"Thank you," I said and went back to my room.

I rang the bell and a boy brought in my luggage. I realised I had to find quarters elsewhere immediately. The dark place in the midst of that October brilliance smelt of the abuse of sullied nights and furtive days. I could imagine what the bathroom was like in such a house of gloom. Therefore, without having the sorely needed wash, I went out, locked the door and, on my way to the steep staircase, met the gold-toothed girl standing at the desk. She could have been a statue in ebony, a madonna without a child, an Ishtar of Babylon: her face was so impassive, her stance so motionless, her eyes so wide and black, that she evoked in me a thousand associations. I climbed down the stairs, and, at the entrance, looked up to see what the hotel was called. *Queen of Sheba* was written in Arabic and English on a yellow sign. Queen of Sheba! What would Solomon have thought?

There were colonnades on both sides of the street. Tawdry and haphazard, they stretched wilfully all the way down, over angular shops with men sitting in the doorways, drink-

3

ing tea in small glasses, and people walking with a swagger that suggested the motions of the Arab cloak which few of them actually wore. I was struck by the strange dark faces, invariably blemished, pock-marked, or bearing the scar of a terrible boil that ate into their skin, across the cheek, in the middle of the forehead, on the side of the nose. It was like the imprint of some savage flower. Some days later I heard a young man express his longing to "pile his kisses upon the lovely 'spot' that adorned his sweetheart's jaw."

The street, with its erratic design and colour—the colonnade columns were never alike for long—seemed patchy, as if it had been built extempore. A tall, very dark policeman with a gaunt face stood against a column.

"Where is the main street, please?" I asked.

"This *is* the main street!" he answered with astonishment as if to say, "You don't think it's good enough?"

I looked out for hotel signs and presently there was a long row of them: *Hotel of Flowers*, *Hotel of Happiness*, *Hotel of the Lily of Dawn*, *Good Morning Hotel*; then a very modest sign: *City Hotel*. It had a long balcony over the street, and I liked the idea of sitting up there in the evenings to watch the flood of traffic rushing below.

The stairs I climbed were not so steep or numerous as those of the Queen of Sheba. I wondered why those hotels had no lobbies on the ground floor, then realised that they actually occupied the top stories only, since underneath them were the shops. After all, I was not entering the air-cooled Shahrazad, where I could envisage a garden looking out on the river, sparkling with clean waiters and pretty girls in sleeveless dresses.

There was a desk behind which a middle-aged man was dozing. He was not only barefooted; he was in his vest and underpants. I coughed, and he jumped to his feet.

4

"I want a room with one bed," I said curtly.

"Yes, sir." He had a face reminiscent of an ikon—but an old one, chipped and scratched. It was a face I liked immediately.

"I can give you a room on the northern side, but the windows are high," he said and showed me one. "Or a room over the street"—and he opened the door of one—"but it is a little too sunny. Of course you can draw the blind; the balcony-door has a blind too, and there is a wash-basin here. If you find it too hot I'll give you a fan."

"Do you have clean sheets?"

"I'll get you a clean pair right away."

He put out his head and called out "Yousef!" then spoke to Yousef, who had responded to the call, in a strange tongue.

"What language is that?" I asked.

"Assyrian," said he briefly and did not seem pleased with the question.

"Are you Christian?" I had thought Christians were too few to be found in their underwear running 'travellers' inns'.

"Yes."

"Chaldaean?"

"Yes." He looked as though he had made a confession that might displease me. But I was absurdly delighted. Chaldaean—three thousand years after Babylon!

"Do you have any luggage?" he inquired, as if to change the subject.

"It is at the Queen of Sheba Hotel," I answered.

He opened his eyes wide.

"Have you been there long?"

"No. I arrived an hour ago. I didn't like the place."

"I am glad. Did you see any women there?"

"Well. There was one——"

5

"Well, she was a prostitute." He said it with great confidence. "You probably didn't know."

Could I tell him what associations she had evoked?

"I rather suspected it," I lied.

Yousef appeared, and I had to suppress a laugh. A young man of about twenty-five, he came in dressed in his vest and underpants too, but he had sandals on, which emphasized the shagginess of his legs and knees. On outstretched forearms he solemnly carried some sheets as if they had been a holy manuscript and offered them to me for inspection. When I approved he set about making the bed and I went back to Solomon's Mistress to collect my bags. Shukri could have murdered me with his looks, but he got a full day's rent before I left him. The girl was not at the desk. Could she be in some 'traveller's' arms in that heat? I wondered.

# 2

When you arrive in a big city you are so excited that you do not deliberate too long about what hotel to stay in, because the streets are crying out to have you walk in them, and you feel an air of expectation about the city as if all these years it had been decking itself out for your benefit. You want to rush out and see it all in an hour; and within that hour are compressed the adventures of your dreams. Nothing is so exhilarating as the sight of unknown buildings and unfamiliar faces, after the eagerness that has worked up in you during the long journey and the longer preparations before it. And was Baghdad a big city? I had asked someone in Damascus. "It certainly is," came the answer. "There are fourteen cabarets in it."

I, however, on that first day of October, 1948, felt little exhilaration and less excitement on my arrival. It was not because I had seen London and Paris and Cairo and Damascus. I had forgotten my travels and could not remember what any city in the world looked like—any city, except one. Only one city did I remember, and remember all the time. I had left a part of my life buried under its rubble, under its gutted trees and fallen roofs, and I came to Baghdad with my eyes still lingering on it—Jerusalem.

Some eighteen months before, we had moved into our recently built house on the Katamon hill in New Jerusalem. The house was the fulfilment of my father's dream, and the result of a lifetime of toil and saving. On my return from England after World War II, I had chosen the spot myself on an eminence which on one side bordered on the hills of the country, and on the other on the beautiful road that wound its way to the heart of the city. But it also overlooked the Jewish quarter of Rehavia, whence I often saw from the balcony odd couples coming up and ringing our bell. They were attracted by the arched entrance, they said; by the geraniums on the white-stone staircase; by the three-pillared tall windows on the second floor which, catching the sun, rose like a flame over the valley. Did we let rooms? they asked. Sometimes we offered them coffee and they commented on my furniture and books, and left effusive with admiration for the 'Arab way of life'.

Next door to us lived the Shahins in a house twice as big as ours. They were a patriarchal family: the grandparents, the parents and the children made the house noisy and suggestive of tribal happiness, on which my brother and I commented freely in our quiet rooms. But hardly had two months passed before Leila Shahin, the eldest of the children, and I took eager notice of each other. The first few times we met we were as secretive about it as we could

7

be. We walked about the rocky unbuilt-up part of the hill in the dark, often defying the mad barking of stray dogs, until I said, "Look here, Leila, I love you, and I can't keep it secret any longer."

She had long chestnut hair always rather untidy, brown eyes, a large mouth and fair skin. We went for long drives in my small Morris, careful not to be seen by too many people. Two or three times I took her to a Jewish café in Rehavia where we could dance. Much to my surprise one evening her mother called on us, introduced herself and had a long chat with my mother. I understood. When she left I told mother about Leila and she said, "Isn't it shameful of you both to have an affair behind our backs? Is that what you learned at Cambridge?"

"But I love her," I said.

"I will not hear such shameful talk. If you love her, do something about it. But remember, having just built this expensive house we've got no money left for a wedding just now. Besides, your father has been only eight months dead."

After that Leila and I met openly and our families exchanged visits. More often however we met when they could not see us, until Leila once said, "Will you ever kiss me enough? It's terrifying." And I said, "I want you like mad. We must get married soon. Will you come and live with us?" "Yes, yes, yes!" she said jubilantly. "It's like going to the neighbours and not coming back ever after, isn't it?"

Some nights later we were woken up by a succession of violent explosions that rocked our house. Jewish terrorists had been killing the British for several years, blowing up government offices, army barracks, officers' clubs. Now they had started on the Arabs. United Nations had recommended splitting Palestine in two, and the terrorists were determined to achieve the bloody dichotomy. Barrels of

T.N.T. were set off in market squares, killing about fifty people at a time, and now it was the beautiful white and rose stone houses of the Arabs they were after. When we went out, trembling with fear, to see what had happened, we saw three great heaps, about three hundred yards away, smoking into the cold air of early dawn. Some British soldiers were soon there to investigate the rubble.

Our quarter, being on the fringe, was in the grip of terror. Three or four people produced revolvers with which they said they would defend their homes. A villager offered me a rifle, an old German Mauser, with exactly five rounds. My brother bought it on the spot, but neither he nor I had ever fired a shot in our lives. The villager showed us how to fire, but we could not spare a single bullet for a live try.

That night we did not sleep. The terrorists did not come. Three nights later there was a mad howling storm. It thundered and rumbled and rain fell ferociously for hours. The power suddenly failed, and the whole quarter was in foul darkness. Every now and then the lightning gave us a glimpse of the hills through the uncurtained windows. The rifle stood on its butt in the corner.

Nothing could be heard but storm and thunder. And we dozed off, dressed in our overcoats. It was December. Then there was a blinding flash, and the house shook as in an earthquake, and the glass was blown in, crashing on the floor. I was stunned. My mother screamed. Yacoub dashed to the rifle in the corner and through the now paneless window tried to fire—at nothing that he could see, but he thought he had heard a car shooting off at the same time as the explosion. But no fire came out and he pulled the trigger again. The rifle might have been a toy. It jammed.

When I looked out, I cried in horror. The Shahins' house was a great heap of masonry, faintly perceptible through the black night. We ran downstairs and out into the howl-

9

ing wind. What could we do? In a few minutes other people came. We started turning the stones over to see if there was any life trapped underneath. "God, keep Leila alive, keep Leila alive," I was saying to myself, and like a madman I skipped about the rubble and the great stones and the iron girders in vain hope. Then I felt something soft hit my hand. I dug it up. It was a hand torn off the wrist. It was Leila's hand, with the engagement ring buckled round the third finger. I sat down and cried.

During the next day the engineers of the British Army unearthed eleven corpses piecemeal. Leila's hand was returned to her battered body. One funeral was enough for the collective family burial.

What was I to do to the faceless anonymous enemy? In our impotence, unarmed and defenceless, we vowed revenge. But the quarter on the hill was open and exposed to the nocturnal terror, like a helpless supine woman. In twenty-four hours it was evacuated. We found a two-room house in nearby Bethlehem. We had not spent three nights in our new refuge when our house, pillars and all, was turned into another large weird mass of ruins. Yacoub and I went to see the iron girders sticking out of the wreckage and pointing twisted fingers to a cold blue sky. The ruins of blown up houses stood in a row, as in a nightmare.

Jerusalem was an embattled city. The most unorganised, the most unarmed collection of volunteers, trying to stop the fanning out of a highly organised, well-armed and ruthless force: a few erratic bullets against mines of gelignite. Soon the British Army left the fighters to their fate, and hell set into the vacuum on its trail. We were cut off from Jerusalem and the Arabs of the city took shelter behind the great Ottoman walls, where their rifles could keep off the armoured cars of the Jewish Skull Squadrons. Night and day were filled with gun-fire.

10

Arab villagers were massacred in the treacherous dark by men they had never seen, and nothing saved our town of Christ except the desperate volunteers who entrenched themselves in the hills and declivities around the town, and grimly waited and sniped and forayed and retired. We all bought our own rifles (I had to buy another one) despite the exorbitant prices (who knows what group trafficked with those rusty outmoded weapons and came out with fearful profits?), and we would take our positions in what we considered strategic points, to keep the enemy off until the Arab Legion came to the rescue. On clear nights, as we went down the terraces of the Valley of Bethlehem, I could not help wondering what diabolical irony made of such a lovely place, thick with olive trees, the scene of our ill-equipped defiance of hate. Where the angels had appeared to the shepherds two thousand years ago to sing of joy and peace to men, we daily faced the ever-spluttering messengers of death.

And time dragged and sorrow came upon sorrow without relief. Despite all our fears we had preserved a little hope, but each new day ate further into our hope. It was a war, we were told. It was the greatest practical joke in the world, and the most tragic one. There were armies; there were guns; there were generals; there were strategists; there were mediators. But the dislodged and the dispossessed multiplied. There was a truce, yet the refugees came in greater numbers. They carried their rags and their bundles, and buried their children unceremoniously under the olive trees. Amidst the wild flowers rested the torn pieces of flesh, human and animal inextricably twined. In the spacious courtyard of the Byzantine Church of Christ's Nativity slept a tangled tattered mass of peasants and mules and camels, and only the braying of asses was louder than the hungry crying of the children.

11

In the town square an enterprising café proprietor had installed a battery radio with a loudspeaker. Wireless sets were becoming cumbersome pieces of furniture since the cutting off of power in New Jerusalem. So the people would congregate in thousands in the town square to hear the news on the small café radio, three times a day, at 8, at 2, at 6, and when the hour was announced by the broadcasting station with its usual six pips, a hush would fall upon the listening crowd, all eager for one item of good news. Every day at the appointed hours the thousands gathered in hope and fifteen minutes later dispersed in agony. "When Jerusalem is open again . . ." that was the phrase on every tongue. "When Jerusalem is open again. . . ." They would climb up the mountain of Beit Jala to have a look at the city they loved spreading over the northern horizon in a haze of pale violet, no more than six miles away, but as good as a hundred thousand miles away, a city of dreams looming beyond a valley of death.

Summer had come. The thousands—they all seemed to have the same face and the same voice—who could not afford the rent which the limited number of available rooms in the small town had made exorbitant, had pitched their tents in the orchards and the vineyards and on the slopes of the hills. Some slept under the olive trees, which became a common habitation. Those who were lucky had a room for each family. We had managed to find two little rooms that had originally been one. In the morning friends and acquaintances would call on us bringing along their friends and acquaintances, and as the little coffee cups were passed round the interminable conversation twined in vicious circles. In the afternoon other people called and the same conversation was set gyrating. Rumour was news. Wishful thinking was argument. Jerusalem would be internationlised, the Jews would soon be defeated, the United Nations

12

would certainly enforce its decisions. More houses had been blown up. More villagers slain. The Jews were using four-engine bombers. When were we to work and earn some money again? Should we stop the custom of serving coffee to guests? After all, we were together every day, we were no longer host and guest. And Abu Hilal's prognosis would be dropped in our lap like a golden apple.

Abu Hilal dabbled in magic. He was a tall thin man with small piercing eyes and a mysterious air, who carried a heavy cane and went on long solitary walks. He charmed the illiterates with a medieval jargon interspersed with theological quotations. He spoke about primary and secondary principles, about chaining the devil and holding communion with the spirits from beyond. He had a 'book' which he consulted and which no one was allowed to see, they said. He made a prophecy: "At the ninth hour of the tenth day of the seventh month Jerusalem shall be open again." Who would not believe him? Those who doubted it in his presence did so under their breath. When the forecast hour came without the projected relief a new prognosis had already been made. Abu Hilal had miscalculated the figures. The happy event was actually to be at the seventh hour of the tenth day of the ninth month.

Discussions and prognostications went on in every house, on every street corner. The farmer, the carpenter, the teacher, the priest, the bootblack, met and talked together. Everyone held opinions, all equally weighty. At first, most of us appeared with rifles slung across our shoulders and guns in our holsters. Day by day, however, the habit lost its force. We were in the hands of superior powers who organised the fight and relegated us to a useless background. Only Simon the Martyr (that was what everybody called him) had no use for weapons. His eyes were poor, and his tatters and periodic hunger made the possession of a very

13

costly rifle impossible. Instead he had a lute. A very old and battered lute, but his own. He was our regular visitor. Not all the motley patches in the world—and he seemed to have them all on his few clothes—could dissuade him from telling a funny story to the most worried of assemblages. When everybody laughed he, being a natural artist, was flattered, and then there was no end to his stories. (Wherever did he get them all from?) Finally he would sit down, take his lute and tune it and, as he listened with an intent ear for the right pitch, his red moist eyes goggled as if they had seen visions. And then off he would go strumming and singing with a lilt to which his body swayed. He might even stand up and dance to his own music, which earned him a good meal.

From one day to another the monotony was sustained, interrupted by occasional news of fresh rapine and slaughter. We were the prisoners of the little town. Cut off from the north by the Jews, if we wanted to go east we had to go through a tortuous, precipitous road in the arid mountains which had been built in haste to facilitate the movements of the Arab Legion of Transjordan. Where should we go east, anyway? Amman, capital of Transjordan, was already flooded with refugees. So was Damascus and so was Beirut. If we went south the Egyptians, who were still fighting, would not allow us an entry into Egypt. We were not allowed to fight—we had no ammunition, and nobody wanted us. The monotony, that repetitious ever-widening emptiness, was as devastating as the carnage itself. We organised a refugee committee, wrote petitions to the authorities on behalf of the homeless multitudes—we never knew exactly whether we should refer to the Egyptian or the Transjordanian authorities, both of whom had adminis-trative control of the place. We wrote long letters in different languages to people abroad requesting aid: money, food, clothing, medicaments. And although I was the treasurer of the committee, I received exactly nothing to register in my books.

"It's now a question of primary needs," my brother Yacoub said. "We're gradually driven back to where the race started at the beginning of time."

"Whoever is behind this Jewish campaign, he must be awfully clever," I said. "They've changed the whole thing from a political issue to a 'refugee' issue. Very clever. Instead of worrying about the restoration of our land we have to worry about feeding the refugees."

"We've got to eat. Even our one decent meal a day is in danger. How much money have we still?"

"About thirty pounds."

"Well?"

"Back to the hunting stage," I said. "The trouble is there aren't enough wild animals around."

"Don't you think we'd better sell your Morris?"

"With those three big holes in it who would want to buy it?"

"It'll fetch fifty or sixty pounds."

"And we'll never go back to Jerusalem again?"

"What, to our mouldering pile of ruins in Katamon? It doesn't look like it."

"And Leila—Leila will remain unavenged—do you remember her hand—her lovely hand resting on a stone, without her arm, without her body?"

"For God's sake don't talk about it. We've suffered enough. More suffering may be waiting for us in the months to come. But we must be practical. We want life, however much death wants us for his own."

"Do we really want life?"

"Didn't you often say in the past, life is resilient and not easy to destroy?"

15

"I suppose I did, with a roof over my head—and a roof of my own at that. I could say it when I knew I was going out in the evening with Leila to send her crazy with love and talk. But now—ugh! When starvation looks you in the face you have to qualify your statements about life."

That morning Father Isa called on us. We passed him the box with the cigarette paper and tobacco, and he rolled himself a cigarette. Cigarettes had disappeared, when suddenly the streets were full of stalls which sold loose brown tobacco and tiny booklets of cigarette paper, with gadgets for rolling the cigarettes. So we took to the custom of passing round the tobacco with the little roller to our visitors, and every guest manufactured his own cigarette.

"I can't understand the West," said Father Isa. "It is supposed to be Christian. Look what it is doing to Christians and to the land of Christ."

"They've sold us out," Yacoub said. "For thirty pieces of silver."

"But how can they do this to the Holy City? How can they allow Jerusalem to fall into ruins under the hoofs of Zionist terrorists?"

"I know what you mean, father," I said. "But may I ask you how you think of Jesus Christ?"

Father Isa was alarmed. He sipped at his coffee, took a pull at his cigarette, let out the smoke through his large grizzled moustache and beard, then said, "My son, I don't know what you mean by your question. He is the Lord of Light, the Redeemer, the Comforter——"

"Very good, father. But I think of Christ as a man walking our streets with a haggard face and beautiful hands. I think of Him standing barefooted on our cobbles and calling all men to His love and His peace. I think of Him here, in

16

these very streets and hills and houses and hovels. For me
Christ is a part of this place. But how do you suppose they
think of Him in the West? Do you suppose our Christianity
is like theirs? When they sing of Jerusalem do you think
they mean our own arched streets and cobbled alleys and
terraced hills? Never. Christ for the West has become an
idea—an abstract idea with a setting, but the setting has
lost all geographical significance. For them the Holy Land
is a fairy land. They have invented a fanciful Jerusalem of
their own and made it the city of their dreams. But for us
the geography is real and inescapable. When they sing of
Jerusalem in their hymns they do not mean our city. Theirs
is a paradise, ours is hell, Gehenna, the city of no peace.
Nor is their Jerusalem the city of Christ any more. It is the
city of David. What does it matter to them if our houses
are destroyed, if a thousand Leilas are blown to bits and our
city gates are turned into shambles? They've stolen our
Christ and kicked us in the teeth."

"No, my son, I don't agree. They may kick us in the
teeth, but they cannot steal our Christ from us."

"For fifteen hundred years Christianity has been exclu-
sively European. What have we, Arabs, Asiatics, Levan-
tines, to do with it? We originated it, but the Greeks and
the Romans took it away from us. All we have left of it is
an antiquated set of rituals to which we have contributed
nothing in a thousand years. What creative, civilising part
has our Christianity played in the midst of a Moslem world?
After the eighth century we should have surrendered ourselves completely to the new forces of Islam, not partially
as we have done. So we have neither enjoyed the full benefit
of belonging to our fatherland—don't you hate the term
'religious minority', the survival of which is always to indicate the tolerance of the 'religious majority'?—nor have we
distinguished ourselves by the creation of some great or even

17

different civilisation out of our different faith. Europe has always been afraid of the Moslem East—but the Christians in it, always looking out towards Europe until their necks have ached, have earned no more than its benign contempt. That is why the West will let Jerusalem fall into ruins under the hoofs of Zionist terrorists. Don't think for a moment, father, they have any love for you. I tell you, they took our Christ from us and kicked us in the teeth."

Father Isa looked at me in silence. At last he said, "You've puzzled me, I'm going back to pray."

A few days after that I sold my car for £60, and went to Damascus where Palestinian teachers were being registered for employment in the neighbouring countries. I had a Cambridge degree with which, after inquiring and waiting and knocking on a dozen unsmiling doors, I managed eventually to secure a teaching post in a college in Baghdad. I left most of the money with my brothers, and set out for the city of the Arabian Nights, with little joy.

"Remember," Yacoub said when the car was about to start on its long desert journey, "life is resilient. Give it another bounce."

"Not through further treachery, I hope." I said.

"Through further love, Jameel. Farewell! And send us some money when you can."

# 3

In the afternoon I turned the fan on and slept. City Hotel was no great edifice. It was constantly rattled by the heavy buses that passed underneath. As there was a bus stop immediately below the balcony, the great red cars would creak as they came to a stop and, a few seconds later, snarl mightily as they started again. The floor shivered and the iron bedstead transmitted the shiver to my skin.

When I went out to the balcony at about five o'clock the heat had subsided—but what noise filled the street, what din, what riotous masquerade! A flood of cars honked and growled incessantly. Whenever there was a halt in the flow, the cacophony of horns was deafening. On either side of the street, on and off the sidewalks under the meandering colonnades, great crowds moved as though in a festival. Hawkers cried their wares, newspaper boys yelled, some shouted obscene oaths, others emitted laughs as loud as the motor car horns, and in the variegated uproar a voice reiterated: "Five thousand dinars! Five thousand dinars!" It was the cry of the barefoot lottery boys selling their tickets, offering their golden promise to all. "Tomorrow's the draw! Five thousand dinars!"

The stupendous sight shocked me out of my lethargy. Women passed by, mostly in black abas. They walked through the commotion with the elegance of mannequins and the dignity of nuns. In the cars could be seen bare feminine elbows resting on their doors. No two men were dressed alike. The head-gear varied from a hat to a turban to a bedouin black coil, and the majority of the young men, in trousers and open-neck shirts, were bare-headed. Arab cloak and European suit moved side by side, and horse-cabs jogged along-side Buicks and Cadillacs. At least two different songs floated electrically over the din from different wireless sets at full blast. When I leaned over the balcony I found that on our side of the street, less than twenty yards up, there was an open-air café already crowded with men, where a voluble radio was determinedly active. The other radio was in a shop on the opposite side: shopkeepers were fond of music behind their counters.

19

"Five thousand dinars! Five thousand dinars!" The lucrative shout penetrated all other sounds.

Yousef, the proprietor's son, appeared at the other end of the long balcony.

"Would you like something to drink, sir?" he inquired. He had put on a shirt and a pair of trousers.

"Yes. Some tea, please."

"Shabo!" he shouted.

Shabo, the hotel's only servant, came through my room to his master. He was without shoes, but what strong, titanic feet! Such feet needed no shoes. Magnificent toes with nails like tortoise shells, and strong firm insteps that seemed to impress the ground with the importance of their load. They might have been carved in granite.

"Tea for the gentleman," ordered Yousef.

"Yes, sir," said Shabo, and his granite feet carried him away with the lightness of wings.

"Do you know Baghdad?" Yousef asked.

"This is my first day here. Are there any interesting places to see?"

"Lots. There are cinemas and cafes."

"No. I mean——" I just did not know how to put it to him.

"I see. You mean cabarets where you can have fun. You just go down this way, to South Gate."

"Suppose I want to walk about for an hour, where would you recommend me to go?"

"Well, sir, there is this one long street, Rashid Street, which you will want to see. It is so straight that you can't get lost in it, and so varied that you will love it. Just walk up this way," he indicated the direction, "until you get to North Gate, and you'll have seen almost everything."

"Rather a lot for one street, don't you think?"

"Y . . . yes sir."

20

"Can I get a map of the city?"

"I don't think so. Prohibited by the Government. What's a map for, anyway?"

"You're right, Yousef. What's a map for when there is only one street to see?"

I went down and joined the crowd. The hot sun, going down, left behind a hard, crystalline light. My senses were invaded by an unexpected invigoration. I looked at faces and hands and clothes and cars and shop fronts as if I had not seen such things before. The colonnades, underlined by the shadows of their long perspective of pillars, seemed to house a fantastic gaiety. After those frustrating months at home, this was a place of laughter.

I passed through King Feisal Square—a mælstrom of movement. That all those cars and horse-cabs and pedestrians and pedlars did not collide with one another was a miracle. Tall dark policemen, in white jackets and black trousers and large helmets, manœuvred the milling process with arms going up and down and sideways with the elegance of ballet dancers. It was not difficult to guess that if you wanted to see somebody you knew, all you had to do was to stand at such an hour on the kerb round the circus and wait: your man was sure to pass there, because everybody in town sooner or later passed through that uproarious bottleneck, which was fed further by numerous tributary alleyways. When in the following months I had learnt more about the city I knew that many young women were driven by chauffeurs up and down that street and through that circus, as if they had been promenading in an avenue. For they would watch one another's cars and with trained eyes spot who was with whom in them and go home replenished with topics for conversation. An unpredictable source of gossip one did well to remember.

On the left was the Feisal Bridge over the Tigris, on the

21

right were hotels and shops topped by a vast open-air roof café filled with a gesticulating clientele, all men.

Presently a shop-window arrested my attention. Books— new English books. Eight months had passed since I had last seen a bookshop. I had wearied of my own books at home arrayed amidst a world of misery. But here were new books—I entered the bookshop—and the latest magazines (only a few weeks old anyway) and Penguin books. The bookseller, a portly fellow whose age was anybody's guess, watched me with a benign smile as I handled the books and smelt their print. When I finally chose a couple of paper-bound books and a magazine (although I knew I could ill afford it) I went over and spoke to him. He was interested in the choice I had made. When he knew I was a college professor, he became expansive on the subject of text-books. He then gave me a discount on what I bought and intro-duced himself. I discovered after some weeks that Matheel, which was his name, was indeed a byword in academic circles. They were almost at his mercy for reading material.

As I walked up the street, the crowd was getting thinner, and the place progressively chaotic. The side-streets, badly illuminated in the oncoming darkness and conspicuously dirty at the corners, were like narrow ravines which seemed to suck in or disgorge the anonymous figures. And most mysterious of all were the girls, the ones black-clad from head to toe, who walked like figures in a dream, hiding in their folds a world of incommunicable secrets. In the slit of a passage, against a pile of garbage, two such black apparitions stood—looking like two enormous flies  Yet others had the eyes and mouths of goddesses. In the next few months such impressions were to come to me with ever-renewed intensity: perfection and vermin, butterflies and scorpions, eyes refulgent with loveliness and eyes dripping with poison.

22

I went through at least two more squares, past one café after another, all over-flowing with men. In a doorway stood a man with a naked torso, whose fat breasts sagged like those of flabby-skinned negresses one sees in pictures. Over him a sign said it was a public bath. Two or three hundred yards up I came to an opening on the right that ended abruptly with a wall in which there was a narrow door. A great flux of men moved through it, and I caught a glimpse of red and yellow lights from within. Driven by curiosity I joined the eager mass of men going in.

There was such a crush at the small entrance that I had to push and be pushed about before I got to it, generously inhaling the pungent odour of human sweat. At the door stood a policeman who frisked everyone from chest to knee. Repelled by the thought of an unnecessary search, I was about to withdraw, whatever the pleasures beyond that narrow gate might be. But, pressed by the gathering throng behind me, I abandoned myself to the policeman's quick search, and was made to pay ten fils before I was shoved into a passage which opened on to an alley, the strangest alley a city could invent.

I had no time to think before I found a woman, heavily painted in red and white, pulling my arm. Another, her blouse revealing a stray breast, got hold of the lower end of my jacket and tugged at it. When I pulled myself clear, two other women attacked me. A woman—I could only see a smudge of cosmetics for a face—cried: "For no money, my love, for no money." Another jostled her off and said, "No, with me." "With me," "with me," "me," "me"—that was all the articulation one could hear. It was a long alley, with doors in rapid succession on both sides and a little café where some men sat calmly with women sipping at their istikans of tea. The gaudy bedraggled females covered the cobbled floor, filled the entrances and the windows. Embrac-

23

ing couples stood around, and every man was avidly assailed. I felt terribly lonely in that living morass in which I seemed to have fallen without gaining contact. I was an alien incapable of response, despite all those violent pulls and nudgings. The women sat on thresholds, on chairs, on the ground. The place was planted with thighs and breasts and faces like hideous masks. There was a girl with one leg, and a girl with one eye stretched out her arm in my way as I struggled through, filled with a thrilling disgust and, having observed in my grip the books I had just bought said: "Have you come here to read or to——" and let out a deep-throated guffaw at my expense.

The alley led to a passage which curved into what seemed a circle. When I managed to go a little farther down, a woman stepped out to face me and said menacingly, "Let me see that magazine!" Very politely I offered it to her. She flipped the pages. "English, hm . . ." she shook her head. "Can you make love in English? I bet you can teach me a few things." I took the magazine back and answered apologetically, "Perhaps—but not tonight." When I walked away I heard her say—I did not know whether to me or to her neighbour: "I don't know what's come over our educated boys these days. They're not much better than women."

The circular passage led me back to the original alley. A young man, whom I had noticed standing alone near the entrance, beamed at me on my way out.

"You don't seem to've done anything," he said.

"No," I said briefly. But he accompanied me out.

"You look like a stranger," he went on, solicitously.

'Hell,' I thought, 'he is probably a pimp—but he is too young—and rather good-looking.'

"Well, yes," I said.

"Where from, if I may ask?"

"Palestine."

24

"I am honoured to meet you. Didn't you think that was a wonderful sight?"

(He couldn't be a pimp, I thought.)

"One of the strangest I've seen. Did *you* do anything?"

"Oh—no. I had merely brought a poem to show to Samiha. She is one of the girls there. But she was busy too long upstairs."

"What poem?" I was intrigued.

"A poem I've written about her. In fact I've written many poems about her. She is extremely good-looking, which is unfortunate. She gets too many customers."

"So you're in love with a prostitute? Original, isn't it?"

"Not really," said the stranger. "It's a pretty common thing in the history of literature. I always remember Baudelaire writing poems about that horrid Negress."

I imagined Baudelaire, the Satanic top-hatted dandy, side by side with my grimy ill-dressed companion, emerging from a whore-house. I refrained from disillusioning him.

"Does Samiha like it in there?" I asked.

"Not much. She can't leave it, you know. Government rules. What's more she lives in horror of what her cousin might do to her."

"What do you mean?"

"Weren't you searched when you went in?"

"Yes."

"You were searched for weapons. You might want to kill one of the girls."

"Is that why there is a policeman there?"

"Yes. In fact there are two or three of them, and they're always armed. Nevertheless, an outraged brother or cousin might still manage to smuggle a knife in. Quite a few girls have been murdered in that colourful alley. Do you see this spot here?" And he pointed to the ground just where we had arrived on our way back. "Last week Samiha's room-

25

mate, having left the closed brothel area to buy some clothes, was surprised here by her brother and stabbed to death. To wash off the disgrace, you know. But the blood wasn't so easy to wash off the ground and the base of the pillar where the girl fell."

"What irony. Poor girls."

"Irony?" he repeated, then went on in that strange dialect of Baghdad that combined the crudity of the desert and the voluptuousness of an old civilisation. "To preserve the honour of our wives and sisters we must create a whole class of honourless women. Who said that? There's irony for you. But they're necessary. And that's even more ironical."

We had come to a square at one corner of which was a large café—or 'casino', as such places were called.

"How about an istikan of tea in this casino?" he said.

I hesitated at first. I was not sure I wanted to listen to a dissertation on prostitution. But the café was attractive, and I wanted to talk, or be talked to. My friend must have been no less lonely than I, for he repeated his invitation and I accepted it.

We went in past a round-bellied beturbanned man in *zuboon*, who sat at the entrance behind a small cracked table. On it lay a big brass plate in which money of small denominations was arranged in parallel worm-like lines that curved in a semicircle within the ridge of the plate. He was the proprietor. The customers paid the set price of 20 fils when they left and received with their change lavish words of thanks which the fat cashier voiced with convincing sincerity. I watched him after we sat at a table, also small, cracked, and covered with the circular traces of many istikans of tea. Occasionally he would look solemn, an image of wisdom, a Buddha, until some departing customer would tell him something at which he roared with laughter

26

and Buddha changed into Silenus, letting forth a rollicking flood of words.

"My name is Husain Abdul Amir", my friend said.

"Jameel Farran," I said, and we shook hands across the table.

"How are things in Palestine?" he asked.

"Oh, I'd rather discuss Baghdad," I said.

"I understand. Of course you know how we feel about it."

"Yes, I do. Your papers must be full of news and articles about us."

"The things we've done for Palestine! But it's all gone down the drain. Dishonesty right and left, within and without. I work on a newspaper, the *Morning Telegraph*— have you seen it? Our papers find in Palestine a rich source of material to fill up their columns. It's repetitious, uninformed, hot-headed, high-worded, and the people are sick of it. But how else can we prove to them we're patriotic?"

"How else indeed? At least I should feel I am no stranger here."

"Stranger?" The thought seemed odd to him. "We're all brothers. We're all in the same boat."

"In spite of my dialect?"

"To you it will be an advantage. Once we hear a foreign dialect we prick up our ears and become more attentive." Looking round, he shouted, "Boy! Tea, tea!"

"Right away," came a loud answer from somewhere. And in no time a waiter in a red apron came with a large tray full of istikans of strong tea in small porcelain saucers that had a Persian design in blue and white. As a considerable amount of the tea had spilled over into the saucers, the boy would take up istikan and saucer together in one hand, tip the saucer down to pour out the tea spilt in it on the floor, then place them in front of us. He repeated the process twice, and went on to the next table.

27

"Do you write much poetry?" I asked him, and he answered enthusiastically, "Yes. Do you?"

"I used to—years ago. Now I only teach it."

"That's very sad. You teachers have a way of teaching old things and thus perpetuating old forms. I am afraid I am very free in form and style. In fact I am a surrealist. I like to shock my readers. They hate my poetry but they read it all the same. I once recited one of my poems to a taxi-driver in the brothel, and do you know what he said? 'I don't understand a word of it, brother,' he said, 'but it makes me shiver all over.' Now isn't that the best definition of poetry? Have you by any chance seen my book of poems?"

"I don't think I have. You see, as far as this country is concerned I am utterly ignorant. I want to know about your poets, your journalists, your politics, your painters——"

"You've begun at the right end—the whore-house, I mean. It's in the centre of the city; some of our most respectable schools are in this area, too." He laughed. His teeth were brown with nicotine. "We are a people of extremes. Our greatest buildings stand in the midst of mud houses; our best poets write the trashiest prose. We use the most devout language only to lapse into the obscenest drivel a language is capable of. In between the extremes you'll find all shades of frustration. Pay no attention to them."

I could not make up my mind about my interlocutor. His appearance did not justify his authoritative airs. He obviously had not shaved for several days, and his clothes were weary and faded One could guess he was wearing his only suit, which had probably been worn for many years now. His collar was dirty and had never been ironed, and he wore a tie the knot of which shone with sweat. It could not have been untied for weeks. He was good-looking, and that was his saving grace. He had almond-shaped black eyes which sparkled through long lashes, and his lips, when closed, were well-moulded. Only he laughed too often, and his brown teeth spoilt his face.

I was getting hungry, and I asked him what restaurant I could go to.

"Plenty of restaurants. But you can eat here too," he said.

"Do they serve food here?"

"No. But have you heard that fellow shouting 'Hearts, livers'? We could ask him to bring us some sheep's hearts and livers with some string beans. They're awfully filling and cheap."

"But where are they cooked?"

"On a stall down one of these alleys."

"All right, I'll try them."

They were served hot on skewers, with plenty of raw onions. "Onions," Husain said, "save one's soul. They whet your appetite and make it possible for you to swallow any food in the world." He pulled the meat off the skewer and said, "So you want to know about us? Have you heard of Adnan Talib?"

"I'm sorry, I haven't."

"Well, you should meet him. He is my friend, you know. He will correct the views you are bound to get about us from the useless, lazy college professors you're going to see around you."

I tried to look pleased. "Come and pay me a visit, both of you, at City Hotel," I said.

When we went out I paid the tutelary Buddha at the entrance, who bestowed on us a hearty "In God's peace."

We walked down the street and Husain plied me with questions, and in between told me a great deal about himself and Adnan Talib. Obviously Bohemians were not peculiarly European. The city of Haroun al-Rashid was full

29

of them. And if I was to believe my friend, the creative arts were only a few of their obsessions.


# 4


At about midnight I returned to the hotel. The turmoil of the earlier hours had subsided and the serpentine street was lonely. The lights, which were not so numerous now that the shops were closed, seemed to guide one into a melancholy world, with the successive pillars casting long dolorous shadows. A man sprawled in the gutter. He writhed in silent agony, tossed then writhed again and his hands passed tensely over his sides and stomach. Thinking he was epileptic I stood by to help him. I stopped a passer by who had only given him a cursory glance.

"Couldn't we help this poor man, please?" I asked. My strange dialect made people eye me twice before answering.

"What's wrong with him?"

"He probably has an epileptic fit."

"Oh, no. He's drunk." He bent over him. "He stinks of arak. Look," pointing a few yards down, "he has vomited."

"I see." I must have looked ridiculous. "I am sorry."

In the hotel Yousef and Shabo were playing cards in the little office. I took my key and went to my room. There were five rooms on each side of the corridor, and they were all quiet.

When I turned on the light and opened the balcony door, a great beam of light fell across the balcony's floor and on one of the closed windows of the opposite building. I went out to the balcony and smoked a cigarette. Behind the opposite building, I knew now, the great Tigris flowed silently away. I sensed its flow each time a whiff of air touched my face.

At last I was there. Only then did I realise how far I had come. 'God, what am I going to do here?' I thought. The street had bewitched me. I kept looking at the lights and the pillars. And out of the profundities of its sorrow, with the river breeze, came to me Leila's face. "Poor, poor Leila—God, what shall I do in this place?" A car zoomed past and the balcony shivered under my feet.

That night I dreamed that I saw Leila dressed in a black aba, like the girls of Baghdad. I was struggling with her all night desperately. I tried to remove her aba, but it would not come off. Again and again I tried, but the black robe clung to her body unyieldingly, and she laughed, laughed, as she had always laughed before that Jewish T.N.T. mine put an end to her laughter and mine.

# 5

The days that followed were occupied with visits to various government departments to get my appointment finally approved. You would kick your heels in a lobby or some clerk's office for an hour or two in order to obtain a few minutes' interview with an important official, only to emerge, like Khayyam's philosophers, as enlightened as when you went in.

The college in which I was to teach was in the throes of birth from a pile of blue-prints: departments and institutions of every kind seemed to be at the nascent stage all over the city. There was much politeness everywhere, attended by endless istikans of tea. No one was in the least bothered by the thought that a whole staff of lecturers and professors, drawn from half a dozen different countries, were left idle week after week. There were meetings to be sure, perhaps too many of them, and discussions of college departments and curricula which achieved very little, since each professor, jealous about his academic standing, was prone to overestimate the particular university system that had produced him. The names of Beirút and Iowa and Oxford and Kansas and Sheffield and London and Cairo were bandied about with zest and determination. But most woeful of all was the haggling over the salary of each lecturer. My money was running short and there were more and more infernal formalities to be gone through before I could receive an advance on my yet undetermined salary.

City Hotel in the meantime was a happier place to be in. I was never sorry to leave the dim musty corridors and small file-choked rooms of government offices, where the walls had been flaking, God knows, ever since Ottoman days, enough to reveal the rotting brick underneath, and be back in my under-furnished room over Rashid Street. Under-furnished? I should say unfurnished, but then I had: a bed with a mattress, sheets and a pillow; a small narrow table whose top was made up of odd boards in reluctant juxta-position; a chair with a bottom that did not match. And there were three metal pegs on the walls for my clothes. From such a room most things looked superfluous. One saw the barefooted in multitudes and wondered if the possession of more than one pair of shoes was not extrava-gance. I even contemplated, stealthily, Shabo's magnifi-cently chiselled feet and remembered Michelangelo's statues.

Husain Abdul Amir lost no time in calling at the hotel. On his second visit he came up together with a young man whom he introduced with much pride as his friend, Adnan

32

Talib. Adnan was Husain's superior in every talent the latter possessed. He was obviously the dark spirit that had driven Husain out of school and out of home in Najaf into the precarious life in Baghdad's streets of a journalist, loafer, whore-lover and poet. Life-long poverty was impressed in Husain's gaunt though well-shaped features, whereas Adnan had known a boyhood of some affluence, which gave him at least part of that grace and self-confidence of his. On a hot summer night, when he was barely seventeen, he had seduced the maid, a firm-fleshed young woman from some southern tribe, with green tattoos on her face and hands and an avid desire for smoking which she indulged on the sly. The seduction was effected by Adnan's slipping a couple of packets of English cigarettes into her hand in the kitchen when everybody in the family had gone to sleep on the roof.

The girl got pregnant and presently named her dear lover. To her surprise, his choleric dipsomaniac father married her off to a man she had never seen and drove his son out of home. Colonel Talib, a gentleman of the old Turkish school who drank arak by the bottle, spoke very little and hated women, thought his son might thus learn not to touch women, let alone a green-tattooed servant. But nothing could have been closer to Adnan's heart. He had shown a precocious talent for writing strange acid poems, and so he considered being thus uprooted from family life a dramatic event well-timed for enhancing his reputation as a poet.

He aggravated matters (when his relatives had intervened on his behalf) by refusing to return home, which intensified his father's irritation, and by borrowing money from several sources that relied on his father for payment, until the old retired Colonel disclaimed any responsibility for him. Most of all, he resented his son's new acquaintances whom in Ottoman days one would not have acknowledged even to exist. The father had been suffering from cirrhosis of the liver of which he died later; the mother, so gossip had it, was playing poker with a group of women when she heard the news of her husband's death, but she insisted on finishing the game before rising from the table. It transpired that not much money had been left in the Colonel's name, but at his mother's death some months later Adnan inherited a sizeable two-storey house in Baghdad and a citrus orchard at Baquba. "That's why my enemies class me with the reactionary landlords," Adnan would sarcastically say.

At cafés and tea-shops his admirers and maligners, flatterers and detractors, clustered about him to hear his latest poem, his latest adventure, his latest political fluctuation. No one knew for certain whether he was a 'progressive' (young aspirants to fame usually started off by calling themselves that) or a 'reactionary'. Some even had the viciousness to accuse him of being an informer who reported his admirers' political opinions to the secret police.

He seemed to have no work to do. He often came up alone—when Husain was probably seeing his employer's anæmic paper through the press or dropping in at the brothel. He entered one afternoon with a batch of English books under his arm and said, "Would you like some dynamite?"

"I prefer actual dynamite, thank you," I replied.

"You're a man after my heart. I know what you're thinking. Still, ideas to us are dynamite, aren't they?"

He threw the books on my bed. "Have you seen our public baths?" he asked.

I laughed. "Is it a baptismal initiation you want to give me?" I said.

"Yes, life begins with water. I must take you along to the one I know best."

"Any connection between your dynamite and public baths?"

"None whatsoever. Except that dynamite reminds me of my father, and my father—if I am happy—reminds me of the baths he used to take me to. I was only ten, I think, at the time. He taught me how to cover my pudenda while washing. Going to the baths in those days was an important occasion performed with great ceremony. We met our friends there, well-provided with oranges and bananas and apples, and turned the dark place into a festive hall. There wasn't one who didn't sing. What wonderful voices they all had in those overarching rooms filled with the sound of gushing taps! Has it struck you, Jameel, that there is some mysterious connection between nudity and song? When we emerged, after the tea and the cinnamon, a miracle had happened: we had shiny faces and soft white hands, and we felt so light that we could fly if we wanted to."

I was not reluctant to go to a public bath with Adnan. But as soon as I saw the fat attendant with the bare drooping breasts standing at the humble entrance I realised that public baths had had their hey-day. How many baths did Rome have? Alexandria? Byzantium? Baghdad of Haroun al-Rashid? However inexact the number, it would attest to the significant place they occupied in the lives of great cities. They expressed men's love of sensuous abandon by alabaster troughs while, in a voluptuous mist, philosopher and merchant, pimp and angel, found communion in nudity, water, and conversation.

The baths we visited, however, were not the fabulous rooms of ancient days with blue and gold mosaics shimmering under the water that spouted in fountains and fell into shells of marble, whence it cascaded from shell to shell on to the floor. Baghdad had decayed before it betrayed the signs of a new growth. The soft brick of the great structures of the Golden Age had fallen to dust centuries ago, and the desert had reclaimed the vast areas once irrigated and taken for the Paradise of Eden. What monuments would the holocaust of Hulago have left behind after his marauding armies had ravaged the city, blackened the Tigris waters with the ink of libraries pitched into them, then turned them red with the blood of the myriads slain? All that the succeeding rulers could do was to hold the pieces of Baghdad together against the ruthlessness of oblivion. Internal strife, sectarian massacres, foreign oppression, flood and plague, all had failed to obliterate the city completely. Babylon had not lasted a thousand years before it became a great mound of ruins. But Baghdad, long after its thousandth year, suddenly heaved into life and energy: the roots reached deep down and—struck oil. And there was blossom burgeoning in the sun.

We had undressed and rolled our clothes up in two bundles to be placed in a box under the long bench running round the walls of a large vestibule. Many men were drying themselves, or sitting, after their ablutions, wrapped up in towels and sipping their tea with conspicuous luxury, when I observed a fair-haired, blue-eyed foreigner. Already undressed, he was saying something in English to a naked pot-bellied servant with a red cloth round his middle. The servant asked me if I could translate for him.

Our friend was asking for soap, and I told the servant so. The Englishman was delighted to find someone to talk to in that limbo in which he said he was a lost soul. The three of us together, having secured our loofas and cakes of soap, opened a creaking door that led to the bath chambers. Brian Flint, our new friend, and I stood back in surprise. The place was a thing out of the dark imagination of a Gothic rather than an Arab mind. We were on the threshold of a large rectangular hall dimly lit by a shaft of tremulous, vaporous light from a round aperture in the arched ceiling. Naked figures (how sad, how forlorn) were hazily seen

36

crouching by their troughs or gingerly moving on the soap-slippery floor as though towards an unknown doom. In the small alcoves round the central chamber human limbs glimmered and vanished as they moved. A man, all bones and flaccid skin and stooping with age, was weighted by a hideous large swelling under his groin as he hobbled towards us, holding by the hand a small boy who seemed to be guiding him. "This is not hell, by any chance, is it?" said Brian, and bravely we stepped forth into the circle of the ghostly men.

We found a free alcove and squatted by the small round troughs with taps hanging over them. Other rooms and cubicles, for those who wanted privacy, spread out in a labyrinth round the chamber.

"This must have been designed by a man with a tormented soul," I suggested, turning on the taps.

"Piranesi might have been proud of it," Brian said.

Adnan spread out his bony corpse and said, "I'm told Italy has better baths than ours. They provide you with hot water and sex."

"I haven't been to one there," Brian said, "but I shouldn't be at all surprised if they still enacted the more salacious parts of the *Satyricon*."

A little exasperated, Adnan said, "What is the *Satyricon*?"

"A book mostly about pederasty—at least that's what you remember most when you've gone through it. A most delightful book."

"I must read it," Adnan said solemnly, and rubbed his chest slowly with his loofa.

"Is this where people in the past ate oranges and apples and sang while they bathed?" I asked.

"They prefer their own bathrooms these days. Though I must admit very few people can claim to have bathrooms in

37

their homes. All the same, washing has become a duty, not a joy."

A tall muscular figure with very dark skin, whose torso was naked but whose lower half was draped in a red striped cloth, looked in at us. He was one of the attendants.

"Does any one of you gentlemen want massage?" he asked.

"What a splendid physique," Brian exclaimed. I told him what the fellow had asked and added that I preferred my own leisurely wash.

"I'd love some massage," he yelled and jumped to his feet. The dark attendant led him across to a cubicle on the other side.

Adnan roared with laughter. "I think I know what our English friend is after," he said.

"Experience," I said.

"Have you ever been massaged in other baths?"

"Yes, once. I didn't like it. I was handled like an inanimate object."

"I don't think our friend will be handled like an inanimate object. The masseurs round here have an eye for the right sort. Did you see the glint of triumph in that masseur's eye?"

"Adnan! You're awful!"

He laughed and emptied the trough's water over his head.

"Listen! So people still sing here," I said.

From a distant part of the central chamber a long mournful note wafted across the steam and the tremulous light. It was a drawn-out sigh, a long sustained melodic awwwwwff...

"There," Adnan muttered through his dripping hair, "you have the sorrows of a whole race in one long syllable. . . ."

It was one of those ineffably sad songs which begin with the lover's desperate sigh for the lovely one beyond his reach. Awwwwwff . . . went on the singer and cursed evil fortune that was never kind to him.

38

"Careful, Jameel!" Adnan said. "That fellow is laying bare the heart of the whole race—a melancholy race to which denial is the one everlasting pain. So—careful with that emotion of yours!"

"You don't have to tell me that, Adnan, I've known enough denial myself." In that absurd posture of mine I was seized by the agony I had been struggling to overcome. "But it was a different kind of denial. A totally different evil imposed its will . . ." I thought of the evil that had presented me with Leila's hand torn off the wrist.

Awwwwwff . . . awwwwwff . . . the voice suspired.

Adnan came over to me, soap suds all over him. "We want to put a full-stop to that denial."

"Are there many people like you here?" I asked.

"Thousands. But we don't have the . . . wherewithal . . ." he answered cryptically.

"Which is more important than all your thousands."

"All right. That should be our concern now." The conspiracy was on. The low voice, the solemn look. "If ever it gets too difficult for us to meet anywhere, remember this place—possibly this very alcove. Right?"

"Right," I answered automatically, and took a good look at Adnan.

Brian came back, stepping carefully on the slippery floor.

"How was it?" we asked.

"Terrific, simply terrific. I'm coming here again."

"A good masseur?" I asked.

"My dear fellow, there's nothing about human skin that the black man doesn't know."

"Be charitable. That man isn't black," Adnan said.

"But he's a perfect demon with a demoniac face. He doesn't understand a word of English, and yet he understood every thing I said. He didn't say much though, apart from an occasional noise he uttered to express his interest

39

in my remarks. He has a chest fit for Apollo." He sat down on the edge of a trough while we still scooped the water at leisurely intervals and soused ourselves.

"How long have you been here?" Adnan asked.

"This is my fourth day."

"Teaching?" I asked.

"Heaven forbid! I am in the banking business."

"You sound as if you were fifty years old."

He laughed. "I left Oxford only last June."

"And you thought a journey to the barbaric East," Adnan said, squeezing his sponge-like loofa over his thighs, "would complete your education?"

"I am a student of Arabic and I have always wanted to see the Arab countries. I look forward to the day when I can read the Koran fluently, like an Arab. Nor do I think a country that can design a public bath like this one is barbaric."

Adnan was not impressed. In Arabic he said to me softly, "The son of a bitch thinks we believe him. God knows he'll be reporting all this to his embassy tonight."

"What was that?" inquired Brian innocently. His knowledge of spoken Arabic, if any, did not go as far as the Baghdadi dialect.

"Oh, I said I'd love to teach you Arabic." Adnan was not unresourceful.

"Would you both like to come and have a drink with me at the Shahrazad?"

"Yes," we said.

Just when our obscure singer had embarked on another song of lover's despair we got up and as decently as possible walked through the flesh-sodden atmosphere back to the chamber door, where we were received by an attendant holding up large thick towels which, with a graceful flourish, he placed on our shoulders as though they had been cloaks.

40

We dried ourselves, got our clothes out of their boxes and dressed. We were invited by the *chaichi* to sit on the long moist bench. The sad song was still in the background as customers uttered loud greetings and gave loud orders to the busy benign attendants, and I had a sense of well-being and voluptuous lassitude. "Tea or cinnamon?" the *chaichi* asked.

"Cinnamon," Brian and I replied. Adnan asked for tea.

When the hot istikans arrived and with conscious delectation we sipped at them, Brian said, "I don't think I shall have much occasion to drink cinnamon tea in the future, but I am certain if ever the smell of it hits my nostrils, I shall remember this damp heavenly limbo."

The dark masseur with Apollo's torso stood by and gave Brian an adoring grin. Brian slipped a paper-note into his hand.

From behind the closed door I could still hear the long tormented sighs of the singer, and Leila's yellow fingers splayed like a fence before my eyes.

# 6

Brian Flint appeared to love everything he saw, even the dirt in Rashid Street.

"At least," he said commenting on it, "it's authentic. There's no garbling of facts here. Perfection and imperfection are all there for everybody to see. And garbage is an essential part of humanity. When men are not all morons, they're likely to be a little slack, a little indifferent about what they leave behind once the business of life itself has been attended to. I imagine only such men are capable of passion, the kind of passion that could be harrowing and

41

deadly. Life is their creation: they make it, they are not made by it."

"If passion is what you're looking for," Adnan said, "I can give you tons of it. But where does it all get you?"

"Into further passion. What greater blessing do you want?"

"That's all very well for a nation given to analysing its emotions and its attitudes," I said. "But I can't help feeling that passion here is mostly a symptom of putrescence. It may be creative putrescence, of course, if such a thing is possible. I live in a hotel right in the midst of it all. It's on our way to the Shahrazad Hotel. How about dropping in for an istikan of tea?"

"Very good. I hope you have one of those delightful tottering balconies with plenty of friends in bedouin dress."

"Tottering balcony. That is the title of one of Adnan's poems."

"Lovely! What other titles do you remember, please?"

"Titles?" Adnan said. "Er . . . *Dream and Death*, *Senile Scent, Treadmill*——"

"Good Lord! Your poetry can't be about wine and roses and secret love, can it? You belong to the despairing Twenties."

"You're putting it in European terms. Actually I may not be even that up-to-date. But I know I belong to this street the way every shop in it does, up-to-date or otherwise."

"Wonderful! I love this street myself. Do you think I would prefer the straight, perpendicular, disinfected thoroughfares of modern cities in the West? Not me! The great poets and artists in Paris do not live on the broad immaculate Champs Elysées. They live in the tortuous smelly alleys of Montmartre and Quartier Latin. Who could have a soul, living in a rectangular shiny tin? The long

42

glass-bright avenues of New York still import their talent from the dim, mazy and squalid streets of the ancient cities of Europe."

When we entered my hotel's narrow doorway Adnan said softly to me in Arabic, "Do you think he's honest?"

Brian's face shone with excitement as we went up the stairs and met on their way down a couple of tall tough-looking Kurds in their national costume, complete with a mighty roll of a turban with tassels and voluminous blue trousers that rustled as they moved. Both Yousef and Shabo were in the little office. Shabo stood up delighted to see a fair blue-eyed foreigner, but Yousef looked up without a gleam in his eyes, then looked away and seemed depressed. I took my key and we walked down the corridor to my room, followed by Shabo. I turned round and ordered three istikans of tea.

It was about six. From the balcony the longest stretch possible of the street could be seen, wild with human move-ment and motor traffic. The peak hour was approaching. The radio song from the neighbouring coffee-house merged with the general clamour and the honking of motor cars. But one cry was always louder than the rest: that of the lottery boys. "Five thousand dinars! Five thousand dinars!" The phrase beat a meaningful rhythm to the rising tumult.

"Can you sleep in the midst of this eternal jubilation?" Brian asked, leaning over the balcony. We had to speak fairly loudly to hear one another.

"You get used to it," I said, "the way you get used to the sound of a waterfall. The street often sounds like a great river with rapids and weirs."

"Anything may drift on it," Adnan said, enjoying the metaphor. "Certain things, however, if not properly managed will sink."

43

"It's parallel with the river all along, even when it lapses into the calm of residential areas," I said.

Shabo came in with our tea. From under his arm he dropped some clean sheets on the bed, then came out to the balcony. When we took our istikans he made for the bed and was about to change the sheets. I went in and told him not to do it until we left.

"Azima, Yousef's sister," he said in a soft voice, "has brought in the clean sheets just now. She wants the dirty ones to take home, and she can't hang around too long, sir."

"Well, if you have to." I was not going to argue with him. I went back and said to Brian, "Have you noticed his feet?"

But before Brian could answer we heard a high piercing shriek from within. Another followed, accompanied by heavy trampling down the corridor.

A girl in a black aba flew in terror to my door and screamed, "Shabo!" Shabo rushed out to her. But Yousef was there before him. He pulled the girl back and plunged a long knife in her belly. Brian turned pale. Adnan, leaning against the banister, took another sip from his istikan unmoved, as though he had always seen such sights.

In the corridor there was another shorter, choked scream. Shabo's voice rose in a horrifying yell. I ran to the corridor. The occupants of other rooms poured in. The shouting and confusion were brought to a hush by Yousef's hoarse agonised groan, as he fell limp in Shabo's strong arms.

The girl was on her back in a pool of blood which was slowly trickling towards my door. Her arms and lègs gave violent jerks every now and then. Her black aba had fallen under her twisted head and shoulders, surrounding them like a mount in a frame. Her eyes were open, her mouth gasping for breath. Yousef, with a white drawn face so

44

filled with horror that he was almost unrecognisable, remained pinioned in Shabo's arms. Suddenly he burst into tears, bellowing with fearful groans that came up from the depths of his bowels, and collapsed by the body on the floor. It was his sister. He had ripped her abdomen.

We did not know whether to call the doctor or the police. A tall fellow in bedouin costume, however, shouted to Yousef over the girl's corpse: "Is it a matter of honour? Well done, man! It's good to see we haven't lost our sense of honour yet. Well done, man!" With the upright carriage of a victor stepping on his prostrate foe, he held the rims of his cloak together and walked away.

"There's honour for you," whispered Adnan. "Of course the honourable sheikh is going on a visit to a prostitute right now, but no matter."

It was no time for moralising. I remembered that in the barber's shop below the balcony there was a telephone. I went down and telephoned to three or four doctors whose names I picked at random from the Doctors' section of the telephone directory. One of them finally consented to come. In a few minutes a policeman appeared on the scene, who went out and came back with a couple more. When the doctor arrived the girl was dead.

The inquest that followed on the spot was long and wearisome. But then, as Brian kept saying, a human life is worth two hours of discomfort. Embarrassed though at first he was—as everybody looked on him as an outsider— he seemed later to have enjoyed being there.

"I hate to sound callous," he said, "but I have witnessed a sight which Swinburne would have paid to see. Talk about passion!"

"What I can't believe," I said, "is that Yousef, of all people, would commit such a murder. He is a most gentle creature."

"And he'll get away with it, too," Adnan said. "Don't look so surprised, Brian. The girl had obviously slept with a man, and the outraged brother got to know about it. This was the only thing for him to do. If he hadn't done it he would have been the laughing stock of his family and friends."

"But she wasn't his wife," Brian said. "Surely he won't get away with that?"

"Three or four years in jail, at most," I said.

"We live in cities and yet we follow the law of the desert," Adnan explained. "We're caught in the vicious meshes of tribal tradition. You heard what that bedouin said, didn't you?"

"Love here must be very exciting, very exciting," Brian said.

# 7

Going to sleep that night was not an easy thing. I kept remembering the pool of blood out in the corridor, although Shabo had already washed the floor and Yousef had been taken away by the police. Shabo had come into my room while I was undressing, exhausted and still shiny with perspiration from his labours, and I had tried to find out from him if there were any especially significant facts pertaining to Yousef's crime. All he could tell me was that the proprietor's son had killed his sister "because her belly became that big," and he indicated with a gesture how big.. Then as I got into my bed he waxed philosophical. "It's dreadful, Mr. Jameel," he said. "God gets you into trouble and you can only get out of it by greater trouble. Man is a miserable thing. Shall I turn out the light for you?"

For hours I courted sleep in vain. I had opened the window and the balcony door for some cool breeze. I found myself in a welter of objects and struggled through vast rooms cluttered with furniture and animals and large insects that kept coming under my feet. Through the wide windows peered hundreds of faces. They laughed as I endeavoured to avoid the tables and chairs which constantly fell across my path. A door banged, then another, and yet another. Many doors were banging shut and open while a crowd of women streamed in and filled the rooms. Through the windows heavy rain was driving in, and harrowed by a sensation of thirst I opened my mouth to receive the rain drops against my throat only to find they rested there like ashes. The women sat down on the furniture and turned into clay models with yawning eye-sockets and mouths wide open but filled with silence. Then the slamming doors went into action again as I reached out to one of the windows, and Shabo's voice boomed over the dead statues: "Shut the window! Shut the window!"

I awoke at Shabo's voice shouting behind my door. Turning on the light I was terrified to find my room was one enormous ball of dust. I jumped out of bed and looked out, but the atmosphere was dense with cloud upon cloud of sand, and the street lights, as in a heavy fog, were a dim yellow blur. The sandstorm, the first I had ever seen, was an extension to my nightmare. Where could one go out of that choking grime that went down the lungs, seeped into the bronchial passage-ways and tried to stop one's respiration? Where could one fly, what depths penetrate, to find one whiff of clean air? I shut the window and the balcony door to have a foretaste of being buried alive.

My blankets were covered with a layer of sand. I caught a glimpse of myself in the mirror, though I could hardly see myself in the thick atmosphere which the electric bulb

47

failed to illumine. I was white. My hair, my eyebrows were thick and white with dust, and so were the books on the table, the clothes on the chair. When I moved my pillow the sand rolled down on to the mattress. The inmates of the neighbouring rooms asserted their presence with a steady staccato sound of coughing, and I heard Shabo say there was no turning away from God's curse.

The cold season thus began. As the dust ravaged the city and sleepers writhed and wheezed, the temperature fell considerably. Morning came in labour and torment, but once it came the dust had settled and a gentle wind began to blow. At about eleven I sat on the balcony in a sun whose fires had at last abated, when Adnan and Husain from the sidewalk down below saw me and came up for an istikan of tea.

"Our weather is just like us," Husain said. "Hot one day, cold the next. We too flare up until you think the universe will fall to pieces, then subside until you think not a spark is left in us."

"I thought the storm last night was going to sink the whole city in sand," I said.

"It never will. I tell you it's just like us. It always funks it at the last minute." Husain laughed, relishing his own humour.

"Poor Husain," Adnan said. "He's sorry he missed the murder of Azima yesterday."

"Not entirely," Husain said. "After all, it's one of those repetitive things, you know. I shan't even bother to write a story about it for my paper. Now, had the girl been the murderess—well——"

"It's all over now with Azima," I said. "It remains to be seen when repetition will catch up with your Samiha."

"The angelic harlot, hey?" Adnan said.

"It's the evil in Samiha that I love," Husain said with a look of great satisfaction. "She's not easy to destroy. In

48

fact, she is like last night's sandstorm. She gets into your lungs and chokes you. Without any motive, without any comprehension."

"Aren't you romanticising her!" I said.

"Certainly not. Because she doesn't know how wonderfully evil she is. She sticks right in the throat of our society and, what's more, she'll see to it that she doesn't fall in a puddle of blood until she has corroded with boils the flesh of a good segment of society."

Obviously Husain, like his Samiha, owed little to society. Yet at any monent he might dilate with all the enthusiasm and naïveté of a green dreamer on love and justice and equality for the preservation of that society. Under a coat of bitterness lay the excessively sweet core of sentimentality.

"Husain loves everybody, doesn't he?" Adnan said. I felt Adnan was behind Husain's very thoughts as though from behind an invisible screen he prompted him into a performance for my benefit.

"I love everybody except humanity," Husain said. "You can forgive its weakness, its misery. But what can you do with its hypocrisy? Even in the humblest slum you have enough hypocrisy for a dozen diplomats. What can you do to a people that cultivates hypocrisy as a profession? Hypocrisy devoid of art, mind you, devoid of elegance, of some kind of wicked beauty. Hypocrisy in politics, hypocrisy in friendship, hypocrisy in virtue, hypocrisy in religion, hypocrisy high and low and everywhere. I could tell you I love you in sixty different, extravagant ways, without meaning it, but I would actually destroy you by one subtle phrase, as sure as an adder's tongue. But don't you believe everything I say, Jameel. Even as I self-righteously attack hypocrites I might be the one who is the most hypocritical of all. The devil knows what we're going to say to the next fellow we meet as soon as we've left you."

49

"We could say," Adnan put in, "that no sooner had Jameel Farran found a room in City Hotel than the proprietor's daughter was killed by her brother. And where? Right in his room. You should have seen his books, we'd say, all smeared with innocent blood."

I laughed. "What grotesque minds you have!" I said.

"You laugh, do you?" Husain said. "You wait until you see such a story in your file at the C.I.D., with a copy in your college secret file! He seduced the poor hotel proprietor's daughter, the story will go, and walked over her body. . . ."

# 8

The saddest man in Baghdad during the next few days was Tobia, the hotel proprietor. "It's terrible to lose a daughter like that," he said. "But if I lose my son as well, it will be even more terrible." Without Yousef it was difficult for the old man to run the hotel, since he was illiterate and could not keep the books as required by the authorities. "Do you think they'll consider the extenuating circumstances at the trial?" he would ask, then in a sudden fit would add, "The bastard, the heartless infidel, the dog son of a dog, knifing his poor sister under his father's roof. I hope he'll hang. But you don't think he'll get more than three years, do you? That's what the lawyer has promised. It'll cost me all I have though, all I have. The dog son of a dog . . ."

One evening he came into my room distraught and careworn. "Forgive me, Mr. Jameel," he said falteringly "But could you pay me the rent for the last two weeks?"

"As it happens," I said, "I am being paid tomorrow. I

50

promise to settle the account by lunch time. Is that all right?"

"You see, sir, the first of Moharram is coming. I have to pay the year's rent in advance, as the custom is here." Moharram is the first month of the Islamic year. "I am very worried," he went on. "I've spent most of what money I had on my son's case. Meanwhile there's a dirty fellow who's been after the landlord to rent him this building. He's offered him fifty dinars more than I, but if I pay the rent in time I'll probably divert the blow."

But Tobia failed to divert the blow.

One night a new sound filled the city. I was in bed when I was awakened by a strange golden voice chanting a long prayer. It was a lament upon the assassination of al-Husain, the martyr saint of the Shi'a Moslem sect. It came from amplifiers installed on the minarets of a near-by mosque. In the streets in the next ten days, there were processions of men and women celebrating with doleful gasping songs the Passion of Ali's Son, as they had done for the last thirteen hundred years. Through many windows women could be heard weeping as they intoned the funeral chants, and in many a mosque crowds of men tore their hair and beat their chests, as through their tears they listened to the story of the holy man's martyrdom. For ten nights the city reverberated with lamentation as though the great bright stars of Baghdad's sky had shed sorrow upon the heads of men. Thus was the new year received—and how fittingly! And I remembered how Tammuz, three thousand years ago, had been lamented by a kindred people throughout the Land of the Two Rivers, when the Tigris, 'river of palm trees', and the Euphrates, 'river of fertility', heard the shrieks of the maidens as they went down the highways with loose locks and bare breasts to weep for the god who had died and who was to rise again with the green corn and the red anemones.

51

Tobia also wept, but for a different reason. I saw him in the morning, on my way out, sitting in his little office, holding his grey head between his hands, no longer looking like a Byzantine ikon. His sobbing was painful to hear. He was to vacate the hotel, as the new occupant was moving in on the same day.

On my return at noon the corridor was cluttered with bedsteads, armchairs, wardrobes of all sizes and shapes with full-length tarnished mirrors. The change-over was effected with remarkable promptitude. A couple of new servants, unshaven and slovenly, were putting things in order together with Shabo who, I was told, was to remain under the new management.

Dawood, the new proprietor, was introduced to me.

"Mr. Jameel," he said, clicking a string of amber beads, "I'm going to make you more comfortable than you've ever been, so you won't leave us. Come and have a look at your room." He led me to it. "Look, two brand-new armchairs, a bed with wooden ends. Now, this is what I call a bed. See? And what a magnificent wardrobe for your clothes! No more dust collecting on your suits. A rug? But of course. I'll get you one in a second. And you won't pay a fil more than you've been paying." Click, click, went his beads.

I had started working at the college and thought I must settle down in a reasonable place. For a day or two I was tempted to stay under the new dispensation. Shabo, however, lost no time in telling me what I was in for. Bringing in my breakfast, he carefully shut the door and seemed to have something to confide.

"Are you happy here, sir?" he started.

"I'm all right," I said noncommittally.

"The proprietor likes you and wants you very much to stay."

"As long as I pay the rent I don't see why he shouldn't."

"Well, he likes people to stay here who are of good class, as you might say."

"Understandable, isn't it?"

"Yes. But do you know what Dawood used to run before he moved in here? A brothel. It was closed down by the police, so he had to find another place."

"I'm afraid, Shabo, I can't go into the history of the proprietor of every hotel I go to."

"Of course not. But he's turning this one into a brothel too. A secret one, naturally."

"What?"

"You see, sir, he's been doing this for the last fifteen years. Actually he is a pimp. Fifteen years ago Dawood and I came down to Baghdad together. We came from the same village. I worked as a servant, he worked as a pimp. He is a rich man now, worth several thousand dinars. I am still a servant, worth all the lice in my hair." He chuckled in resignation. "I'm sorry to keep you with my gossip," he added. "Your eggs are getting cold."

I was disgusted. But I was also amused. Suspecting, however, that Shabo spoke out of envy of his successful friend and master, I thought I had better talk to Dawood himself about it when I came back from my lectures at the college. At about four that afternoon Brian called.

"What a transformation!" he exclaimed as he lay down on my new bed. "A rug even in the corridor! It's no longer the haggard inn made for saints and cut-throats, but a common bourgeois hotel."

"It has got an appearance of respectability, hasn't it? That banal appearance behind which all vices may be indulged with impunity," I said.

"Jameel!" Brian was gloriously happy. "You don't mean you've acquired a mistress, do you?"

53

"I am afraid it's not as delightful as that. I am told on good authority the place is to be turned into a—bordello."

"How wonderful! You're going to have a gay time, watching the naked aphrodites performing their rites."

"I can just imagine them," I said and rang the bell.

Shabo appeared to tell me that Dawood would like to come in for a word with me.

"Very good. Ask him to come in, and bring tea for three."

Dawood walked in carrying his long string of amber beads. When I introduced him to Brian he showed great affability but could say nothing in English beyond 'how are you' and 'yes'. Brian's spoken Arabic was not much better.

Easing himself into an armchair, Dawood dangled the string of beads between his knee and clicked them, as though he counted them, one by one, two by two, three by three.

"I don't want to disturb you, professor," he said, "but I've been wondering if you could help me choose a suitable name for the hotel."

Brian, I noticed, watched him closely, fascinated by his beads, which acted as a metronome to his speech.

"I'm afraid I don't know much about hotel business," I said.

"You've travelled abroad, professor, you must have been in dozens of hotels."

"You don't want to call it the Ambassador or the Rialto, do you? Of course you can call it the Garden of Eden." I couldn't help pulling his leg a little. "Many people believe Eden was in these parts."

The tea was brought in, and I was amazed to see it served in a proper pot with porcelain cups. I poured it out.

"But seriously, professor," (he seemed to elicit a positive enjoyment from calling me professor) "what do you think of, say, the Rising Sun, or the Rising Moon?"

54

I translated the suggestion to Brian. "Poor old goddess of chastity!" he exclaimed.

"My friend thinks the Rising Moon is a good name," I interpreted. "Yet I think you could call it simply after yourself: David's Hotel, Chez David, you know."

"As a matter of fact, the last two hotels I owned were called each after one of my two sons. Haven't you heard of Micha's Hotel? It was a famous place."

I leaned forward in his direction and said in a low voice, "But I understand it was closed down by the police."

"In a way, yes."

"You had girls there, did you?"

"Your friend doesn't understand Arabic, does he? Well, to be honest with you, we did have girls. And—er—not only girls. To suit our clients' tastes, you know. It was such a fine place. . . ."

I was struck by his outspokenness. "This sort of thing is prohibited, though, isn't it?"

"Professor, may God give you long life, you should know a little grease in the right palm can go a long way. Yet it was by no means little, really. It cost me no less than fifty dinars a month to keep the hounds off. Unfortunately we got too many customers at the end, and the place became too well known for anybody's liking. There was a raid, of which I had been warned well beforehand, of course, and though nothing was proved I was advised to close the place for good. But I am starting a new life, professor. I've made enough money to run a clean honest establishment. That's why I'm giving this place a new name, though it's too small for my purpose. I should be grateful if you would tell your friends about it. Have you seen the telephone I've installed today? I have even discarded my old number."

"Since that is so, I think the Rising Moon should be an appropriate name."

55

Dawood gulped the last drops of tea in his cup and rose to his feet. "I am glad you agree with me," he said. He shook hands with Brian and myself and left.

For us it was all a great joke. On hearing the gist of Dawood's conversation Brian said, "The only honest thing about old Dawood is his beads. They're simply wonderful. The rest you can take with a pinch of salt. He wants a few respectable people to stay here as a cover for his profession."

Before the week was over I had observed two or three suspicious looking females slinking into the bedroom across the corridor.

Both Adnan and Husain were watching out for news of the prospective fornications and were sorry to hear that I was looking for an apartment elsewhere. Two days before I left, Shabo came into my room dressed like a prince, with a colourful turban and a brocade *zuboon*. He extended a mighty hand with horny fingers and said affectionately, "Jameel, I've come to say good-bye. I'm leaving for home."

"What a wonderful costume," I said.

"That's how I want my friends to see me when I arrive in my village. They'll probably envy me. They won't know I've had enough of this city. Good-bye and God bless you."

I quickly dug into my pockets and took out a dinar which I left in the palm of his hand as I shook hands with him.

"Give my best regards to your wife," I said.

"Thank you, thank you so much, Jameel. Look after yourself and let nobody in this city know what you think or do." With that piece of fatherly advice he went out, no longer on bare feet. No doubt before putting on any shoes he had shaken off his feet the dust of the city that for fifteen years had kept him a servant in a poor man's hotel.

On that very evening, coming out of a restaurant I glimpsed an old man sitting on the threshold of a closed shop, carry-

56

ing a small board covered with an array of lottery tickets. "Five thousand dinars . . ." came out his weak miserable voice. "Five thousand dinars . . ." he said, brandishing the tickets for me to look at them as I approached him.

"Mr. Jameel!" he exclaimed. "I nearly didn't recognise you."

It was poor Tobia, broken and abandoned.

"Four years they've sentenced him," he said, referring to his son Yousef. "Who says I'm going to live four more years selling these dirty tickets?"

# 9

In Rashid Street was the essence of all the cities of history, and the Tigris which cut the city neatly in two held in its expansive unhurried flow the memory of civilisations thousands of years old. The street and the river ran parallel to each other, like substance and reflection: the street, overcrowded but leisurely, was the embodiment of the vital forces of the river. No wonder the waters overwhelmed their banks in the spring and flooded the street and its wild extensions.

I spent long hours walking along the muddy banks of the Tigris, pursuing its course from north to south, from Kadhimiya where, beyond a long wobbly pontoon bridge, the golden minarets of the great mosque glittered in the sun, down through the vast lettuce fields and palm groves, through the gardens and the mud houses (grey dusty honeycombs, sores on a diseased limb, whose survival like that of their inmates in the merciless heat of long summers was nothing short of a miracle) swarming with black-vested barefooted women. They had jewelled rings in their nostrils and green arched lines tattooed in place of their plucked eyebrows. Naked children wallowed in the dust while their mothers poised on their heads large pots of brown cow-dung to be caked into fuel and heaped in little mounds around the huts. Next came the Royal Bilat and the modern residential areas. Then, further down, the bazaars: rugs and silks, calico and rushmats; the red of pomegranates and the green of emeralds pitted against the yellow of arid wastes. The blue minarets tilted against a dazzling sky on either bank and sent forth electrically amplified calls to prayer throughout a city of nearly a million people to whom the brown of dung-surrounded slums was no more strange than the flame-hued patterns of ornate carpets from Tabreez.

"But we do not accept things as we see them any more," Adnan said to Brian as we went on one of our perambulations through the sooq. Adnan wanted Brian Flint to know Baghdad from within. "Not your imaginary city of sheikhs and harems, but the earthy poverty-stricken city of men who hunger and love and hate and kill. You know what we've gone through for centuries. Centuries—that's our conception of the primary unit of time! For seven hundred years we have struggled with an ungenerous soil. Yes, we've got two mighty rivers, but the irrigation systems were destroyed by wave after wave of marauders until our earth was exhausted and our people learnt to accept their interminable servitude. Rulers from abroad came with their hordes and swept over the country; they brought little prosperity and less resilience. At last even the vestiges of historical pride were nearly obliterated, and the great city of the Abbasid empire was reduced to an ugly little place choked all about with shrubberies which only sheltered snakes and thieves."

"But it is not doing badly now, is it? Should I say thanks to oil?" Brian said.

58

"Oil, my foot," Adnan was irritated. "*Your* interest in us is because of oil. But we didn't know the importance of oil to us until very recently. It was mentally that we woke up, and that was at the turn of the century when we opened our eyes and had a nasty shock. Poverty and disease had ravaged us: from thirty million we had been reduced to five million, and the country had been turned into a waste land. This city, which had prided itself on its great university when Europe was in darkness, had fifty years ago. only a few primitive schools. But the last fifty years have been years of ferment. The intellectuals of Lebanon and Syria had breathed into the Arabs everywhere a first breath of regeneration shortly before the First World War. Nor was it easily done. The Ottoman Turks hanged one nationalist after another, but every corpse that dangled from the gibbets in the squares of Beirut and Damascus infused us with further pride and determination."

"And now?"

"Now? Well, you can see for yourself. We're caught in the web of power politics, oil politics, East and West politics."

"But you can't deny, Adnan, you've begun to have freedom now."

"Freedom? A wonderful catchword."

"Surely, it must mean something to somebody?"

"To me, freedom means release. We woke up with a bang and discovered the material progress of the West, its ideologies and political theories, and were horrified at our own stagnation. So we wanted release, flow, movement."

"Haven't you achieved some of that?"

"You know very well we haven't yet, Brian. Don't pretend to be ignorant when, like every other Englishman, you know more about our politics than we do ourselves."

Brian laughed. "We're always credited with far more wisdom than we could ever hope to possess. However, free-

59

dom is no easy thing, I imagine, after the servitude—as you put it—of so many centuries."

"Exactly. A double servitude: to evil masters from without, and to diseased powers from within. And both closely related. Now that the West has planted Israel on our doorstep, it'll get even worse."

We entered the Coppersmith Quarter where the clang of hammer and plate, in a dark arcade permeated with the smell of fire and metal, was like a hundred gongs going on at once. "As far as I can see," Brian said, "the forces at work in your lives are so numerous that they probably clash into futility. Just listen to this gay pandemonium!"

"They result in murder and waste," Adnan said in a loud but unemotional voice to be heard over the brassy din. "In strikes and uprisings and indefinite imprisonments and assassinations and hangings. There are forces that often pull back more mightily than those that drive ahead. Aren't these lovely pitchers?"

"These people, at least, are making something, freedom or no freedom. I must buy some of these delightful pots. Do they just beat them out of sheets of copper? How wonderful."

From one coppersmith to another we went handling shiny pots and ewers with long necks and curved beaks, and bargaining about prices. "It's sinful to bargain with artists," I said.

"But great fun, my dear fellow, great fun," Brian said.

# 10

"Mr. Farran," my landlady said, "your telephone rang a

dozen times to-day when you were out. You must have lots of friends."

My landlady was an Armenian widow of about forty-five. After her husband's death, she had occupied herself by running a pension. Her apartment in a building on Rashid Street was too small for more than two lodgers, one of whom was myself, but it was enough for her. I was given a large room with blue curtains, a broad bed without ends which in daytime, with its many cushions, looked like a comfortable divan, and a telephone.

Adnan called in the evening. "I'm angry with you," he said as he walked in. "I rang you up several times to-day. Aren't you ever in? I'm angry with you."

"I know." I said. "Because after the lecture yesterday I went away without talking to you."

"I wanted to congratulate you on your lecture. To think that anyone would want to listen to a lecture on Byron in Arabic! There must have been at least four hundred people in that hall. Aren't we a wonderful people? But I liked the . . . what shall I call it? . . . 'twist' you gave to Byron's satanism: you developed it into a thirst for freedom which made Byron want to fight for others' freedom. Am I right?"

"More or less," I said. I was tired of the subject.

"And it was a good thing you gave it to Husain to publish in his newspaper."

"He was so insistent, I couldn't avoid it."

"It might please you to know that they printed 300 copies more than usual to-day, and they were all gone by midday."

"But I won't be paid a fil for it."

"Of course not. You know, this is the second lecture you have given, and already a lot of people are talking about you."

"I'm getting popular," I said delightedly.

"God help you." His voice dripped with pity. It annoyed me.

"But I like being popular."

"I should avoid it like poison. Popularity in this city is the first sign of ruin. First, you'll draw too many people to you, women will get interested in you, you'll talk a great deal, everybody will know what you eat, what you wear, what you think. You become an actor, and everybody watches you. Then someone gets jealous. Another begins to worry about his daughter. A third finds you unduly influential. Someone will suspect you're a communist. Another will swear you have three different mistresses comprising the three different faiths. The police will watch you: you're seeing too many people, your politics are not exactly the right shade. Rumours will spread. Rumours will fecundate. Ten eyes dote but a thousand spy on you. At last, lo and behold, the great man, who was everybody's idol, has fallen. And when an ox is down, as the saying goes, the knives in his side will multiply."

"O Adnan, you're a God-damn pessimist!"

"Pessimist? Anyway, I rang you up today to tell you that Salma Rubeidi wants to see you."

"One of my admirers?"

"You don't know Salma. She collects people. Brian Flint is already in her collection."

"Who is she?"

"One of the leaders of society."

"Married, of course."

"To Ahmad Rubeidi, a silly old fool who must be now in his late sixties."

"And she, I suppose, is in her late twenties."

"Don't be absurd. No woman of that age could be a leading socialite. Still, she is under forty."

"I can imagine the rest, Adnan. She's a young woman

62

who is no more really young. She gives a party every night and sees to it that the guests are all young and good-looking. Right?"

"More or less. Mind you, we are related, and we are great friends, and her parties are impressive."

"Do you go to her parties?"

"Two or three times I did. But I didn't like the experience. All those top officials and oil men and ministers and diplomats and what have you. English is spoken as a rule, and I find it trying to speak English two hours at a stretch. Once I horrified Salma by insisting on speaking Kurdish to her guests. I'm Kurdish on my mother's side, you know. I went straight to a blond man who was saying something in English to a lady. I addressed him in Kurdish, thinking I might outrage him. To my utter surprise, he answered me in perfect Kurdish and quoted for my benefit a few verses from a Kurdish epic! Of course, he was a member of the British Embassy. But I'm forgetting about Salma," he went on. "I went round to see her this morning. Nothing in the world I hate more than my relatives. They don't like me very much, they just about tolerate me. I don't even tolerate them and I look forward to the day when I shall see them all blasted. But Salma is an exception. I love her and go round to see her whenever she is alone. In fact, intellectually she is my benefactress. She has an enormous library, two thousand books at least, most of which she brought with her from the States. If I know anything I owe it to her library. Well, I happened to mention your name to her, whereupon she immediately said, 'Do you know him? I want to get in touch with him!'"

"May I consider this the beginning of success?"

"She wants to see you."

"You might have given her my address and telephone number."

"I have already. She asked me to take you along one morning for a cup of coffee at her home."

"How about Friday morning?"

"Good. Friday morning at ten. I hope her husband won't be there. A stupid old man. A senator too. He owns thousands of acres of land and has been in politics all his life and travelled abroad a dozen times and is married to the most intelligent woman in town, and yet I don't think he's read more than a couple of books in the last thirty years."

"Perhaps if you owned a thousand acres of land you wouldn't want to read more than a couple of books every thirty years. Come, now." I laughed.

Adnan's voice suddenly changed into something harsh and unpleasant. "Shortly before my father's death, old fox Rubeidi had a quarrel with him over some land. What with his influence and cunning and my father's alcoholism, he took legal action against him and got the land. He hasn't managed to produce a son—or a daughter for that matter— although he's been married to Salma over fifteen years now. The land that should have been mine is now the property of an intolerable eunuch."

"You should try and wheedle it out of Salma," I suggested. "But knowledge is one thing, property another."

"Unfortunately." He paused. Laughing he added, "And yet, she recently gave me Karl Marx to read. Actually she gave me Karl Marx and the Bible. I found *The Capital* impossible to comprehend, so I took up the Bible. You know, were it not for the Jeremiahs and the Ezekiels, the Bible would be an extremely entertaining book."

I never knew how seriously to take Adnan. I thought he would have found his kinship with, if anything, the Jeremiahs and the Ezekiels. But I always felt that he deliberately gave an impression of himself as frivolous and cynical. I

64

was not certain that he had not spent many long nights over Karl Marx. I never forgot our short 'conspiracy' in the public bath. What was he up to exactly? For a moment I even wondered if he had not made up the whole thing about Salma and her husband. After all, I was seeing him almost every other day, and yet I did not know where and how he lived. And when somebody brought up the subject of women, he hardly ever spoke about any of his own recent experiences, although Husain often hinted that Adnan was a notorious lover. Where would he meet women, when he practically lived on the street and in coffee shops?

# 11

Friday morning, 10 o'clock. The gate was opened by a man-servant who led me and Adnan into the house. Salma made her appearance with the effective timing of an actress. I was startled to see a young-looking woman, tall and well-shaped, perhaps too well-shaped. Her make-up was a shade too heavy, and her breasts a shade too firmly thrust forward. Obviously she was a woman who would not give up youth easily.

I was duly introduced and we were taken to a large drawing-room, sparsely furnished but in very good taste.

"My husband would have liked to meet you, Mr. Farran," she said, "but he had to go out on some urgent business."

"I am very pleased, madam, that Adnan has made it possible for me to meet you," I said. "He told me so much about you that I wondered if he hadn't entirely invented you."

She laughed and offered us cigarettes from a box inlaid

65

with mother-of-pearl. "His imagination is always running away with him," she said.

"Salma!" Adnan said in a voice ringing with delight. "Nothing I say about you will ever do you justice."

"I'm very fond of you, too, Adnan," she said, as he jumped up to light her cigarette. Then turning to me she added, "But I wish he would look for a decent job somewhere. He never seems to tire of this life of the 'noble savage'."

"Quite a luxury, I should think," I said.

"I have the gutter in my blood, that's all," he commented.

"Don't we all?" said Salma.

I could not envisage the gutter behind her expensive clothes. "Surely not you, madam?" I said.

"Why not? Of course one can't always help one's circumstances, and, what's worse, one has to mature sooner or later."

"Only one doesn't know when maturity has been attained, does one?"

"Oh yes, one does," she said with melancholy. "Once it's there, you can't mistake it."

"Dear Salma," Adnan said impishly, "I am the eternal adolescent. I'll never mature. I am determined not to. After all, look at our society. It's so mature that it's rotting. People around here are born grey."

Salma laughed. "If ever I see you unadolescent, Adnan, I shall warn the world. It would mean a catastrophic change was threatening the order of things."

Suddenly Salma switched over to English and said, "Mr. Farran, I understand you're a college professor. Would you care to give some private lessons?"

My pride was deflated at once. "Private lessons?" I said, my voice replete with disappointment.

"Yes, private lessons in English. Not too elementary. Poetry, drama, Shelley, Keats, the moderns, you know, the

66

sort of thing you might do at college with a fairly advanced group."

"To whom?"

"To a young woman who, for special reasons, can't go to college."

I immediately thought of a girl with large suffering eyes and proudly curled lips upon a crippled body, a sort of Elizabeth Barrett, complete with the poetry, too. I groped for the way in which to say no. "Is it important to you that I should teach her?" I asked.

"Very."

"May I know who she is?" asked Adnan.

"Well, my niece Sulafa," she answered reluctantly.

Short of asking a point-blank question I could not see why she was so secretive about the matter. I suspected Adnan's colour changed a little when with a facial grimace and a nod of the head he expressed his understanding. Salma made it worse when she added, "I don't want you to tell anybody about it, please."

"Does she live in this house?" I inquired.

"She lives with her parents in a lovely house in Jafar Street. A perfect house right on the river."

"Frankly, Mrs. Rubaidi, I'm intrigued."

"You see, she is the daughter of Imad Nafawi. You've heard of Imad Nafawi, haven't you?"

"Not *the* Imad Nafawi, the Arabic scholar, who I believe was a Minister once upon a time?" I seemed to remember a book of his on an ancient Arab poet which I had actually found very tedious.

"Well, he will not allow his daughter to go to college. He's against the mixing of the sexes, no matter where. I've been getting private teachers to educate Sulafa all the same. To that he has no objection, as long as I pick the teachers myself. He's my brother-in-law, you know."

"But you've gone to college. I can judge by your American accent."

"Yes, I went to Wellesley in the United States. Years and years ago, when for a woman to be educated was a deadly sin."

"What does he say to that?"

"Oh, he's reconciled to it by this time. But he worships his daughter, and you will like him when you meet him. You see, he has little faith in our theories about life and change. As far as he is concerned, if there is any change it's for the worse, a sort of sliding down to chaos."

"Men," said Adnan in a pompous voice, "are a compound of different kinds of evil, and nothing but the greatest discipline could instil a drop, just a drop, of goodness into such a compound. Such is Imad Nafawi's opinion of humanity."

"You have reason to remember that," Salma said with a smile.

"I certainly have." Adnan said. "The compound that's me, according to him, is evil through and through. But the corruption, the cruelty, the poverty, the evil rampant in our lives, Imad Nafawi prefers not to comment on." Adnan's voice had soured.

"Don't be wearisome, Adnan."

"I'm sorry. My argument is as old as the Creation. All great arguments are."

"And one day, I suppose, all you young people will give point to your argument by hanging us in our gardens." Salma laughed.

Adnan also laughed. "If that becomes necessary, well. . . ."

"That's just where you and all your street protegés are wrong. You fancy yourselves as rebels, capable of the greatest bloodshed. You think it's all like these idiots who go around knifing their sisters and wives, thinking they're serving the cause of virtue." She stood up, seeming to have suddenly remembered something. "But you're fooling no one. You don't have the guts to undertake one task which requires tenacity or self-sacrifice. You're all self-willed and self-motivated, exactly like your rulers. You can't even be as functional and serviceable as they are. In fact, you're worse than your rulers. Excuse me." She walked out to the hall and I heard her dial the telephone.

In a subdued voice I told Adnan that Salma had given him a piece of her mind.

"Rubbish!" he said. "This is the voice of fear." He got up and offered me another cigarette from the box with the mother-of-pearl inlay and took one himself.

I looked at a large reproduction of one of Monet's lovely cathedrals hanging over a bookshelf. Out of the luminous Gothic windows emerged the stark twisted girders of Leila's ruined house and ours. My imagination never stopped playing that trick on me.

Salma was back in a minute or two. "They're all nihilists, Mr. Farran," she said, "they're all nihilists." With all the inconsequence in the world she added, "I've called Imad Beg to tell him you have agreed to teach his daughter."

I did not recall that I had agreed, but I did not correct her.

"Would 5 p.m. tomorrow be all right?" she asked. "If you wait in your apartment, the Nafawis' chauffeur will collect you. I've given Imad Beg your address."

# 12

As arranged, at five the following afternoon I was called for and driven in a black Humber to Jafar Street. Imad ud-Deen Nafawi, or Imad Beg, as everybody respectfully called him, received me at the entrance of a large two-storey house standing in the midst of palm and eucalyptus trees. It had an extensive well-trimmed garden with a lawn and tiled path edged with flowers. Imad Beg, tall, stern and pale, with a long nose and a large bluish mouth, was wearing a voluminous brown cloak under which, whenever he moved his arms, I could see his European clothes. He offered me a soft delicate hand to shake and was effusive in his welcome. Though never good at this kind of ceremony I exerted myself to match the generous words of the old gentleman with words of my own. He took me to a small room whose walls were covered with books all, I could tell by their appearance, Arabic, Persian or Turkish. We sat on a divan with a Persian rug for cover and a boy in a long gown brought me a cup of Turkish coffee.

"You must forgive me," Imad Beg said, "I am not allowed to drink any coffee or tea. Now tell me please, where were you educated?"

Try as I could, I failed to conceal my excitement. After all, I argued with myself, I had gone there merely to give lessons to a girl. But the elaborate manner with which the preliminaries were conducted heightened my expectation. I was being seduced into an illusion, and I was conscious of giving way to it.

When finally I was conducted by my host upstairs to a neatly furnished room—the river glistened through a couple of windows that faced me—I wanted to reassure myself I had not been hypnotised. Against one of the windows in silhouette stood a girl with her back to us, against the light of a setting sun.

"Sulafa!" her father almost shouted. "This is Professor Jameel Farran."

She was slow in turning round. She bowed her head a little and said, "*Ahlan wa sahlan.*"

"Sulafa has friends at the college where you teach," said Imad Beg. "I want you to teach her exactly the same subjects as those you teach them. What's more, I want you to see that she learns the stuff better than they do."

I could not help laughing. "I teach English only," I said. "Her friends are likely to be studying many other subjects."

"English will be enough for the education of any lady. Our ancestors used to study nothing more than grammar and theology and yet they were a hundred times more civilised than we are. Please be seated," he continued. "Sit down, Sulafa. Allow me to leave you now to discuss your work together."

On his way out he turned on the light, and I discovered that a servant was standing by.

When we sat down at the opposite ends of the room, the servant squatted on a stool by the door. And ever after that he stuck to that stool to keep us company. He was the third party, the chaperon, God's ruthless eye. Indeed, he was there to obey our slightest whim: to open the window, draw the curtains, move a table, put a book back on the shelf. But he was there positively, irremovably, however unobtrusive he made himself by his silence, his vacant look, his occasional dozing. His name was Abed, which means slave. It was probably the short of Abdullah, 'the slave of God', but no one bothered to go beyond the first syllable of his name. It fitted his posture, his movement, his soul.

It was his duty to receive me at the gate. The Nafawis' Humber took me to their house and back each time without fail; if Imad Beg was using the car at the particular hour of Sulafa's lesson, Abed collected me in a taxi. He would open the door for me, accompany me with infinite respect to Sulafa's study, perch on his seat until the hour was over, see me off to the waiting Humber, open its door and intone the

71

same reverential "In God's peace!" as he shut it at last behind me.

But what of Sulafa? Did I need to be interviewed by her aunt and her father before I could see her, protected as she was by that relentless slave of God? I had fancied her as an Emilia Viviani, imprisored like 'a bird in a cage', to be visited by an ethereal Shelley who would soon find in her misery, let alone her loveliness, a cause for love, spiritual or otherwise. But she soon dispelled such unwarranted fancies in me. She possessed the loveliness but seemed to lack the misery I had preferred to imagine. She had the infernal pride of an ancient family, though I could not see on what achievement such a family did actually pride itself. Family pride often becomes a habit whose origins are difficult to determine. With her finely chiselled nose and large black eyes in which emotion was as difficult to see as in the wide-eyed sockets of a mask, Sulafa at first exhibited all her haughtiness and none of her misfortune. She was always smartly dressed, her room was full of books, and even during our lesson hour she would receive several telephone calls from her girl friends. She could at any time use her father's car but only if she went out in the company of a female relative or a trusted female friend; otherwise humble unobtrusive Abed would sit by the chauffeur to obey every wish of hers, ostensibly, but more likely to prevent any contact with men.

During the first few weeks Sulafa, whatever I thought, never revealed so much as the shadow of complaint or resentment. Twice a week I went to that room of hers hanging over the Tigris to find each time that she had done more work than I had prescribed. But I was beginning to be restless. I was careful never to be personal with her. Each time I trod on that tiled path that led from the gate to the house I knew that I was treading on explosive ground. I was too

72

busy, I thought, with my work, with the effort to reconstruct my existence and reintegrate my life. Back in Bethlehem, among thousands of hungry refugees, I had my family to keep alive, so I could ill afford to embark upon an adventure that might make life for them and myself more uncertain still. In the midst of all this I hugged the memory of Leila, of the ruins in Jerusalem that had once buried the torn body I had loved. Was it not possible after seeing Sulafa a dozen times and reading Shakespeare's tragedies with her to fuse the two women into one, to imagine the lifeless hand of Leila quicken into the dark hand of Sulafa? I had to remind myself over and over again that in this strange resuscitated city there were whirlwinds of custom and creed that admitted of no personal whims and threatened with death all that stood in their way or foolishly attempted to stay their course. Sulafa was therefore to be no more than any other student I taught, for whom the only significance I should have was in my power to stimulate her mind. Her mind, and no more.

But Sulafa's eyes were inescapable. Although I sat yards away from her and only occasionally was I close enough to her, usually near the bookshelf, to hear her breathing or smell her faint perfume, I knew that we were becoming necessary to each other. I wanted to overstay my time with her, and no sooner had I left her and walked downstairs and got into the waiting car than I wished to be back again. The days between one session and another began to acquire a feeling of emptiness; they became an odious gap that had to be filled. And once Sulafa looked up at me and laughed. "You called me Leila just now," she said. "Is she a girl friend of yours?"

"Did I? I am sorry," I said. It was the easiest error to make. Oh, Leila, Leila! She had become a symbol, a symbol of woman. And whenever in an hour of loneliness I was visited by the thought of woman, it was still Leila who came

73

to me, until I wondered whether the love of women would always be for me an echo of her love. Would the sign never change with the passage of days and the change of the objects of desire? Would Leila's long hair falling over her eyes remain a constant image of other women's hair even when styles had changed? Was she to remain like Eve, a prototype, a reference, an everlasting legend?

Baghdad, at least for a stranger, had an atmosphere charged with sex. Whether it was the unavoidable association with the Arabian Nights, its dry air, or the scarcity of normal contact with women in it, I could not tell. Venus never had easier employment than on the banks of the Tigris. Leila, however, would not desert me. Even when I longed for Sulafa's touch, it was Leila who often posed for my longing in the rooms of the mind. Whenever I caught myself perpetrating this act of imposture upon myself I said to myself, "Why don't I leave the dead to death and uproot this yellow hand from my brain?" But she had become the embodiment of temptation, of sexual beauty, and love for me had meant her hair, her lips, her thighs, her hands. And then I saw her in pieces and touched her blood with my fingers. How could Sulafa replace her?

But the victory of the living over the dead was a foregone conclusion. Or was it? For the dead had strong allies even among the living themselves. One barrier after another stood between Sulafa and myself. Barriers of faith and custom and tradition. Was a Moslem woman ever allowed to marry a Christian? I, though Arab from remotest time, was Christian. Would a father like Imad Beg, keeping his daughter away from common gaze, allow a stranger to his family to express his interest in her? People here have been killed for less. Let Abed, the irremovable, implacable Abed, lurk upon his stool in order to pounce upon the slightest love that might move from its hiding place! If Leila's ghost could

74

be laid, how was this three-headed Cerberus to be blinded and put to silence? Society had placed him there as a guardian spirit and, like all guardian spirits, he was ever awake.

# 13

"Although the women glorify you," Adnan began. He cleared his throat and looked significantly at the small circle of young men around him. Immediately they knew he was about to recite his latest poem: his face lit up, his eyes expanded and became tense. The 'casino' by the river was bursting with men and hoarse with noise. Istikans clinked, domino pieces fell on tables with successive smacks, trick-track dice rattled, and the radio brayed mightily over all. But Adnan's circle was hushed, each trying to exclude from his hearing all sounds except that of Adnan's voice which rose like a shout over a booming sea, as his hand, with extended fingers, rhythmically rose and fell:

> "Although the women glorify you,
> A symbol of their ancient lust,
> Upon a palm-tree they'll crucify you
> With mouth wide open for midday dust.
>
> They'll dance around your quartered limbs
> And pour their arak at your feet
> And tell you of their secret whims
> And seize your genitals to eat.
>
> They'll eat your eyes in their despair
> And cry to see your lips unkissed,
> And as they dance their backs they'll bare,
> And thorns will grow where they have pissed."

"Magnificent!" the listeners roared in unison. "Repeat, repeat!"

With an even greater boom in his voice—it was his usual histrionic trick ("What's poetry reading if not dramatic and oracular?" he would say), Adnan declaimed his poem again.

"But how bitter," Abdul Kader Yassin said. He was a long-haired sallow-faced fellow with theories of his own about everything, from poetry to rebellion.

"Not bitter enough, I say," Husain answered. "You must remember the age of roses and dawns of pearly dew is gone. We want a caustic, harsh, provocative kind of poetry."

"I'm afraid it's no more than a pose," Abdul Kader said. "Which means it's false."

"False, false!" Adnan mimicked. "It's new; it's the summing up of a hundred experiences. The experience may be yours or somebody else's, what does it matter?"

"I mean it's false," Abdul Kader said, "in the sense that it is not true to life."

"And what is true to life? The tedious wisdom of ancient books? The realism of modern novels? Who was it who said, 'The sweetest poetry is that most charged with lies?' It would have been more profound to say 'The *truest* poetry is that most charged with lies.' For centuries our poets have invented their lies for the sake of sweetness: I'd rather invent them for truth, my kind of truth. And since the truth of life is dirt, bitterness, treachery, evil—who of our sweet old poets would have dared to admit it?—bitterness shall be the end of all poetic falsehood-truth. I leave the roses and the dews of dawn to you."

"Who wants them?" Abdul Kader's lips were taut, cruel. "I want art to be the voice of the people, not the ramblings of crazy individuals. The poet should worry about the ail-

76

ments of his people and suggest a cure for them and tell them a great future awaits them all."

"He should be guided by political principles," piped in Kareem. "He could then act as a guide to his people."

"I know all your theories," Adnan said.

"The usual bla bla," Husain added.

"I am inclined to agree with Adnan," I said. "Humanity has always had prophets and religious teachers and political leaders and learned economists to advise it on what to do, what to avoid, what to think, where to go. And yet humanity is in a sorry state. I don't think poets and artists could achieve much in that respect either. So we can have them create their art for our delight, if nothing else. Perhaps through delight man may achieve a higher state of grace."

"Delight in bitterness," Adnan said.

"I want understanding, not delight," Abdul Kader Yassin said. "If understanding comes through bitterness, bitterness may perhaps be forgiven."

"And it must be put to the service of our people," Kareem said.

"It should aim at creation through destruction," Abdul Kader expounded. "How to do that is our problem. It's a problem which we must face." Abdul Kader had big deep-socketed eyes undershadowed by crescents of blue. His bony cheeks and square jaws suggested a living skull. Everything for him was a 'problem' to be tackled mercilessly and with purpose. With every statement he made his eyes flashed. "Our problem," he continued, "is how to harness the arts to the cause of the poor and the ignorant. The blight of our literature has been this excessive futile individualism of authors who remove themselves from contact with the masses."

"Individualism, rubbish!" Adnan said. "I don't think

77

we've had enough individualism in our authors. They're all general, flabby, sentimental: just the right thing for a public with the modicum of literacy such as ours. They even try to teach us, the idiots. Nor do they remove themselves from contact with the masses. They merely have that passionate delusion that the way to elevate the populace is to revive ancient learning. They simply wallow in antiquarianism. They're not satisfied with the scholars whose job it is to bore into the layers of buried thought, they want us all to do the same. Can there be a greater confusion of historical amateurishness with creative thought? That's why you can't tolerate them. No one can, either, and they are gradually falling into healthy silence. But the only literature that will survive is the work of obstinate minds that don't care two hoots for your masses."

"Such minds are like acrobats among a crowd of cripples. We don't want them. We want those who know how to use their limbs profitably, so they can teach others how to use theirs. The problem, of course, is not entirely literary."

"No, it is not entirely literary," Kareem echoed. "It is political."

"The everlasting bla bla," Husain said. "So whenever I go with a poem to Samiha at the Brothel I must go with a political message, hey? I'd much rather go, as I always do, with a poem about herself. I don't touch her, mind you. I don't think gonorrhœa on an empty stomach is a healthy thing. I am simply moved by beauty and pity, by the curse of evil on the lust of life, as you might say, that's all."

"You're decadent, Husain!" Kareem said.

"So I am decadent, am I? I live in a palatial house, I have two cooks, three servants and a chauffeur. My Cadillac is next year's model, and I keep four mistresses. Of course I am decadent."

78

We laughed. Even Abdul Kader smiled, holding his pipe between his teeth.

"You deserve an extra istikan of tea for that," Adnan said. "Boy!" The tough, bare-chested, unshaven waiter jumped forth. "Another istikan of tea, and see that it is one of your best!"

"Immediately, sir," the waiter said and disappeared in the throng.

"I saw you again," Adnan said to me in a whisper. "You keep looking at your watch."

"You know I am invited to dinner at Salma Rubeidi's tonight," I whispered back.

"Plenty of time. It isn't eight yet. You can walk there in ten minutes."

"Yes, yes, I know."

In the previous few weeks I had seen Salma three or four times at Imad Nafawi's, each time for a few minutes on my way out after Sulafa's lesson. She left me a written invitation to dinner with Sulafa herself. When I asked my pupil whether she would be there too, she laughed, actually laughed. "I hear a lot about dinner parties," she said, "but that doesn't mean I may go to them."

"Why?"

"For obvious reasons."

"Well, you're not missing much."

"I don't miss a thing I've never known. But is it true that at such parties guests speak in innuendo and that . . . intrigue . . . love intrigue . . . gets very active?"

"That sort of thing is highly overrated by people who only hear about it."

"I've seen it in films. I just wonder. You should see one of our women's gatherings at home. You would think from their conversation there was nothing in the world but love, apart from gambling."

79

I was glad to see her digress, however little, from the grammar I was teaching her at that moment, but I was not ready yet to discuss with her whether there was anything in the world but love, apart from gambling. I dismissed the subject with a laugh to which she did not respond.

Judging by my companions' conversation in the 'casino' tonight, there seemed to be one or two things to occupy some people's minds other than love. Wherever they went they carried sweat-soiled thumb-worn books on which they sat or placed their tea glasses, but which they read and re-read, and argued about as if they had been their own great productions. But what often wearied me in such gatherings was the way in which they became excited and querulous about elementary ideas. It was with an exertion of the will that I put myself in their place to experience the thrill of discovering such creaky ideas for the first time. They were like someone looking at the Tigris and suddenly yelling, "Look, it moves! And there are fish in it!"

Abdul Kader was holding forth on the view that all stories from now on should be taken from the lives of farmers, beggars, criminals and whatever society held in contempt or considered as its refuse, in order to disclose what he called the sickness in our blood, when everyone of the listeners screamed with joy at the sight of Towfiq al Khalaf passing by, and invited him to come in and join us. I had never seen him before. He was tall, thin, with narrow eyes which in the dim light I suspected were blue, and sharp as the point of a knife. He wore a bedouin's cloak which, as soon as I was introduced to him, he parted to reveal a cartridge belt he had on underneath (he might have just come back from the wars), and said, "My pride and my disgrace!"

"I think it is superb," I said.

"It is superb," he proudly said, "but whenever I meet a brother from Palestine I realise what a disgrace it is that I should wear it here and not on the battle front in Palestine."

We were all moved, and he knew it. He sat down and tea was ordered for him.

Kareem, Abdul Kader's ineffectual shadow, appeared to know what would provoke our guest. "We were talking," he said, "about literature and the people."

"I am happy each time I come back from my tribe to see you are still talking," Towfiq said and laughed. "Trust us for talking!"

"We were talking about poets and writers," Kareem persisted. "Abdul Kader thinks that all our stories should——"

"I know, I know. One thing, however, you never seem to learn. That stories, painting, music, and the other appendages of your impotent life, are the mere fabrications of civilisation."

"So you think we should or should not encourage them to thrive?" I asked.

"You don't have to encourage them," he said. "Civilisation will do that for you. You know civilisation means deterioration?"

"Oh?"

"It means a sickness, a corruption. Art is the outcome of such corruption. It is the poisonous exhalation of the vast swamp that so-called civilisation is."

Nudging me, Adnan gave me a significant glance as if to say, 'Let him go on.'

"You therefore think there should be no art?" I asked.

"It depends whether you want your civilisation. Obviously every artist, every story writer, every novelist, stabs with his poisonous dagger at life's healthy body, since he serves the cause of 'civilisation'. What is civilisation? It is, as you can tell from the derivation of the word, the life of cities. Cities thrive at the expense of the countryside, far away from the real sources of human energy. And what do you get? This. . . ." He made a wide gesture with his hand to imply the great crowd in the café. "Sitting on their buttocks, talking all day long, getting bored, getting restless, getting impotent—so impotent in fact that most city women are either lesbians or whores, because they are never sexually satisfied by their men. That is civilisation. The artists come, and out of their sickness and impotence they spin out gorgeous dreams. Dreams? It's rather a vomit. You want your civilisation? You get the vomit. Ha ha ha!" He looked around and shouted, "Boy! Water, water!" Then with a vigorous grunt he cleared his nose and throat and shot a large blob of phlegm on the floor.

"Your nonsense again," Abdul Kader said. "Isn't it bad enough that the desert has been devouring our cities and fertile lands for centuries that you want us now to stop resisting it?"

"I don't care in the least whether you stop resisting it or not," Towfiq said and gulped the glass of water poured out for him by the waiter from a brass pitcher. "I only said art is the vomit of civilisation, which itself is a disease. Each time I go back to live in God's pasture lands, amidst the bleating sheep and the barking dogs, I get more convinced of it. Have you ever been on horse-back?"

"Why should I want a horse when I can ride in a car?" Abdul Kader said with the pipe in his mouth.

"A car bought from America with the sweat of your arse, when you may have a fine Arab horse? Have you ever ridden a camel? Of course not. Have you ever slept in a tent? Have you ever prayed the dawn's prayer in the middle of a boundless circular horizon? Have you ever spent a night of vigil with a loaded gun? Ever known a raid, a real honest raid that depends purely on your personal courage and enterprise? Ever had some exploit to tell—or ever listened to one, *listened*, not read one? Of course not." His tea came

82

and he drank it in two gulps. "That is the genuine way of Arab life, and that alone will survive."

He cast a sudden piercing look at me and continued: "Do I understand that you are a professor? You're most likely to have studied abroad, and people who have been contaminated with European thought will not stomach my kind of belief. But you agree, don't you, that the Arabs lost their force and drive only when they settled in the cities they had conquered. They were softened up by the luxury of the infidel. But where had they got their original force from? The desert. The desert is our stronghold: it is our bread and our water. What, then, would bring vigour back to the Arabs? The answer could not be more obvious: a return to the desert. A return to the desert's austerity and moral code. A return to the simple ideas of honour and courage. A return to the age-old conflict between one tribe and another which would keep us healthy and alert. There your stories will not come out of the dreams of frustrated moronic individuals, who think love is the latest discovery of man and who, nevertheless, out of the whole domain of love will only get a bit of masturbation." He forced a laugh. "Forgive my language. We sons of the desert have no use for euphemisms. We call a spade a spade: our stomachs are good and our enjoyment is direct and physical. Our stories out there are the stories of real men and authentic incidents. We don't have to record them in books, we keep them alive by word of mouth. We are our own works of art, and everything else is dead and worthless. Do you know the story of the bedouin who once felt the urge to make a statue? He wanted to make a statue for a dead woman he had loved, but he had no material to work with. But he had a quantity of dates. So he made it of dates. Next morning he was hungry, so he ate the statue! And rightly too. Sir, we are our own works of beauty, thank God, the one and only artist."

At that Adnan burst out into a resounding guffaw. "We are our own works of beauty indeed!" he said. "O heavenly piece of self-deception! The ugly, emaciated creatures of al-Asima's slums are their own works of beauty too."

"It is your city that has degraded them, your vile civilisation," Towfiq rejoined.

"And the peasants of the Southern Swamps, who live immersed in the rice bogs until their flesh peels off their feet and ankles—they are works of beauty too!" Adnan said.

Abdul Kader gave Towfiq no time to rebut when he said: "Our enemies would simply love every word you uttered, Towfiq."

"What the hell do you mean?"

"The Zionists would love us to believe we should all go back to the desert."

Towfiq's eyes glared in a rage. "You son of a bitch," he yelled. "We've seen the likes of you in the Palestine War. I know the number of hairs on your backsides, each one of you. You filled the world with talk, talk, talk, but at the moment of action your pants fell off your backs. And why? Because the British and the Americans disagreed with you. Had it not been for us, the tribesmen, the British would be on your backs in this country even now."

"We've had no proper political organisation," Kareem said. "But we don't advocate a return to the arid wastes to bury our heads in the sand."

"You don't have faith, that's what is ailing you. You're full of words, but not a touch, not a shade, of faith in them. You may have all the organisation in the world and yet remain the poor insignificant lot that you are. Come and live with us in the desert tents for but one month, and I'll teach you what it means to possess faith and pride in your impotent little selves."

Towfiq was a live wire, dangerous to touch. He could

out-talk all those whom he condemned for excessive talk, and despite his hatred of civilisation he must have spent a number of years in the midst of it when he went to college, which he obviously had done. Though they disagreed with his views, the other boys admired his eloquence and seemed to love to hear him speak. They probably pulled his leg a little too, merely to make him talk further. But they knew they could not dispose of his remarks very easily. With their hesitant probings and questionings they must have found his gigantic self-confidence quite withering. "Towfiq al-Khalaf is a problem, a big problem, you know," Abdul Kader said to me, and struck a match to light his pipe again.

Already it was half-past-eight, and I had to keep my dinner appointment at the Rubeidis'.

I should have hated to find I knew nobody there but the hostess. But Brian was there, having come back the day before from his trip to the North where he had seen the Assyrian ruins of Nimrud and the tough warlike Kurds. Ahmad Rubeidi, to whom I was introduced by Salma, was listening to Brian's remarks on Kurdish hand-weaving. He was a little wiry silver-haired man, sprucely dressed, who spoke with the rapidity of a man answering a question as if he had answered it a hundred times before. I must have been the last guest to arrive and Salma, having got me a drink from the tray held by a servant in white clothes, stood next to me while we listened to her husband's talk on rugs (a blind spot in my education, I confessed) which was illustrated by his reference to the carpet on which we were standing. I was then introduced to Professor Braithwaite, an eminent Assyriologist, who together with his wife joined us in our scrutiny of the stitching of the carpet. Salma took me round and introduced me to the other guests: a couple of Englishmen, an American from the U.S. Embassy and his wife, and two bright-eyed girls just back from college in

America. The Rubeidis' drawing room betrayed good taste and many servants. I noticed three paintings on the wall which had not been there on my first visit to Salma, and I told her so. We walked away to examine them separately.

"I got them last year from Italy," she said. "When you came here some time ago I had sent them to be re-framed. This is by——"

"Don't say it. Let me guess," I said. "Chirico! Right?

"Right! Have you seen it before?"

"No, but I think I could guess his style. Let me see if I can guess the others." Unfortunately I couldn't: twentieth-century impressionists are so numerous and so unmemorable.

"They are my husband's choice. He is terrified by the moderns."

Presently the two girls back from America joined in the conversation, and Salma withdrew to perform the functions of the good hostess. One of the girls said she painted a little whenever she could afford the time: she had learnt how to handle oils from a painter in Madison when she was a student at the University of Wisconsin. Soon Salma was back. Almost in a whisper, she said: "How is Sulafa doing?"

"Very well," I said. And dinner was announced.

The conversation during dinner (with much white wine) was steady, varied and crisp. It changed almost with the change of courses, I felt, and was now personal, between one guest and another, now general, for all to hear. (Against the wine and the sophistication I remembered the disputants in the 'casino' by the river less than a mile away and wondered where they had got in their arguments.) Professor Braithwaite, the Assyriologist, spoke about Tiglath Pileser II and Ashur Banipal as if they had been his pals: a gap of some three thousand years was certainly nothing to him.

"There are fires in Kirkuk," Ahmad Rubeidi said, "which have been burning for sixty thousand years. What is time?"

"The eternal fires!" Brian said. "The burning furnace into which the Babylonian king threw Daniel's three prophetic friends, or so I was told. It is sad to learn that such eternal fires are not an entrance to hell but merely the burning of a natural gas seepage."

"The scientists spoil one's fun," the American diplomat's wife said. "I'm sure, though, Nebuchadnezzar—I can never pronounce his name properly—did not eat grass with the swine in Babylon. What do you think, Professor Braithwaite?"

"Even if he did," the archæologist said, "no inscription to that effect has been found."

We laughed. And Salma said: "Which reminds me of Jerusalem." The servant was holding a silver dish at my left for me to help myself to a piece of turkey, when Salma added: "I spent a wonderful week in it three years ago. I've never seen a more beautiful city."

."The most beautiful in the world," I said.

"Silver Jerusalem, golden Jerusalem," the archæologist seemed to chant.

"Jerusalem of the emerald and the violet," I put in gratuitously.

"How does that poem go? My memory is really hopeless," the archæologist said.

Prompted by a wicked whim I recited lines I had written during my undergraduate days: "The city whose sky is a vast sapphire, a shell washed by the sea, fit for the birth of a new Aphrodite every morning. . . . I don't remember the exact lines, I'm afraid."

"That's an Arabic poem, I suppose," one of the Englishmen said.

"Yes," I said.

"So the Arabs have mentioned Aphrodite in their poetry?" the American diplomat asked.

87

"The moderns among them are most eclectic," explained Professor Braithwaite with a conniving glint in his eyes. "Do you remember any more?" Deliberately he made himself my accomplice.

"Er . . ." I hesitated for a second. "The land of brown earth and rose-tinted stone, of the olive trees since the Flood evergreen, and blood-red anemones: has not the soil been sodden with the blood of Adonis and of Christ? . . ."

"Gee," the girl back from Wisconsin said, "it must be a wonderful place."

"I've never known narcissi to grow in such abundance as in Jerusalem," the archæologist said. "In the spring the hills and the valleys are strewn with millions of wild flowers. Disgusting, what happened there last year."

Mr. Rubeidi at the other end of the table said: "The British played a foul game there. Very foul, if I may say so."

"Ah—but they were not the only ones who did," Professor Braithwaite said and cast a meaningful glance at the American opposite him.

Suddenly I became aware of the sound of our knives and forks hitting the plates: it was eerie and hostile. But the awareness did not last long. As the conversation progressed ideas were flying off at tangents. All the horror I had known was reduced to a witty remark here and there. When our plates were replaced by the servants and crêpe suzette was served, Salma with delightful inconsequence said: "Let me see who can guess what liqueur has been used in your sweet."

"Kummel?" Mrs. Braithwaite said.

"No," Salma said.

There was a happy buzz of conjecture and comment, and someone compared the sweet to a thing he had eaten once in a superlative restaurant in Place St. Michel in Paris. Paris: each one seemed to sigh over his memories of Paris; if he had no memories of it, he had dreams. But although

I had spent a whole summer in Paris, at that particular moment I could not remember a thing. Instead, the streets of Jerusalem unfolded simultaneously before my eyes, rising, falling, bending, with the white-stone buildings refracting the light, shedding the glow of silver and gold which shimmers in the imagination of all lovers long parted. Salma Rubeidi's sweet, however, was delicious and I did not deny it. They all declared it was very delicious indeed.

It was nearly midnight when the guests began to leave. I had drunk some brandy after dinner, but in spite of feeling inwardly warm and well-fed, I was disconsolate. I wanted to see Adnan and talk to him again, so I walked back alone while a soft cold wind blew across the river, moist and refreshing. At the 'casino' where I had left my friends I found the café had turned into a vast empty hall, with the chairs placed legs up on the tables that were ranged in lines along the walls. Tattered newspapers were blown about on the soiled floor. In a corner lit by a solitary naked light a few men sat chatting quietly amidst the litter of cigarette butts. Husain sat alone there reading a magazine.

"Where are the boys?" I asked him.

"They've gone to 'The Golden Nights' with Towfiq to drink arak," he said. "I couldn't go. I have to lift three or four articles from these magazines for my paper."

'The Golden Nights' was a neighbouring bar. I was going there when I saw Adnan and Towfiq come out, laughing loudly. They were reeling conspicuously.

As soon as he glanced at me Adnan yelled, "So you're back from Salma's are you? Lucky boy!"

"Lucky bastard!" Towfiq said. "Salma is such a beautiful woman."

"And if you have Salma Rubeidi for a friend you needn't worry about a thing," Adnan said and limped forward.

"You're drunk," I said.

89

"Drunk? Salma is my relative. I love her and honour her. But she has shoved herself into that hateful, false atmosphere, in order to have herself surrounded by guests day and night . . . day and night . . . and she won't speak a word other than English. I've a mind to call on her tomorrow and give her a piece of my mind."

"Excellent!" said Towfiq. "We'll carry her off to the desert and veil her and keep her in a tent with the women and the goats. Let her speak English there to her heart's content."

"What desert, Towfiq? Won't even arak wash away the sand from your brain?"

"The sand? It's cleaner and purer than all these houses, stuffed with God knows what diseased human beings, and all these miserable streets about which you've been writing love songs all your life."

"Oh, if only you knew what I should like to see happen to these streets which I love. I should like to see them blown upside down, our houses torn empty, our women filling the alleyways with drunken orgies, and blood running knee-deep everywhere. No cities, no art for the people, no politics, no brothels, no dinner parties. Nothing but a howling chaos, while Abdul Kader Yassin removes his pipe from between his teeth to drink from the piss of the masses, and Salma pours out her French wine to ten carcasses around her, and I croak with my latest poem over the ruins."

Adnan's voice vibrated in the deserted street like a bell in a valley of rock and thorn. He was pushing us along the tree-lined sidewalk as he spoke, pausing between one step and another, his hand going up and down as though along with it his words would rise and fall.

"And then," Towfiq said, "I'd mount you on a thorough-bred horse and give you a rifle and teach you what it means to be a man at last."

"I leave all manliness to you. But you are obstinate, Towfiq. You prefer your goat to our women, and yet you cannot keep away from whores three weeks on end. Come to me and I'll teach you what it means to be angry and yet afraid, and you'll know how despair can tear the heart, the brain, the bowels to pieces. Oh no, Towfiq, I want none of your 'works of beauty', I want none of Abdul Kader's art pimping to the poor and the illiterate. Ough . . . I want, I want . . . heaven to topple down upon the earth, while people hold their bowels and groan, and files of policemen level their guns at the women's brains, while you and I and the others perch on the street ruins yawping like crows . . ."

He hiccuped and apologised, then hiccuped again. He leaned against a tree and said, "And then . . . we shall be immortalised by the secret files of . . . ough. . . ."

His mouth burst with vomit. We held him up: he was soft as a piece of dough. Towfiq reproached him affectionately. "Didn't I tell you," he said, "not to drink too much arak if you hadn't had any supper?"

Adnan vomited again, and Towfiq whispered to me: "Poor boy. He hasn't got a penny for a decent meal."

We then helped him to sit on the sidewalk and rest.


# 14


After that evening, each time I went to give a lesson to Sulafa I was likely to see Salma with her, and she would stay for a few minutes to talk about a book she might have recently received from a bookseller at Oxford or tell me about some of the people I was getting to know—largely through her. Once you entered the magic circle of the cocktail society of Baghdad, you were in it for as long as your energy held out. For I was soon asked to parties by people to whom I had hardly said how-do-you-do, and in most cases found Ahmad and Salma Rubeidi there—inveterate party-goers, as it seemed. Adnan and Husain delighted in making fun of that mode of life: Adnan consciously rejecting it—"There are more people I can talk to with profit in the cafés by the river than at any cocktail party," he said with conviction, and Husain feeling left out of it because society had totally ignored him.

Adnan was one day in my room when the landlady ushered in a man with a bunch of yellow roses. "The lady says she hopes you will soon recover," the fellow said and handed me the sweet bouquet like a lover, and I blushed to my hair roots because the lady referred to was Salma and the man was her driver, and the Lord knows what Adnan thought, since he knew who the man was. In Sulafa's room, the night before, I had merely said, "I love yellow roses," and Salma, who was there, said, "We have masses of them." Nor was I sick. But the roses had to be delivered under some pretext, for the benefit of the driver, at least. "Wine, roses, and seven carcasses," Adnan said and shoved his sizable nose into the bunch.

"Aunt Salma unhappy?" Sulafa said during one of our hours together. I had asked the question most warily. "Never. She knows everybody, everybody knows her. Everybody loves her. She goes to Europe almost every year——"

"Alone?" I asked.

"No. With her husband. He's rather old. But he sent her to college in America soon after their marriage. He is good to her. She is younger than my mother, and he is older than my father. Imagine. But he is very fond of her. And very rich, too. Salma is a very happy woman."

With the whole vista of the room between us I looked in Sulafa's big black-lashed eyes, outlined like eyes in an Assyrian bas-relief, and courting mischief, since I enjoyed listening to every word dropping from her lips, though in basic English and closely guarded by Cerberus Abed, I said: "Don't you envy her?"

Her dark cheeks turned wine-red. "Why should I?"

Abed's head as he sat on his stool hung over his chest with a fallen jaw. "For her freedom," I said.

A gleam of challenge shone in her eyes for a second then she turned her face away and did not answer.

At about midnight two days later I was undressing to go to bed when the telephone rang. I took up the receiver.

"Jameel Farran," I said.

A tremulous feminine voice whispered, "Hello."

"Yes?"

"Jameel Farran?" came the whisper.

"Yes."

There was a pause.

"Well?" I said. "Who is it?"

"Never mind."

"Oh?"

"What's that noise?"

"A motor car's horn, madam. If you hold that receiver long you'll hear many horns." Silence. "My room is right on Rashid Street."

"I know."

"Who are you?"

"Never mind. Good night." The telephone clicked.

For a moment I was mystified. Then I laughed. It must be one of those silly tricks some idle girls like to play on people. I had heard it was a common practice since the advent of the automatic telephone—such a wonderful penetrator of homes and barriers.

93

The following evening the telephone rang again around midnight, and the same suggestive silence came to me over the wires.

"Who are you?" I said as coaxingly as I could.

· "Say something," was the illuminating answer.

Suddenly I suspected it might be one of my college pupils. Perhaps if I kept up the game I might recognise the voice. "I wish *you* would say something," I said.

"I can't."

"Have you nothing to tell me then?"

"Ummm, no."

"Did you call last night?"

"Yes."

"What do you want?"

"Nothing."

"Well, look, this is a very silly game, and I have other things to do."

"Sorry."

"You ought to be."

"Good night."

I hung up sharply.

The next afternoon I was collected by the Nafawis' chauffeur and received at the gate by Abed, who conducted me to Sulafa's room and then perched on his seat.

"I've been looking at the river," Sulafa said and looked out of the window. "It has been rising, but I don't think there will be a flood this year." I stood beside her and looked at the broad expanse of the Tigris which flowed past the house, grey and muddy on our side but silken blue in the distance. It sparkled restlessly like a vast sheet of brocade. A seagull dipped, skimmed the water then shot away.

"You never see it actually move, do you. Like a lake," I said.

"But it flows, flows, flows, like the minutes and the hours. Like life itself."

"In my undergraduate days I was so fascinated by water, so obsessed by it, that I was afraid I might drown myself in the Cam. Fortunately the river was too small and shallow."

"I've never been afraid of drowning. I'm sure the first thing I saw the moment I was born was the Tigris. How I wish I could swim in it. Still, I love watching it. It reflects my moods. Sometimes I reflect its moods. Isn't it funny? It can look so unhappy, so sulky. It flows. It has flowed for ten thousand years, like life. Down to the ocean. Where does life go?"

"To an everlasting darkness, I suppose."

"The ocean, then, is darkness. It is death. The river is life. The Koran says, 'We have made of water everything that lives.' Have you read the Koran?"

"In parts."

"My father told me, when you were suggested to teach me, if you weren't Christian he wouldn't allow you to be alone with me."

"Alone? How about the gentleman on the stool?"

"He could hardly be considered a third person. Poor Abed."

Abed, hearing his name, stood up immediately, Sulafa told him to sit down. And we opened *King Lear*, Act III, Scene I.

*Kent: Who's there besides foul weather?*
*Gentleman: One minded like the weather, most unquietly. . . .*

When in the evening the telephone rang at the usual hour I was infuriated. I took the receiver, knowing for certain whom to expect, and shouted: "Who is it?"

The mysterious voice laughed. "Jameel?" it said.

"Yes!" I expected silence at which I should hang up.

"Can't you recognise my voice?"

"You've scarcely said anything beyond yes and no."

"The river is life. It flows like the minutes and the hours. . . ."

A shiver seized the back of my neck then shot through every part of me. "Sulafa!"

"I found your number by accident."

"I'm not in the telephone directory. Did you call the operator for it?"

"No. I found it in Salma's bedroom in a list of names and numbers."

"You are wicked." My heart, quite against my wish, thumped wildly.

"Aren't you angry?"

"No, I'm not at all angry. But why didn't you tell me it was you on the last two occasions?"

"I wanted you to do some guessing first." There was a cheerful note in her voice of which I had not known her to be capable.

"Well?" I said.

"Oh, nothing really."

I wanted to shout into the receiver, "You are the loveliest creature this side of the Tigris." But I couldn't and was lost for anything else to say. "Er . . . are you alone?" I finally said.

"Yes. Mother is in bed, and father is out and hasn't come back yet."

"And Abed?"

She laughed. "Your enemy goes to bed very early when I don't go out."

Her voice transmitted a luxury, a delightful shiver of guilt, as if we had met in carefully guarded secrecy. I wondered what her father would have thought had he known about it.

"Father was in when I called the last couple of times," she said.

"How silly of you!"

"I am sorry. Am I bothering you?"

"No, no."

"Never mind." She suddenly sounded angry. "Good night."

"But Sulafa——"

The other end was dead.

I collapsed on my bed. Frightened, elated, agonised, I felt utterly stupid and powerless.

About ten minutes later the telephone rang and Sulafa was on the line again.

"I am sorry for being rude," she said.

"Are you still alone?" I asked, as if the knowledge of her being alone at that late hour would end all the misery.

"Yes. And I can't go to sleep."

"Is there a telephone in your bedroom?"

"No, unfortunately. It's in my father's library. Why?"

"I just wondered. Do you hear any horns hooting?"

She laughed. "Not just now," she replied.

"You will in a minute."

"Don't they disturb you at night?"

"Not any more. But I must admit they pierce my dreams and get mixed up with my nightmares."

"Our house is dead quiet. But every now and then the river gets restless and I hear it lashing our wall. I didn't wake you up, did I?"

"I wasn't in bed."

"Well, good night."

"I hope you'll be able to sleep now," I said.

"I hope so."

"Good night."

"Good night."

There were no more calls from Sulafa until I saw her again. She made no reference to them, but I could not pretend that I had forgotten. "Have you been sleeping well?" I asked.

Her eyes widened, alarmed. "I don't know," she said.

"You didn't call me again."

"I was silly. I am really sorry."

"There's nothing wrong with your calling me whenever you're bored or can't go to sleep." "Whom are you fooling?" I said to myself.

"I'll never call you again."

"Don't be absurd. If you like I can call you once in a while."

She was horrified. "Don't, ever! I may not be here to answer the phone. If my father knows about it he'll go mad. It'll be the end of our English lessons."

Presently she added, "Please don't tell Salma I called you either."

She was struggling against the net in which we had been caught, but the net was closing in more tightly every day. My flesh hung heavy on my bones. I could not endure the unexpressed agony. Abed squatted in his corner and wielded the invisible sword over our heads. Through the windows the Tigris glittered as if it had been planted with a million fluttering eyes.

Presently I heard Imad's voice, strident and self-confident, outside the room. Sulafa's father walked in towards me followed by Salma, and my heart sank into my stomach weighted with guilt.

"Professor Jameel," he said, shaking my hand, "I am sorry that all these weeks we haven't had a chance to sit down together for a chat. Abed!"—he turned round to his servant—"Get us some tea and cakes." Abed went out obediently.

98

"Is the lesson over for today?" Salma asked.

"Off with your books," Imad said with benign gruffness. "This room is much too small. Let us go down to the drawing-room."

On our way down he put his arm round my shoulder—he was very tall—and with great affection said, "I've been sick for weeks, you know. Did Sulafa tell you? My heart isn't much good, it seems. But I shall see all doctors in their graves before I die." He was brimming with recovered well-being.

We passed through the library, with its heavy black shelves set with mother-of-pearl, which led to the drawing-room. The walls were flaked in several places with the dampness that either seeped up from the river-sodden ground or filtered down the roof after the occasional spells of rain. It was a musty cold room whose armchairs and settees, upholstered in bright floral patterns and lined round the four walls, promised little comfort or warmth. Small tables with big ashtrays were placed between one seat and another. A large Persian carpet covered the whole of the floor, and two small rugs were hung lengthwise on the walls. On a low table in the centre a green vase held a bunch of fresh roses. To complete this interior, there was facing me, as I entered, a painting about four feet by three of an old man in a turban hanging on the wall in oblivious solitude. It must have been done by one of those hack painters who work from a small faded photograph by enlarging it a dozen times and colouring it in an idealised manner; the result was something like a doll in cream and cherry-red, with whiskers and beard attached.

"My late father," Imad said. "He was a member of the Ottoman Parliament in Istanbul and a famous speaker. Please sit down."

"We want to see how well Sulafa is doing," Salma said.

99

Noticing that the object of our interest had not come down, she went out to call her in.

"She is a good scholar," I said. "You should have sent her to college, like most of her friends."

"No, no, I am afraid I don't agree, Professor," Imad said. "I know you and Salma think I am a reactionary old fool. But I have no faith in all this craze for modernisation and westernisation. As long as there is life in me I stick to my family's tradition. Perhaps you don't know I come from a long line of gentleman scholars, and some of my forebears were governors of this city. I will never have people say my daughter went to school with a lot of roughnecks. Besides, what is wrong with a private education?" Salma and Sulafa came in at that moment, and Imad added, "Private education is in the best aristocratic tradition, isn't it, Salma?"

"All right, all right," Salma said with a faint sardonic smile. They must have had many arguments about it in the past.

Imad made his daughter sit down next to him and proudly, possessively, patted her back. "You know why I want this girl to speak English well? My little secret! I am going to England very soon. My heart hasn't been too good. I intend to see some specialists there, and I am taking Sulafa with me to look after her dear old father."

"Father!" Sulafa yelled jubilantly. "You really mean it?"

"Of course, my dear. I was most unhappy when I went there the year before the war, because I couldn't speak a word of English. Had it not been for Mr. Donaldson, whom I had known for many years when he was Political Officer in Iraq, it would have been very difficult for me. So I want my daughter to learn . . . er . . . Shakespeare's tongue." He gave the last two words a vocal caress.

He patted his daughter's back again, and she laughed. "Shall we ask my father to listen to us as we read King

100

Lear's lines in his madness on the heath, Professor?" she asked.

"I know he is a great poet," he said with all seriousness and produced a small string of beads, oddly disproportionate with his corpulence. His hands, however, were small and delicate. "But how does he compare with our own poets?"

Fortunately we did not have to answer, partly because the tea was brought in at that moment already poured out in cups, and partly because Imad was reminded of the poets he himself read and admired. "You know why I learnt Persian?" he said. "In order to read Hafiz in the original. There's a poet for you, my son. Do you know his 'Wild Hart' *mathnawy*? I often think we've never progressed, in spite of all this change in our way of life. Tell me what poet today can equal Hafiz? We have cinemas, noisy red buses, refrigerators. But of matters of the spirit, what do we have?"

I had placed my cup of tea on the small side table. Salma offered me a cake from the tray held respectfully by Abed.

"We are stagnant, sir," I said. "Nor do we have to flatter ourselves about cinemas and refrigerators: we have made none of them ourselves. We merely import them. But we hope our colleges will some day produce some of them—matters of the spirit, if nothing else."

"Please don't be angry if I say I have no faith in our young men. You know why? They've lost the old virtues and acquired no new ones. It's easy to see they've lost all religious feeling, for instance. And once religion loses its force in people's lives, nothing but evil will operate."

"Anything that operates," Salma said with a wicked smile, "is better than nothing at all."

"That's the kind of thing that unhappy wretch Adnan would say," Imad said with conspicuous resentment. "I was telling the Minister of Interior the other day, 'More mosques and more police stations, that's what you should

101

build. Mosques and police stations.' The fear of God and the fear of authority, that's what we need. Mosques and police stations. We are a very difficult people, Professor— very difficult. Mosques and police stations are the only medicine for our sickness." He flicked his beads. I remembered Abed sitting on his slave's chair then imagined him standing up, with a face that looked like Imad's, to shut the door and lock it against a rebellious Sulafa. I could see him walk away with a large ring of keys which clinked with dark, grim authority and lock a row of doors down an endless corridor. Sulafa bit her cake, not even looking at her father who seemed so mild and harmless as he flicked his tiny beads.

"But my dear Imad," Salma said, "you hardly ever go to a mosque yourself!"

"What does it matter?" he said. "Didn't I build a very fine one last year? I can't very well go around building police stations, can I?" He eyed me with a self-assured smile as if to say, "Between us, I could do even that if I wanted to."

Taking another bite Sulafa said very quietly, "But aren't you likely with such means to inspire hatred rather than a fear of authority in the hearts of the people?"

"Nonsense," he said. "What does it matter what the beast feels as long as it is muzzled?" He turned to me again. "All these riots and uprisings on the part of the students and the thugs of the city do us nothing but harm. What I cannot understand is that the more we educate our young men and women the more hot-headed they become."

"You don't want a whole race of sheep, sir, do you?" I asked. "Poets like Hafiz, if we hope ever to have them, are not bred by sheep, are they?" I felt I wanted to roar in his face, but to my unspeakable astonishment it was he who roared with laughter. "How right you are, how right you are!" he said and choked with his weird guffaw.

102

"Narcissi do not grow in the desert," Salma philosophised and stood up. "Mosques and police stations disturb me." She walked towards the door and I knew that was my cue to make an exit too, when she turned round and said to me, "I can give you a lift if you're going my way."

"Please," I said and got up.

When I said good-bye to Imad and Sulafa, the poor girl's face was static and I thought her eyes pursued me. How I wished I could turn round and shake her violently out of that statuesque impassivity to see her face break up into a thousand lines of suffering.

Abed was already ahead of Salma and me. He opened the Buick's door for her to get in behind the wheel.

"Where is your chauffeur?" I asked, as I sat next to her.

"I prefer to drive myself sometimes," she said. "I suppose you know what was on Imad's mind?" The car growled into a smooth run.

"Some political trouble is brewing among college students because half a dozen of them have been arrested. One of them, in fact, is a pupil of mine."

"Yes. But I had come to see Imad about something which might interest you." She gave me a side glance, and I saw a smile on her lips.

"Oh?"

"About Adnan."

"What's wrong with him?"

"He's getting into trouble."

"I never thought Adnan was effectively capable of trouble. What has he done?" I remembered his conspiratorial hints.

"He's watched by the police."

"Adnan?"

"Yes. He's a suspect."

"But he is not a communist," I said indignantly.

"I know he isn't," she said. We had come to North Gate.

We turned right, to Rashid Street. "But if he's not careful he may be arrested any time."

"Disgusting. He can no more be careful than all the other young men we have around who have to cause trouble all their lives."

"Don't be innocent, Jameel. He lives like a vagrant, has no permanent address, is seen everywhere, especially with college students, and is awfully opinionated."

"A good thing, too!" I said and laughed. "Your library has not been wasted."

"Jameel," she gave me a quick coquettish glance, "you mean I haven't made good use of it myself?"

"You don't sit in circles of famished-looking young men to tell them what you've read. You're probably worse than I. You read to weigh and consider but hardly ever to believe. Adnan believes."

"That's just it. They're very suspicious of young men who make use of their beliefs. Once you hold opinions, well, you're damned."

"Wonderful, Salma! In other words all opinions are— subversive."

"Quite. Especially when they are thrown around, right and left, in cafés and under the colonnades. All opinions must be faked here, and everybody knows it and respects others' dissimulation. Haters must appear like lovers and lechers must look pious. It deceives no one and everyone is happy. But once you try to tear down such defensive façades and discover even political meanings in them, you're up against trouble."

"I don't think this is peculiar to this city. I should think it's a common social practice."

"Yes, but when your city is a glorified village where everybody knows everybody and everybody scrutinises everybody, you have to be careful. You see, I got to know

104

from my husband that Adnan was being considered for arrest, so I went to see Imad about it. He has friends in the right quarters. Unfortunately he has very little affection for Adnan."

"I hope you did persuade him to help the poor boy."

"I think I did, although he thinks a short period in a lock-up would be a desirable corrective."

"I am afraid Imad Beg has a jailer's mind, if you forgive my saying so."

For a moment she was silent. We were caught in the usual traffic jam, and importunate horns were blowing behind us. I thought she did not like my remark.

"Do you know Adnan is Imad's nephew?" she asked.

"What? Incredible. Adnan doesn't bear the Nafawis' name."

"He refuses to."

"You mean he refuses to be associated with his uncle?"

"Exactly."

We came to Feisal Square. On the right was the bridge. Four policemen channelled the impatient cars with the rhythmic gestures of ballet dancers.

"Tell me more," I said.

"How about a drive?" she asked,

"Wonderful."

She turned right, on to the Bridge then out into the western outskirts of Baghdad, through coffee shops, cinemas, squalid groceries, until a straight narrow road bordered with leafy eucalyptus trees led to the bottleneck of a one-way bridge, hanging over a marsh and guarded by a police station, beyond which lay the verdant beginnings of the countryside.

"I've crossed the Tigris with you," she said.

"Is it like crossing the Rubicon?" I asked.

"Worse."

I was not certain what she meant, but I had a premonition

105

of what was to follow. She spoke no more about Adnan, and my sense of how alone I was with her was emphasised by the long deserted road. "Is this the road to Babylon?" I asked.

"Yes," she replied. She slowed down, until I thought she was going to stop. But she did not. "I've never been able to make you out." While steering with the left hand she placed her shy hesitant right hand on my knee. Though baffled for a moment I gave way to the silent invitation and put up no resistance. Sulafa's eyes, like Leila's dead hand, pursued me, but I refused to be hunted down.

"Oh, Salma, I am a weary man," I said.

"You're a fool. You're young and the whole world is at your feet." Her hand went back to the steering wheel when she negotiated a curve, then slowly and hesitantly settled on my knee again.

"What world, what world?"

"You're free. You don't realise how free you are. I'll be ruined if someone driving past recognises me now."

"Drive on, for God's sake."

"At this minute I should be back at home."

"All right then, turn round."

"I can't, I can't. Jameel, you're awful."

"Thank you."

"I've been dead ever since I came back from the States."

I slid up to her and put my arm round her shoulder. "I know what you mean."

She trembled all over. "I can't drive!" she screamed. With a powerful jolt the car came to a standstill, and she fell in my arms.

I kissed her mouth, desireless and passionless. Not having touched a woman for many months I enjoyed having the smoothness of her skin and the warmth of her flesh against my hands. My hands, independent of the rest of me, delighted in the contact with her arms and neck and breasts.

106

She kissed me again intensely, ravenously, but my flesh was void of all desire, and in my brain there was a blank—a large cold emptiness. As I kissed her and my hands went subtly and deliberately all over her, I thought I was merely re-enacting a joy of the past: it was an act which I knew by heart, not an event.

"We must move," I said. "A car by the roadside could not be passed unobserved."

"Yes, yes," she muttered. Her voice was thick with her need.

I disengaged myself, went out of the car and got in at the other door and settled behind the steering wheel. I started the car with Salma clinging to me.

"Do you love me—a bit?" she asked.

"Must you talk about love?" "Love, love, love—who wants to love again?" I wanted to say; but it would have sounded hollow and overdone.

"Who was the last woman you loved?"

"That's a funny question, Salma. But I'll give you the answer. The last woman I loved was killed in Jerusalem."

"How terrible. Do you still love her?"

"How do I know?"

"You have never told me anything about her. What was her name?"

"I'll tell you. I'll tell you everything about her. But would you like it?"

"I shall love everything you have loved—even your memories."

What a lie. Would she love Sulafa if I told her about her? It was easy to love those with whom there was no question of competition.

We were approaching a great farm with thousands of palm trees which, when caught in the beams of the headlights, looked like enormous shadows of menace. On the potholed road the car rattled and jolted restlessly.

107

# 15

When I went home the landlady handed me a message. "From an Englishman," she said. It was from Brian: "I am waiting for you at the Café Suisse. If you don't come by nine I shall give you a ring."

I was too distraught to go. I wanted to be alone to see my way with Salma more clearly. I wanted to work things out. I could not simply decide to avoid her. In fact I did not want to avoid her. Only I must recognise the difficulty, the complexity of the situation and see that Salma did nothing desperate in an attempt to surmount it. I had no doubt that she was too sensible to jeopardise her social position, her very life perhaps, for the sake of a mad venture. But I was afraid she would so manage the affair as to implicate me in a labyrinthine secrecy which would encompass her ends without damaging the exterior of her life or mine. The idea of secrecy and amorous intrigue appealed to me, but I could not muster enough passion for a positive role in the game. Feeling more wanted than wanting, any such design would be brutal on my part. I should avoid it. Yet I did not want to avoid it. I rather dallied with the notion that she would go on loving me while I, though within her reach, would watch her feed a futile passion with the idea of our love, yet keep far enough to preserve the clarity of my vision. Monstrous, evil! Insane, too. "Our life here," she had said during our drive back towards the city, "is a loveless one. Dry as dust. But I love you, and I am terrified. Whether you love me or not, I love you. But I am terrified." I would have liked to shout: "But what about Sulafa?"

The telephone rang, and Brian's voice came over the wire with vibrant intonation which became more perceptible, querulous, delightful, when thus disembodied.

"Wouldn't you oblige a lonely man?" he said. "Let's see you. Could you come round to the Suisse?"

I was about to apologise, but Brian's voice by some mysterious connection dragged Adnan's image up: Salma until that moment had submerged him in the backwater of my mind. Now I remembered I must see him and tell him what I had heard.

"I'm coming straight away," I said.

At the Café I found Brian sitting in a circle of young men who thought his Arabic, which he was practising on them, too admirable for words. They were keener, however, on practising their English on him. I joined them for a few minutes, but before I was served I told Brian I had to see Adnan and asked him whether he would like to go along with me. He said he would. We left the group and went down Rashid Street.

"Where does he live?" Brian asked.

"I don't know. But I am sure we'll find him in one of the casinos by the river," I said.

"I am always tempted to sit in one of them. The crowd is tremendously exciting. But I feel too much of a stranger there, and I don't dare to talk to anyone."

"But your Arabic has improved enormously, hasn't it?"

"Oh come, come. It's too halting and too elementary for a decent conversation."

"I hope we'll find Adnan," I said.

We found him. There he was with Husain, Abdul Kader and Kareem. Two or three others, unknown to me, were introduced as law students. Husain received Brian with open arms. I pulled up a chair and sat next to Adnan.

"Have you ever tried boiled turnips?" Adnan asked.

"*Shalgham*, turnips." He charged the word seductively.

"I don't think I'd care for them," Brian answered.

The boys laughed, as if for him to care for them would indeed be funny.

"But you must try our *shalgham*. You too, Jameel. Don't turn up your nose. It's a delicacy you have to get used to."

A *shalgham* vendor was standing outside the rails with his barrow which carried a huge copper pot over a charcoal fire. As the group were seated near the rails, Adnan shouted to the vendor from his seat to bring us some *shalgham*. In a minute a number of little dishes were placed before us, each with a boiled turnip, dirty brown, divided into four sections.

"A delicacy," Adnan repeated, as the salt was passed round.

I was hungry. The mushy vegetable, sweet and salt in turn, was not the best thing I could eat. But I asked for another. Heroically Brian ate his, lingering over each of the four sections until the tea arrived. We washed the thing down with the strong syrupy drink.

But I was restless. The leisurely fatuous talk irritated me. The radio songs, blatant, hearty, doleful, gushed through the uproar of the crowd, and I was seized by a mysterious longing for a breathless hush over a vast high-ceilinged hall where men would fear to talk, lest the silence should be broken. And yet there sat Adnan, part of the noise, competing like the radio with the febrile chuckles and irrepressible shouts. Like many of his friends, like penniless Husain and skull-faced Abdul Kader, he envisaged himself as a hero, a saviour, a conspirator of the people, who would consciously merge in them, who would turn all their wild noise into a hymn of joy for an age of love and justice. In my irritation, in my longing for some vast rolling silence, I pictured Adnan, as I looked at him, suddenly clapping his hands to his lips, looking round with terrified eyes, then as though pursued by a pack of hounds running away, away, in an endless flat desert.

"Adnan," I said abruptly as I stood up, "I want to talk to you."

Everybody looked up at me.

"What is it?" Adnan inquired.

"I am afraid I must go home. Do you mind walking along with me?"

"Anything important?"

"No. But would you like to walk?"

"All right."

"We'll join you," Brian said. When we left the 'casino' he walked with Husain a few yards behind us. They were engaged in an arduous conversation in Arabic.

We sauntered down the esplanade, past a few more casinos and cafés, until there were only the attractive new buildings extending in a long curving line following the course of the broad Tigris.

"Adnan, I understand you're being watched," I said.

"Watched?" he said.

"By the police."

"Really?" He was not startled, which disappointed me.

"So I heard," I said.

"Take it with a pinch of salt. I told you they watched everyone here—everyone that mattered. It's the disease of the age."

"I think it's dreadful."

"Oh, I don't mind it in the least. It rather amuses me."

"Tell me without any quibbling, what kind of political activity are you engaged in?"

"Like every fool in this city, I jabber and waste my breath on everything done and undone," he answered evasively.

"You call that politics?"

"What else is politics for us? You don't suppose we can

111

*do* anything, do you? Everybody wants a change, a revolution; not only the leftists and the progressives, but the rightists and the reactionaries too. But what do we do? Some talk, some organise piddling little cells, some fill acres of paper with sh—y articles. That's about all we can do. We all swear we are fighting for our country against the foreigners. The leftists mean the British and the Americans, the rightists mean the Russians."

"Well?"

"In the meantime we've forgotten we've cheated the people, ourselves, and even God. Why don't we look at ourselves, for God's sake, for a minute? Why don't we examine our faces in the mirror every morning we get up, and scrutinise our hands to see what spots of blood may be on them? But once you say that kind of thing you become an outsider. For then you're siding with neither the top-dog nor the under-dog, you're looking neither east nor west. You're rejected by either side."

"Naturally. It's so much easier to help in hunting down the secret rebels or in yelling out against the corrupt reactionaries."

"And both kinds of activity are meant to impress the poor people with our worth and significance. That's politics for us." He paused, then asked, "Do you know the derivation of the English word politics?"

"Oh, I suppose it is derived from the Greek word 'polis', city."

"I thought so. Politics would thus mean the science of managing cities and citizens. I wonder what the derivation is of the equivalent word in Arabic—*siyasah*."

He looked at me and in the dim light I saw a flicker of delight in his eyes.

"The only thing I can think of," I said, "is the 'care of horses', which is also *siyasah*."

112

"Precisely. The care and tending of horses—that's our politics. That's what our lords and masters have always thought of us! Is there anything so funny in the whole history of mankind? Horses and horse masters." He laughed then stopped short. "Let us hope the horses won't go mad and hurl down their riders."

"What's that you're saying about horses?" Brian shouted from a distance behind us. We waited for him and Husain to catch up with us. "You see, I can tell what you're talking about," he said.

Husain pointed to a bench by the river bank. "Let us sit down for a while," he clearly enunciated in English.

"I wish my Arabic would improve as fast as Husain's English," Brian said.

"Patience, patience!" Husain enunciated again, then added in Arabic, "Nothing has killed us but patience."

"Do you know Towfiq al-Khalaf?" I asked Brian.

"I'm afraid I don't," Brian answered.

"What a pair you two would make!" I said. "Adnan, you must get Towfiq and Brian together."

Adnan seemed pleased to change the subject.

"He is the real stuff," he said. "He is the one to teach you Arabic. A man who refuses to admit he knows English, whose hate is more wonderful than all the love in the world. A real bedouin."

Brian was excited. "But I must make a confession," he said. "You remember the Rising Moon Hotel? Every now and then I go there——"

Husain jumped and exclaimed, "You like Baghdad girls?"

"I don't go there for girls," Brian said. "I spend two or three days at a time to practise my Arabic with the lodgers. Everybody at the better hotels speaks English. So I have to go to a place like the Rising Moon. Dawood and I are great friends now. He's presented me with a string of beads."

113

"Ah, maybe you like boys," Husain said with difficulty. "Many men come to the East because they like boys." He chuckled happily.

"Don't be silly," Brian said benignly and laughed.

Brian, though working in a British-owned bank, was a student of Arab history. He had taken a small house in Alwiyah and had his library shipped to him, with which he covered a whole wall in his sitting room. Husain, in particular, was impressed by his learning and enthusiasm, and enjoyed taking him under his wing. He guided him through the dark corners of the Sooq where Brian bought not Persian carpets but bedouin goat's hair rugs, whose primitive designs and crude texture he admired. His three-room house was rigged with the handiwork of Arab and Kurd, and he was beginning to collect Arabic books. He could already discourse on Islamic art with an authority that both delighted and aroused the jealousy of his listeners. A typical argument was when Husain, listening very intently to one of Brian's expatiations on the 14th century painter Al-Wasiti, blurted out desperately: "We're so obsessed with our present we don't know a thing about our past." Whereupon Adnan corrected him: "We're so obsessed with our past, I should say, that we don't know a thing about our present." A heated discussion ensued before Brian could enlarge further on the achievements of the past. I therefore liked to imagine the active polarity and fertile tension that would be obtained by a friendship between him and Towfiq: one with a well-developed consciousness of chronology and temporality, the other with a faith in timelessness that rejected all chronology as the symptoms of a diseased civilisation. So I said, "If you meet Towfiq, you won't have to go to the Rising Moon so often."

"Some of the servants there, I gathered, are Assyrian," he said. "They keep reminding me of the ruins of Nineveh

114

and Nimrud. I've made up my mind to write something about it. Why don't you write a poem about it, Adnan?"

"What, about the gigantic statues that fill Nimrud with fragments?"

"Yes. And all those great winged bulls and monolithic guardian spirits in the shape of vultures which ornamented the gates of a city that was once the centre of an empire. I can picture the wealth and captives of many nations pouring into it under the protection of those imperturbable large-eyed deities. The strength of the whole nation was expressed in their powerfully moulded muscles——"

"I'm afraid for centuries an entirely different attitude was taken by our people in the North," Adnan said. "They used to break them to pieces and burn them for lime, because they took them to be images of the devil."

"How terrible," I said. "Still, who could help being stunned at the first sight of a winged bull ten times the size of an ordinary animal? You had either to bow and worship it, or apply your vengeful hammer and break it, burn it and get rid of it."

"I don't know," Brian said. "They make you think. You know, the fall of empires and all that. There it is—the whole thing that took centuries to happen is caught in one moment of time, in one shiny marble fragment celebrating in cuneiform a gory conquest: but the fragment lies in a footpath, and the inscription is covered with asses' excrement. It is frightening."

"Have you observed the little villages, all clawed by poverty, that usually encircle such ruins?"

"Yes. It's a sad sight, I am afraid. The villagers squat in the shade, while their children play in the dust with flies eating their eyes and noses, quite unconscious of the forces that lie petrified in those grass-covered mounds."

115

"You will never know how we feel about it, Brian," Adnan said with a hoarseness in the throat that gradually melted into a miserable angry quiver. "You may be a good historian or a wonderful archæologist, you may be able to tell us about all the kings of Sumer and Assyria, the battles they fought, the palaces they built, the cities they razed. But to you, in the final analysis, it is no more than an æsthetic adventure. It is outside you. You can enjoy it with equanimity and organise it into historical patterns. In the end you'll go back to England and remember it all as an experience, a discovery, an intellectual achievement, call it what you will. But to us—God, how different it is. We may or may not know the details of the past. But we know it's there. We're aware of its presence in our midst like a spirit that cannot be exorcised. The very soil, whether it glitters with the green of fecundity or the salt of exhaustion, emits the odour of the past. This river glides past us heavy with memory. The barges, the armies, the wealth, the blood, which have drifted down these waters haunt us, torture us. Even if we did not look at the river, we'd sense them in our blood, like an incurable disease. We are the inheritors of the glory and the squalor, the fanfares and the plaintive laments. With your critical eye, Brian, you may observe the irony of such juxtapositions as peasants with gummy eyes sitting in the midst of their asses' dung within sight of the great monuments of an empire they cannot understand. But to us the irony is savage. It fills us with bitterness. It is an agony that shatters us. It fills us with hatred and despair. It fills us with wild hope, but terrifies us into realising our impotence."

There was a long silence. A shape was floating down the far side of the river, and a song was wafted over the water, faint and distant and sad. Every now and then the sound of a radio came from the coffee shops up the street, while

116

behind us motor cars growled and suspired. The song from the river was long in fading out.

"Let us go home," I said. "It's getting late."

"I'm going in the opposite direction," Brian said. He hailed a taxi and said goodnight to us. The three of us trudged back, until we approached the now dimly lit casino. Suddenly Adnan took my arm and said, "What exactly did you hear about my being watched?" I winced to see his face. He looked worn out, and actually afraid.

I told him about Salma and Imad. He was infuriated. "Oh these sons of bitches, these dogs, these bastards——"

"Whom do you mean?" I said. "Salma and Imad are trying to help you."

"I don't mean them—not them in particular, anyway. I mean—everybody. Everybody under this foul heaven."

"The leeches on our backs," Husain said, and spat furiously.

"Look, Jameel. Would you like to come and see where I live? I feel guilty for not having asked you before."

"It's getting on for midnight and I am really tired," I said, and immediately realised I had to be back in my room if I wanted to hear Sulafa's voice that night.

"All right. I'll see you tomorrow and take you home with me." He then turned round to Husain and said, "How about a last game of dominoes?" Husain concurred.

I said goodnight and left them there.

Although it would have taken me less than ten minutes to walk home, I was afraid that Sulafa had already telephoned, in spite of her earlier determination not to. To waste no more time I took a taxi, and as soon as I got out of it I rushed upstairs. I entered my room panting for breath after running up fifty-three steps.

The telephone looked dead. It wouldn't ring. I took up the receiver to ascertain that it worked and put it down again. I paced up and down my room waiting for it to ring. Oh, how did I forget to be back earlier? Damn Adnan, damn Salma, damn them all. My brain seemed to splinter into a hundred agonies. Leila was dead, Salma married, Sulafa beyond reach. Brian lived on a luxurious periphery, Adnan in a spurious mystery, and I in an exile which mystified and harrowed me. After the monotony of a sterile misery in Bethlehem, the horrors of another kind of misery. "Not misery, not misery," I kept reiterating. "Here are the possibilities of life, of action, even of sensuous experience. I must have the will to become a part of life again: to join in releasing Sulafa, a million Sulafas, a million Adnans from the powers of negation and evil. But am I released myself? I wish that telephone would ring."

It rang, and I pounced on it.

"Jameel?" the voice whispered.

I was horrified. I thought it was Salma.

"Yes. Who is it?"

"Sulafa."

"At last, at last." I noticed my own sibilant sigh.

"Were you waiting for me to call?"

"Yes, yes, Sulafa."

"I'm glad. I thought you did not like me to call."

"I want you to call—as often as you can."

"I wish I could."

"I know, I know."

My voice vibrated with frenzied enthusiasm. But Sulafa's was as calm as ever. It angered me.

"I must go to bed before father returns," she said.

"Won't you say something?"

She laughed gently: I heard the little giggle in her very throat. "I can imagine your throat shimmering with your laugh," I said.

"I have a thousand things to tell you."

118

"Then please tell me one of them."

She paused. Her breath was audible.

"I can't," she said at last.

"You . . . don't have to. . . ."

"I am afraid," she said.

"Afraid? What of?"

"Nothing, nothing. Good night, Jameel."

"But Sulafa——"

"Good night, my love."

"Good night. Sulafa. Sulafa." I repeated her name a dozen times like an incantation—over a dead wire.

# 16

The college corridors next morning were crowded with groups of taciturn students looking resentful and determined. In the Staff Room I was told a delegation of students had gone to the Dean for the third time, demanding the release of their classmate, Wahab Jassim, who was one of the seven students from various colleges arrested by the police five days earlier. The rest were on strike, and unless all the seven students were immediately acquitted, the whole city was to go on strike the following morning. The Dean had promised to do all that was in his power, which was not much.

Among my letters that morning was one from my brother, Yacoub. Yacoub had not received much formal education, which was probably why he never wrote a dull letter.

Bethlehem
10th April, 1949

My dear brother,

We have never seen such a lovely spring. Almond blossom

has burst upon the town, wild and festive. It makes you want to jump savagely and laugh. But nature is unforgivable. It makes you want to laugh just when there is no time for laughter. Simon the Martyr died in his hut among the festive almond trees, and he was given a funeral—of sorts. We were half a dozen men in all and old Father Isa officiated. On our way down to the cemetery we ran into another funeral: Roman Catholic and spectacular. Emile Hubaish, who never sang or danced in his life, because he was busy making money in Bolivia, had a procession of Franciscan monks and choir boys a mile long, all chanting hymns that begged God to rest his soul. A brass band struggled with Chopin's Marche Funèbre, and at least two thousand haggard faces, all Moslem refugees, watched with wonder and fascination. Our own dead man's coffin was too hastily made to look even decent, but no one took any notice of us, coming as we did as an anti-climax after the rich man's cortege. Incidentally, when I suggested we might bury Simon's old lute with him, we looked around and found it had disappeared. We didn't know whether he'd sold it or somebody had stolen it. (As I write these lines I hear chanting in the street below: another funeral. It's Greek Orthodox this time, I think. Every day we have one or two).

We've been recently counted and pigeon-holed by United Nations. They're giving us ration cards, on the strength of which we get so much flour and powdered milk and a few ounces of margarine per head. The flour makes black bread, and the powdered milk is not much appreciated by the refugees, especially when they have to take it every morning dissolved back into liquid. Most of them turn it into leben and sell it dirt cheap to the unlucky ones who have not been given ration cards because they do not technically qualify as refugees. Misery is being classified, and oh, they're so clever at it, U.N.O.'s officials. How miserable can one get?

120

The refugee camps are sprawling wider every day over the hills. You probably know that many more villages in the area have been recently evacuated. Frontier lines are constantly being pushed by the Jews through the most unexpected places, and our poor peasants are as usual terrorised by bullet and gelignite into flight to us—and U.N.O.'s officials have every day some more counting to do. Our emasculation is complete. Old rifles and no ammunition. But that's an old story.

The town has suddenly developed a rash of missionaries. American missionaries, well-heeled and glib, who talk about the love of Jesus Christ to Christians and Moslems alike, and hope to convert the refugees by telling them Christ is the son of Allah, which makes even the starved laugh. They like to visit people in their homes, but only Christians allow them to do so. They preach through interpreters to those who need no preaching, and embark on theological controversies with the Orthodox. People say they're Zionists in disguise, spying on our conditions, and indirectly plugging the old line of the gathering of the Jews in the Promised Land. At least two of them were given a sound beating the other day near the vegetable market. A certain Rev. Ronson came to our house with a cine-camera and expressed surprise at your English books. He thought they were mine. "You're educated, I see," he said, almost deprecatingly. "Not quite," I said. After a long rigmarole about the Prophets— I think he fancied himself as an Apostle declaiming faith to the heathens of Rome, you should have seen his grand gestures—he said something about the necessity of resignation to the old prophecies of Ezekiel, even if that meant the death of thousands of Gentiles. I couldn't contain myself. "You are my guest," I said, "but you are a bastard, Rev. Ronson." He had drunk his coffee, and I showed him to the door. Brazen-facedly, he stopped short and said, "May I

121

shoot the view with my cine-camera from your window?"
"You may not," I said. Pity I did not kick him down the stairs. But my mother wouldn't have liked it. She likes the manna you sent us very much. Look after yourself, and keep out of trouble.

Yacoub.

# 17

In the afternoon I was awakened from a nap by a cheerful Adnan. My landlady had become fond of him and considered him one of the few people who might be let in before being announced. Her femininity, I noticed more than once, would quiver at his greeting her, and a wicked look from him might sometimes bridge for her the woeful gap between middle-aged widowhood and vibrant youth.

"Talk about the sleep of the just!" he exclaimed.

"Is that why you did not sleep?" I said.

"I hardly ever sleep in the afternoon, just or unjust."

"How can you manage, when you spend so many late hours in casinos and coffee-houses?"

"I've got used to it. There's no deprivation—if you can call it that—which you can't get used to. Come on," he added, "get dressed. I'm taking you to my place."

"Good. How are things in the city?"

"Pretty tense. There'll be demonstrations tomorrow."

"Do you expect any trouble?"

"Oh, the usual thing."

Adnan's nonchalance could be most exasperating. "You talk as if nothing less than the Day of Doom could excite you."

"Nothing less, nothing less."

122

I had a wash and got dressed. We drank some tea and went out. After walking up the main street for about ten minutes we entered one of the numerous lanes that joined Rashid Street. You did not have to go far down such a lane to discover the senility of the houses, the decrepitude that hinted at the ungracious years the city had gone through.

Occasionally through an open arched gate one caught a glimpse of a courtyard and spacious rooms in distinct contrast with the narrow street. Often, however, the endless convolution of houses, whose latticed windows that jutted overhead on either side met almost face to face, revealed as they perched on top of one another their shabby closeness and pointed to the human seethings within. In spite of the clear afternoon sky, darkness clung to the corners of the lane, muddied by streams of filthy water emerging from the gateways. Children in dirty long shirts screamed, and flies buzzed over their excrement. Black-cloaked women walked erect with large bare feet and thick anklets, their faces no longer capable of registering happiness or suffering. When I entered through a small, lop-sided doorway, redolent of garbage and urine, I realised I had come to a place where all talk about the human substance of happiness and suffering was meaningless, if not shameful. Here you either accepted life unquestioningly or went mad.

Adnan led me up a steep staircase which ended with the door of his room. When he unlocked it and we stepped in I could hardly believe that a man like him could inhabit such a dingy shapeless hovel. It was not small, but it was so messy, so cluttered up with battered and faded furniture, with odd objects varying from a lovely head in wood resting on the floor, to empty cans and bottles, palm-leaf fans, istikans, tea-pots, glasses, dirty plates. And books, books every-where, some of them still open, in piles, in corners, on the chairs and under the rusty iron bed. By the only window in the room lay a chest with its top tilted up. I could see in it heaps of paper, presumably Adnan's writings. There was one small table next to it with a portable gramophone, whose top was open, with a red-labelled record on the turntable. Under the table was a pile of record albums. When I bent over the gramophone to see what the record on it was, Adnan said, "I was playing that before I came to you."

"What is it?"

"It's a part of *La Symphonie Fantastique* by Berlioz. The guillotine part. Do you know it? The artist imagining himself being guillotined. And then the terrifying *Dies irae*. Like this: tum . . . tum . . . tum . . ." He sang the solemn melody. "A great tune. And the artist's descent into hell . . . I have always loved to see hell."

"With all this, it shouldn't be too difficult," I said.

"To compare notes, of course."

"But, Adnan, how can you live here?"

"Why not? Mind you, I am no St. Francis. I have not given away my things to the poor. I have a steady income on which I subsist."

"I am sure you could find something better."

"Of course I could. Here, be seated. But what for? On the other hand, considering the books and records I buy I don't think I could afford anything much better."

"Are all these your books?"

"Most of them. Some of them are Salma's. You've been seeing her quite a lot recently, haven't you?"

I probably went pale, but tried hard to look composed. "Fairly often, she's a fine woman."

"She is very fond of you."

"Is she? I am fond of her myself. An intelligent woman restores one's faith in things."

Adnan chuckled. "What things? What faith?"

"Now, Adnan, don't put on airs. You're no cynic, and

124

you know it. In fact, I'd be surprised if behind that tragi-comic face of yours you didn't hide one of the most sentimental souls in the world."

"Nonsense. Emotion is not for me. It's the property of people with little awareness of what's going on."

"That's absurd. I bet you often spend long lonely nights wallowing in it. All this slum business which you have adopted smacks of it."

"Slum business? I am only living the way nine-tenths of the human race are living."

"When you can afford better? I call that sentimentality."

"I don't care what you call it. That's my way of life. But don't think I am eliciting any pleasure from it," he said sulkily, believing he had failed to impress me.

"I am sorry, Adnan. But you have intrigued me rather."

"There's nothing intriguing in this."

"What do you do exactly most of the day? You can't tell me you sit in this room and read all the time."

"I do a lot of writing and er . . . a lot of talking. I am keeping a frank autobiographical journal and I want to have the whole of the city in it."

Suddenly he fell back on his resourceful voice: a voice that was many voices, each of which was a mask he would put on and off as the occasion demanded. To those who knew him it was ridiculous and baffling, overwhelming and irritating all at once.

"It's not enough for me to know every nook and cranny in Baghdad. I have sought physical contact with the God-damned race that crawls in them. But God knows I have little love for it. And yet I have gone around hugging all those that seem so impossible to love. I mean, you know, the vulgar, the dirty, the diseased, the ones that can kill for a song. Not the others. The others are well looked after. I know what evil there is in them all, the ones I hug and the

125

ones I spurn. There's nothing but evil in them. But what does it matter? There's as much evil in you, in me, in everyone. You've seen those grim eyes in the streets today. Tomorrow it'll be worse. It's all evil. But it's all wonderful, too."

"I fail to see the connection."

"There is no connection, Jameel. The thing is wonderful in spite of its inherent evil. You see, it is a sign of vitality. Vitality, at last. Not decay. Not stagnation. Not connivance. But sheer full-blooded vitality. Our people can now flare up. They can unglue their rears from their seats and walk down the streets in hordes and actually crack their throats with shouting. It means we're no longer dead. It doesn't matter whom we're rising up against. Sooner or later we'll hit on the right thing, the right person."

"But the injury, the suffering, the blood incurred in such an uprising—they're all wasted?"

"Nothing is wasted. It is part of the exercise in will power. For eight hundred years we've been cowed and kicked about. A little more and nothing of the sort will happen. But we must exercise our limbs, we must hurry, we must learn to face the gunfire. Our poets have sung about blood and fire in their works to the point of sickness. It is time now they saw blood and fire in the flesh. Ten years from now the Palestine disaster would not have happened. We would have learnt by that time how to stir up our vitality, how to tap it, how to direct it against any hostile power in the world."

"Ten years from now. Cold comfort! What are we going to do for Palestine now?"

"That's just another reason why the people, the students, everybody, should bestir themselves. There's much evil in it, I tell you. But there's no other way. Oh how I hate the mob. It's a fearful monster. But that is the way life's energy,

126

life's will, can be asserted. God bless the loathsome monster."

"I'm not convinced," I said. "We have always relied on the mob in vain. That is why we lost the better half of Palestine. One rifle in a trained hand is worth a thousand men shouting slogans in the streets."

"We'll get the rifles too," he said solemnly.

"Where from? America? Russia? It will only mean we're putting ourselves at the mercy of whoever will offer us arms. Look at our soldiers and volunteers in Palestine."

"What else can we do?"

"I don't know. Short of making our own arms——"

"Where shall we get the know-how, the steel, the materials? We'll have to wait for another century, Jameel. We can't wait."

For the first time I felt I could divulge a little secret, a very unimportant one, to my friend. "When at home the Zionists were butchering us like sheep, a group of young men met——"

Adnan made a sudden leap to the door. He opened it and looked out, then, reassured that no one was eavesdropping, shut it, came back and said with great interest, "Yes?"

"Well, we met and decided to retaliate: to infiltrate behind the enemy lines, to blow up their houses and streets as they did ours. But who could spare a penny for an explosive charge? So, we had to go abroad, we said, to collect money in secret, recruit infiltrators, have them trained——"

"A good idea, but it'll take years."

"We gave it three or four years."

"And then?"

"It came to nothing. It was a wild gesture—it came to nothing. Unless it was organised on a large scale, and we had agents in Europe and America, and got the backing of

127

one or two governments, we realised it was even silly to talk about it."

"I wonder." Adnan bit his lip nervously. "I wonder," he repeated. "Still, we have the mob. It's not entirely hopeless."

The door was flung violently open, and Adnan's face went white as a sheet. Husain rushed in looking deeply perturbed.

"She's gone," Husain exclaimed furiously. "She's gone, the bloody whore!"

"I wish you'd learn to knock on the door," Adnan shouted angrily. "You've given me a fright. Who is gone?"

"Samiha," Husain said.

"What, your brothel sweetheart?" I said. "Surely you're not angry to see her get away?"

"Not from the brothel," he said, "but from the room I had lodged her in."

"Good for her," Adnan said. He smiled. "I don't think Jameel knows what you did recently."

"The whore daughter of a whore," Husain continued in a passion. "You don't know what I risked to smuggle her out of that filthy hole. Prostitutes there, being a public menace, are not allowed to leave the brothel. It cost us a lot of money and worry to get her out and teach her some decency. 'I'll never look at a man', she said. 'Just keep my body and soul together, and I'll do anything you want me to.' The damn bitch. I found a room with some people on the other side of the river. Of course I claimed she was my wife. I paid her rent and gave her money for food. I bought her a dress and a good pair of shoes which cost me two and a half dinars. I never paid that much for any shoes that I have worn. And there you are. She couldn't stay respectable for two weeks on end."

Adnan enjoyed the event enormously. "Clever Samiha! So she's had the courage to run away," he said. "There's

128

vitality for you. She wants to go back to life her own way. Of course she'd bite the hand that fed her. But no matter."

"The bitch sent me mad," resumed Husain. "When I went an hour ago to see her, the people in charge of the house said she'd told them she was going away to see her mother in Hilla. And I know both her parents are dead."

I laughed. Husain was in a temper, but even he was about to see the comedy in his situation.

"Think of all those poems you wrote about her," I said.

"Damn her. She didn't deserve them. They're all whores. I've never had luck with a woman I loved, whore or no whore. She had such a beautiful body, though. But I never actually slept with her. Impotent, impotent, she'd say, the bitch. I didn't want to hurt her feelings by telling her I didn't care for syphilis."

"Did she ever read the poems?"

"She just about deciphered them. I am going to publish them when the riots are over. And believe me I'm going to make money on them. They're beautifully erotic. Adnan dishes up the politics, I dish up the sex, and between us——"

"Don't be silly," interrupted Adnan. He was angry at the implied slur on his beliefs.

"Well, I mean, people want a bit of politics and a bit of sex, you know. I'll never forgive her though, never forgive her."

When about an hour later Husain and I left—Adnan was staying behind to do some writing—Husain confided to me with great feeling, "I love that fellow Adnan. I don't know why he insists on living in such a place, when he can live in a decent house in Karradeh. You know, it was his money that I used to save Samiha and buy her clothes and put her up in an honest room. He wouldn't mention it, though. He has an income of about thirty dinars a month. But it all goes on such mad schemes, helping this one and that one.

129

It sounds crazy, doesn't it? There are days when he hasn't enough money for a good dinner. I can't understand him. I think he is the greatest poet alive in this country, don't you? But that whore, Samiha, she really had the nerve to give me the slip. I am going to publish all those poems and dedicate them 'To Samiha, with Hate and Unforgiveness': it sounds good. But I hope the riots won't last too long. The students will go out in a huge demonstration tomorrow. It's very exciting. You never know what might happen."

# 18

The following day tension was in every face. The passengers on the bus I took to the college were silent and furtive. The noise of the street had failed to rise that morning to its usual pitch. The air was charged with a secret desperation, an undeclared fear. In the college corridors there was a peculiar hush, anticipatory and hostile. The whole city throbbed with a sinister grimness, as if the very buildings, the very shops and deserted cafés, had lain in ambush marking time. And I remembered similar days in Jerusalem, days of strikes and demonstrations, days of anger and agony. I remembered the hundred and eighty days of 1936 when, in outraged protest, no shop was opened, no car—not even a bicycle—ran in the streets or on the highways. I remembered the days in 1946 when the mangled bodies of more than a hundred men and women were one by one removed from under the debris of one of the wings of the King David Hotel, which had been blown up by Zionist terrorists, and the funerals that passed in cortege after cortege through the mournful streets of the desecrated city. I remembered all my years in Jerusalem, for they had passed through the same atmosphere of protest, defiance and anguish, under the predatory shadow of police and soldiery. Back there we had contended with alien forces, trying to assert our will against another will that sought our destruction, until it almost succeeded. But here, in this city, the contention was within: it was the act of a city groping in the dark, stumbling upon sharp edges. It was the nightmare that had to be dreamed before awakening.

Truckloads of policemen were stationed at strategic points: in the squares and near the bridges especially, to prevent the confluence of demonstrating crowds streaming in from different parts of the city. The policemen, dark and haggard and taut-faced, were armed with clubs. In their eyes one could detect the fear and incipient ferocity of an animal turning at bay. They probably knew theirs was the most ungrateful task in the world. Like mercenary troops, they did not know what exactly they were out to defend, but they were aware that in an act of violence they would be subjected to the first shattering impact. They received the people's hatred and hurled it back doubled at them. And though they were the visible symbols of authority and inter-diction, they could think of themselves only as unfortunate individuals each with a duty and a physical need for a salary, with a wife and half a dozen children at home who feverishly awaited his safe return. As I looked at their anonymous pock-marked, boil-spotted faces, and their bony restless hands, betraying a poverty of soul and flesh, I wondered if they ever asked themselves, "Why are we not loved a little more?" But such a question would have already verged on the disloyal and seditious.

I was in the college Staff Room—since no students had turned up—when the charged hush that had hung over the city exploded in many parts at once. Outside the central area, on both sides of the river, scattered groups coalesced into crowds, and each crowd after some confusion, after some swaying and milling, ordering and contradicting, presently became a massive body which moved forward in a solemn mysterious rhythm, slow and relentless. Young women, some in their black abas, mingled with men of all ages and professions. But the driving force everywhere were the students, young, angry, full of memories of other rebellions in history.

Meanwhile the policemen, in file upon file, in trucks and armoured cars, waited tensely for the slightest aberration in the movement of the advancing thousands.

Now, in order to experience the savage plenitude of mass violence, you have to be at different points at the same time. One may be thankful that such ubiquity is denied one. And yet in such a crowd you acquire the exhilarating feeling of being one and many simultaneously. Every now and then, as the mob advances or sways, comes the sharp realisation that you are appallingly alone, appallingly average, deprived of the distinction on which you pride yourself. But the realisation does not last long. For you are involved in a battle which, lacking prearranged plans for offensive or retreat, is one enormous eddy, in spite of the shadow leaders, who may or may not be on the spot, who presumably channel the demonstration. In all this you are no more than a tiny faceless unit, flotsam in the torrent. It is the police, as a rule, who will finally select the strategic ground, who will try to get the rioters into a sort of Thermopylæ Pass, where the few can rout the many, if not with clubs then with tear gas or automatic fire.

From the Staff Room windows my colleagues (many of them British) and I could see at least one such crowd. At a distance of less than a mile a vast multitude rolled towards us like an implacable flood. It moved unimpeded with a roar of indistinct cries. After a time the cries, synchronised with the heavy marching, became a regular choral response to somebody shouting words of denunciation. From all over the city similar shouts came, booming and echoing. A small shrill voice would rip the air, and a thunderous yell would follow. When the advance was halted a speaker perched on his fellows' shoulders, and lashed up emotion with fiery oratory. The passion and the frenzy were never more intense than when a young woman in a black dress stood high up amidst the tossing mass and recited some of her verses: every rhyme with insidious magic drew a terrifying collective groan. On the roofs and balconies flanking the street, the huddled spectators were as thick and loud as the demonstrators. With their colour and movement it might have been a feast, had it not been for the anguish discernible in the voices that rose and fell.

When the crowd got to the street on which the college stood, it rumbled through it towards the Square. And no sooner had they got near it than they were warned not to advance any further and to fall back. But as the demonstrators heading from different directions were to join forces in Rashid Street, the Square had to be penetrated. The entrance to it from our street, on account of its narrowness, was ideal for the purposes of the police. And in a few minutes, there was a charge, a counter-charge, the mob swayed, broke up into blocks, and a shower of missiles seemed to fall from the four corners of the sky on the policemen in the Square. The tail-end, unable to engage anyone, was made ineffectual and was already beginning to disintegrate. There were screams of pain and bellowings of wrath. The neighbouring houses were stormed by different groups which immediately appeared on the flat roofs, where they removed the bricks off the ledges with naked hands and hurled them at the Square. Some dropped bricks carefully

133

on the pavements to be collected as weapons by those below. A human sea churned and seethed and roared.

The policemen had so far held their ground with clubs. But they were being overpowered and the bricks were hitting home. Suddenly from a police car in the Square a shot was fired. Then another. A rattle of shots followed. The mass cracked, then fell apart into hundreds of stray individuals running in different directions, the policemen pursuing them with renewed energy.

Almost under our window, a policeman's club hit a girl on the head. She fell in a heap. Half a dozen students fell upon him at once. They stretched him out and clubbed him with his own weapon, stripped him of his gun, and kneaded him with their heels.

Horse-cabs were driven up to the scene and the wounded were carried to them by their friends. At some distance the benches of a café were used as beds for the injured, while others dipped their fingers in their blood and wrote "Long Live FREEDOM" "Down with Feudalism" on banners which were immediately carried to the scene of battle.

Police reinforcements were rushed up from behind the mob. They jumped out of their cars and in twos and threes started seizing anyone that fell in their hands and throwing them into the car with armed guards. Suddenly automatic fire came from an unexpected quarter: the top of a tall palm tree in front of a house near the Square. All heads at once turned up towards the tree. A policeman with a tommy gun perched uncomfortably amidst the long palm branches. At least thirty men stormed the house, but no one appeared on the roof, which was on a level with the policeman in his sniper's nest in the tree. All at once from the house came four or five shots. The sniper dropped like a ripe fruit. Out came the mob with a tin of kerosene, which they poured on the prostrate policeman. They set a match to it. Savage

134

yells rose as the terrible human flame shot up and sizzled.

About midday the Army was called in. At the sight of the first armoured car with the machine-gun turret, the people were quiet, and the shooting stopped. As the Army moved in, the mob began to withdraw, some of them even cheered the Army. In less than an hour the Square, like a change of scene on the stage, was cleared. When I went out of the college building, the street was deserted, except for an odd pedestrian, like me, lurching home. Near the Square my eyes itched and watered, and my nose ran: the clinging smell of tear gas had turned the place into a valley of tears. It was littered with bricks and clubs and shoes, and smeared here and there with blood. Except for an occasional tank rumbling slowly along, it was fearfully lonely. And fearfully silent.

# 19

Although there were no more riots, the tension was not dispelled for a few days. Gradually, however, the city regained its mobility, the cafés were full to capacity again, and the criers of lottery tickets, of roasted water-melon seeds, were back on their articulate rounds. A number of people had been killed, many more injured. In the meantime the jails were becoming jammed with students and suspects. But the voices of protest, under the temporarily imposed martial law, were faint and few.

When the Nafawis' car collected me for the usual lesson, and Abed accompanied me to Sulafa's room and sat on his stool, I found Sulafa gayer than usual.

"I thought you'd never come," she said in English.

"Did you think I was lost in the riots?" I said.

"I was afraid you might be."

"Why didn't you telephone to find out? For seven days you neglected me."

She walked to the window and looked out on the glistening river. "I didn't neglect you," she said.

My knees, as I sat in the armchair, trembled against my will. "Come back to your chair, Sulafa," I said harshly.

She turned round slowly, and said in a calm voice, "I love you."

"I wish you'd throw out that creature on the stool," I hissed through clenched teeth. I wondered if Abed, despite his vacant look, saw my agitation. He had just lit a cigarette, and his blue lips emitted discreet exhalations of smoke. "I feel like shouting at the top of my voice. Here am I, paid by your father to teach you, and I fall in love with you. It's cheap. It's shameful."

Sulafa leaned back against the window. "I don't care," she said. "I love you."

"Out of a quarter of a million women in Baghdad, I choose you to be in love with. You, the acquiescent, the unhurried, the incommunicable, the—prisoner. It's horrible."

"How I longed to join those demonstrators the other day —if only for your sake." Her voice was tremulous, as though she were holding back a gasp.

"Why didn't you?"

"My father nearly had a collapse when I told him. He went mad. Oh, I would have loved to go out there with that screaming mob. I would have liked to have our Humber filled with bricks, so that I could hurl bricks all day long at all the repression, the lies, the cruelty——". She turned back to the river.

Presently I said, "If you won't chuck this fellow out of

136

the room, I think you'd better come back to your seat. Let's do a bit of work."

Obediently she went to her chair. "But I want to talk," she said.

"We'll talk later."

"When later?"

"I wish I knew."

"I'm afraid I haven't written the silly essay you wanted me to write."

I laughed nervously. My colour, changing every second, must have been great fun for Abed to watch. But he looked as uninterested as ever. "It's all right," I said. "And I agree it was silly."

"But I've written something else."

"Good. Let me see it."

"It's very long. And in Arabic." She went to her desk and, unlocking the top drawer, got out a large envelope. I thought it was a love letter. She took out the sheets and said, "It's a long letter. About my life—or should I say, my death?"

When I stood up to take it from her, she held it back. "I'll give it to you at the end of the hour. I don't dare see you reading it."

Unexpectedly, she turned to Abed and said peremptorily, "Abed!"

Abed rose to his feet at once. "Yes, madam?"

"Get us some tea."

"Shall I call Fatima?" (She was the cook).

"No. Go and see if there is any tea ready. If not, make some and bring it in yourself."

He hesitated a little. Then going to the door he said, "Yes, madam."

No sooner had he stepped out than Sulafa looked wide-eyed at me, as though frightened by a sudden thought. I was

137

frightened too. Both of us, simultaneously, swept forward to each other. She fell in my arms violently and without saying a word gave me her lips. It was a hot agonised kiss, as I felt the sweet soft resilience of her lips and the hardness of her teeth. Our mouths were torn apart with the same violence with which they met, and we retired to our respective places, my heart pounding and sending torrents of blood to my head. Sulafa went yellow and red in the face, and her hands were transparent, like alabaster. The numerous sheets of her letter were all over the floor.

Abed was not back yet. Though we did not utter a word, I knew we shared the same thought: could we kiss again before he appeared? With the desperation born of long withheld desire we jumped to our feet again and stood in each other's arms. The hot agonised kiss burnt holes in my head, a thousand windows long shut in it were flung wide open. The room was flooded with a joy maddened by long compulsory silence. I kissed her again and again, on the mouth, on the nose, on the cheek, on the throat, on the mouth again. And only just in time did we go back to our seats. As I consciously tasted the sweet traces of Sulafa's saliva on my lips, Abed was back with the tea. "I wish he'd died in the kitchen!" she said. A husky laugh sounded in my throat.

We had done the impossible.


# 20


When I left the house with the garden of roses and eucalyptus trees, I asked the Nafawis' chauffeur to take me to the Shahrazad Hotel. I went straight to the bar (where as yet there were only two or three people), sat in a corner and impatiently took out the wad of sheets which Sulafa had given me. It was a long letter in Arabic written over a period of some days. But it must have been written at dizzy speed —for there it was, full of indecipherable words, of inadvertent ellipses, of spelling mistakes. As I read it through, my skin, from my ankles to my neck, went through alternate spasms and shivers. For the first time I heard Sulafa's voice: excitable, tormented, feverish. Everything was enlarged in her eyes, and unbearably heightened.

It began thus:

"Last night I called you but my voice was choked. You'd had tea with my father and gone out with Aunt Salma and left me, as usual, on the edge of the precipice. I am clinging hard to the edge. I don't want to fall over. I called you to get some reassurance from you, but I knew the ground was giving way under my feet. I couldn't sleep. I felt hot and was perspiring. The dawn had broken pale and cruel before I slept. . . ."

It went on and on.

"I do not want to love you, because each time I think of your love I tremble and think of death. Then I think of you, of your serenity, of the peace which radiates from your face, and I love you more. I know how much you have suffered, in spite of your apparent serenity. Whereas I was not even given the chance to suffer, unless you call family quarrels suffering. And now I fall to pieces with one blow. I know you think I am cold-blooded and incapable of passion, because my face is hard and my voice never varies its pitch. Perhaps now you'll know how wrong you are. Perhaps now you'll know that there are shadows falling on my face to obscure my expression, and my tongue is tied up in a knot. . . .

". . . I am making you my accomplice in a secret crime. It's all in my mind, of course, My mind is becoming a

139

fertile ground for criminal thoughts. I've seen myself there jumping into the Tigris with you in my arms; I've seen you there dressed in a wide bedouin cloak in the folds of which you hid me until we reached a strange shore where a boat was waiting for us: I've even seen you kill poor Abeḍ. But now my mind bursts forth with much more horrible things, and I seem there to be tempting you to commit a crime so hideous that I don't dare name it. You come to us for an hour and go away, like an angel from another sphere, not knowing what thoughts you leave behind. I must have loved you the very moment I saw you, because my love now seems so full, so ripe, as if it had begun years ago. But for the dark thoughts I can only blame myself, and perhaps my father. Oh Jameel, I am so mixed up, my writing makes no sense, I am sure. . . .

". . . Did you know I had a married sister, and a brother married to an Italian girl (she is so lovely, everybody says she was a nightclub dancer)? My brother lives in the United States now, my sister is happy with her husband in Baghdad. Twice I nearly got married, but fortunately escaped. Three years ago—should I tell you this?—Adnan Talib, whom you know (he is my cousin, too) came to my father and asked my hand in marriage. Father was furious when Adnan left. He thought it was insulting. Uncle Omar had just died when Adnan came to propose, and we had heard all kinds of stories about him since he had rebelled against his family and wouldn't even use our surname. After that I saw him a few times, usually at a distance. At the cinema especially. I noticed how he'd wait for me at the turn of the street whenever I went in the afternoon for a drive: I knew he waited for me by the way he looked at me, straight through the car's window. I pretended not to see him. O trivialities, you'll say. Mother receives a flood of women visitors every Tuesday. From morning till midnight they play cards and drink tea and lemonade and talk, talk, talk, like a thousand parrots about husbands, children, boy lovers, girl lovers, you would think the whole of the Arabian Nights were coming back to life in the shapes of those fat-breasted women. Finally they go away leaving behind their gossip, their stories of sex and money and scandal, hanging over the dirty plates and glasses and remnants of food and shells of pistachio nuts. Trivialities? And you call on me and we read about King Lear and Goneril and Regan and Cordelia. Perhaps Goneril and Regan were right, the way they treated their father? It's a blasphemous thought, I know, but how could they have turned into such harpies if the proud old father had not ill-treated them before dividing his kingdom? Perhaps their subsequent acts were not acts of pure cruelty but of revenge? If he had not ill-treated them, he probably had loved them too much. Love can be as deadly as hate....

". . . This morning Salma came to see my father but he was out. She told me everybody in town was apprehensive. I told her I wished some catastrophe would blow us up, and she was angry. She told me she was afraid of violence, because she imagined all those *shargawis*, with their stained turbans and sweat-soiled shirts, breaking loose and going around dagger in hand to loot and rape. She was particularly scared of rape, and she frightened me the way she talked about it. She also spoke about you and told me what you had refused to tell me about Leila, how at midnight you went out of your house when it was shaken by a fearful explosion to see her house in smouldering ruins, how you went rummaging in the rubble for a sign of life and saw only torn pieces of human flesh. Jameel, poor darling. I wish I had been there to ease your pain—but I am mad, and I know it, because I am jealous even of the poor girl who lay buried in those ruins. When Salma left I went to my study and cried like a fool. When three years ago my uncle

141

Omar died my father made me wear mourning black for twelve whole months, though his brother had been an old idiot who should have died centuries ago. Why shouldn't I wear mourning for a girl you loved, a girl in whose death I see the death of myself, the death of a good part of my country and yours? But she had received your love, you had kissed her, you had walked with her all over the hills of Jerusalem. She had had her share. What have I had from you, or from life? I go to our orchards in Baquba in the company of women and servants, I sing the songs all girls learn from the radio, I have my dresses made by Salma's costly dressmaker. But I have yet to listen to a whisper that tempts my flesh, I have yet to touch a hand that throbs for me. May Leila's soul find solace in Paradise. May Sulafa's soul find solace in her parents' long shadows. Jameel, am I being silly? Am I being immoral? Or is this what love is like—open and shameless and rebellious?

". . . I was determined not to telephone you, lest you should interfere with my decisions. Besides, I begin to be afraid of this black instrument with ten blind eyes. They can look so hostile. . . .

". . . I hear the cries of the demonstrators. My father is furious and has been calling up all kinds of people. It is a left-over from his ministerial days. As soon as he puts the receiver down, the telephone rings. But I am secretly elated. Father nearly collapsed when, as gently as I could, I asked him if I could slip out to join the mob. So I am back in my room. (I wonder where you are.) The din is increasing. I hear shots. I can imagine the battle—though vaguely and abstractly. It's like the tempest on the heath in *Lear*: I wish I could scream like the old mad king for the storm to beat on my unhoused head, but my head is only too well housed. The strife and the terror are within. O for the defiance of a Satan. I won't be resigned, my love. I shall also demand

142

independence, sovereignty, even the freedom of self-destruction. But what shall I do? I can't simply walk out of the door, or fling a couple of bricks through father's bedroom window, can I? I am afraid of the streets, as if they were tunnels that surreptitiously, seductively, led one to a dark mysterious place where one could not breathe. Yet I promise never never to be resigned again. . . .

". . . I am still holding myself back from the telephone. I tell myself over and over again no one has more right than I to use this black instrument of communication with the world outside. But I will have no interference with my determination. My determination is mine alone. I am perhaps bothering you, perhaps tormenting you, perhaps involving you against your better judgment. When I heard your voice a few times over the phone I could hear—or did I imagine it?—your lips touching, your tongue clicking against your teeth. You only said a few words, but you came so close to me that I imagined your lips against my ear, my cheek, my mouth. It was like being kissed—I've never been kissed by a man—and I was afraid. No. I shall not call you. . . .

". . . But what can we do, my love? I don't suppose I shall have the courage even to give you this long wild letter, let alone embark upon a venture more mad and more deadly. We have been deprived of the freedom of choice. Freedom, freedom, everybody talks about it. (Even father does, but with what contempt! A 'free' man, he says, is unorthodox and, consequently, anti-social. A 'free' woman is, of course, a 'bad' woman. And that's that.) But who can be free? Adam perhaps was free in Eden, because his children had not yet been born. If I want freedom I must go against the wishes and unwritten laws of Adam's children. Oh, Jameel, what can we do? Where can we go? I feel dizzy in the head when I think of it. It's like my feeling when I think of being

143

in your arms. I think I should faint. It's like all those demonstrators feeling free for a few hours then succumbing under the hostility of law and order. What law, what order, I do not know. I am terrified. I am the greatest coward in the world. I am afraid of my own love. . . ."

I went over the letter again and again. I had had three drinks already. My head was spinning. My hands shook. I was full of joy and full of venom at once. The city seemed to have peeled off part of its skin where I saw the sore puss-covered flesh. I loved Sulafa; I loved her for her fears and her despondency; at last she could *say* it, she could at last get something off her chest. But what did she mean by her 'decision', 'determination', 'crime'? I was not so foolish as to contemplate for a moment that she meant running away; she made it quite clear herself. Did she merely think she was from now on to try and see me more often, alone, or somewhere out of her house? I did not know. She had also startled me: Adnan had wanted to marry her! The fool had never told me. He had never so much as asked me about her. Did he love her still? What would he say if he knew we were in love? I was so fond of Adnan that I thought I might tell him. On second thoughts, the idea seemed foolish. Obviously I had to keep the whole matter secret. The only person to whom I could talk about it was Sulafa herself; sitting yards away or weeping over the phone. It was hideous. Love had to become a secret mystic passion for the intangible and incommunicable. We might as well have loved the moon or the stars and hoped for an entranced kiss stolen in a dream. Nor could I forget about Adnan. She dismissed him in a few phrases, light-heartedly. Could she imagine what bitterness that incident had caused him? What would she say if she read his poem about women crucifying a man on a palm tree for their lust? But Adnan was out of the picture now. His affair was over, mine beginning.

144

"Jameel!" I winced abominably when a hand rested gently on my shoulder and a voice called my name against my face.

Almost guiltily I folded the sheets of Sulafa's letter while I looked up. It was Brian.

"Don't be startled," he said. "You must have been terribly absorbed."

"Yes, rather," I said weakly and shoved the letter in my inner breast pocket.

"I called you twice from the corner over there, but you didn't hear me."

When I looked in the direction he indicated I saw Salma and her grey husband sitting at a table with drinks. And the memory of my drive with Salma fell upon my mind like a hammer: I saw the endlessly straight bumpy road with the trees caught in the beams of the headlights and nodding like conniving ghosts, while Salma clung to me.

I smiled to them both and bowed a little. Ahmad Rubeidi grinned for a second, and Salma, with her elbow on the table, waved her hand slightly then put it down.

"Come and join us," Brian said.

"Wouldn't you rather be alone?" I said. I should have put that question to myself. For seven days Salma had dropped clean out of my mind, and now I was reluctant to renew the contact.

"Don't be an ass," Brian said softly. "Come on. They're my guests."

We went over to them.

The waiter came and I ordered a fourth brandy.

"You must have been reading something very important," Ahmad Rubeidi said. "We sat here for some time watching you."

"How unkind of you," I said. "You could have at least warned me. Did my expression change a lot?"

"Quite a lot."

"I said it must be a love letter," Salma said.

I laughed as best I could and said "It's nothing very important."

"Have you heard the news?" Brian said.

"What news?"

"About Adnan," Salma said.

My heart sank.

"He's been arrested," she said.

"How hideous."

"He'll be out soon," Mr. Rubeidi said. "We'll see to that."

"I hope so," I said.

"But not too soon," he added. "The boy has ruined himself."

"No one could be more harmless, if you ask me," Brian said. "He's passionate. He is tormented by some utopian vision. An honest frustrated idealist, that's what he is."

Salma took a packet of cigarettes out of her bag and said, "Adnan has succeeded in making of himself an intellectual in a very unintellectual atmosphere." She lit a cigarette. "Are such men always frustrated idealists?"

"Whatever frustration there is in him and whatever idealism," I said, "they are typical of fifty million Arabs."

Mr. Rubeidi was unwilling to subscribe to such abstract speculations. "Adnan is like many other young fellows around. Raw and obstinate. He refuses to accept facts. Self-centred too. And don't tell me the Arabs are idealistic. They are practical and logical. And don't tell me they're frustrated. They're incompetent. There's a lot of difference between frustration and incompetence. I'll tell you what's wrong with Adnan. He was badly brought up. I knew his father very well."

"Give the boy some credit, Ahmad," his wife said. "You

146

have to sympathise with the younger generation to see their point of view."

Mr. Rubeidi resented the reference to the younger generation. He waved a hand decked with a large ruby ring and said, "I don't want to see their point of view."

"Do you know why Adnan was arrested?" I asked Salma.

"In connection with the riots," she said. "And, of all places, in a public bath in Narrow Street."

I was stunned. That was the place he had considered safe for clandestine meetings.

"That was where we first met," Brian said. "Was he found to be a ringleader or something?"

"As far as I know, he took no part in the demonstrations."

"I am not surprised," I said. "He is not actually a mobster."

"You see?" the old gentleman said. "Such men don't even have the courage of their convictions. I hope they'll knock some sense into their heads."

Brian beckoned to the waiter to get us another drink each. I was getting drunk and felt miserable. Sulafa's words were seething in my brain and I kept thinking of her sweeping towards me for a violent kiss. But Adnan also obsessed me. I imagined us all in his dusty cobwebbed room: grey-haired Rubeidi with his precious rings and bow tie sitting on the stained floor to talk about carpets, Brian examining with curious eyes the empty cans and bottles, Salma furtively touching my hand, Sulafa sitting statuesquely on the iron bed to recite her own letter, while Adnan played his record of the scaffold scene in Berlioz's symphony and solemnly went through the act of execution, and I, withdrawing my hand from under Salma's, sang in a powerful bass the *Dies Irae*.

"Which reminds me," Brian said. "Somebody told me

147

Husain had his head bashed in, poor fellow. In the demonstrations."

"What? I must see him," I said.

"You can't. He's in jail too. Incommunicado."

"Well, we'd better move," Mr. Rubeidi suggested. It was nearly eight o'clock.

"Yes, we'd better," Salma said.

"You seem to be in a hurry," I said.

"We're having dinner at the Alwiya Club with the Blenkinsops," Salma explained. Blenkinsop was a member of the British Embassy.


# 21


And on that very evening, about three hours later, when I was in my room, thinking of myself, as I had often thought, hitting an ultimate wall in flight or in pursuit—I never knew which—Salma, whom I always forgot when she was not there, was on the telephone.

"I am at the Club," she said softly. She did not want to be overheard.

"After a good dinner, I trust," I said.

"They're playing bridge."

"Why aren't you?"

"I refused to play. I am bored."

"Boredom is passive. I am positively sick."

"Listen."

"Yes?"

She whispered something, and I said, "What did you say? I can't hear you."

"How about a drive?"

"Oh Lord," I thought. "What, now?"

"Yes."

"Are you serious?"

And her voice gasped ever so softly, "Please. I'll explain later."

"All right. I'll wait on the kerb."

I could never explain my acquiescence. Like a man who is offered a drink, then another, then another, then many others, who accepts them and gulps them down because he refuses to resist, until he is drunk and says all the things he never wanted to say, until he is sick and self-abominating, until he befouls himself and everything around him, I accepted her invitation for a drive. I was not entirely sober, but I knew very well that I was going out with Salma against all the laws of self-respect. (Sulafa was like a wound in my brain.) 'Wait, Jameel,' I said to myself, 'for the woman who wants to rejuvenate her flesh upon your flesh, while Sulafa rages like a fever in your head. Tell that to Salma, the civilised woman who knows and admits and loves the disease and the futility of her life: she will understand.'

In a few minutes she was there in her Buick behind the wheel. I got in and sat next to her.

"I must be back at the Club before midnight," she said. "We've hardly an hour."

"Won't they miss you?"

"Oh, I told Ahmad I was going out for a short drive. He doesn't mind."

"And the Blenkinsops?"

"They were all too busy with their bridge. There were six tables."

"Where did you call from?"

"From the phone in the Club's lobby. I phoned my sister first—Sulafa's mother—just in case."

"You're mad."

149

"I know. But since our last drive I couldn't get you out of my mind."

"You're mad. You're courting disaster."

"Please, Jameel."

She hardly looked at me and drove too fast.

"Where are we going?"

"Will you light me a cigarette?"

I did. She took a couple of pulls then threw the cigarette out of the car window.

We came to a place where the houses were sparse. I had not been to that suburb before, and it was not well lit. We stopped outside a house that had no lights in it. All around us were trees.

"This house belongs to us. It was rented by an American family that left some days before the demonstrations."

We got out of the car. The small iron gate was ajar. We walked up a short concrete path that cut across a small garden. The key was already in her hand. She unlocked the door and we stole into the dark hall like thieves.

"We shan't turn on any lights," she said.

In the dim light that filtered from the street through the muslin-curtained windows I could just see that the rooms were furnished, and Salma knew her way around.

"You're the maddest woman alive," I said.

I sat on a settee by the window and pulled her down to me. When she sat in my lap I wanted to see her naked. I drew a curtain back for more light from the street and she wound her arms round my neck. "We'll be seen," she whispered.

I pulled her dress over her head. I hated her. I hoped I'd see a lot of flaccid outworn flesh in my lap. But she was firm and smooth. She drew away from me and slipped down to the floor, so that I could see her better as she writhed and tossed on the tiles. My flesh was cold and deliberate. But

150

I slipped down too and took her resilient nudity in my arms.

Her lips were savage. My fingers, ice-cold, dug into her body like blind chisels in a hot quivering mass.

On our way back I said, "I can see how well you planned everything."

"What do you mean?"

"It was no accident that you had on you the key of the unoccupied house, that your chauffeur was kept at home tonight."

"I hate you."

"We shall never do this again."

"Do you think I like risking all this horror?"

"You must do your bloody best to get Adnan out of jail."

"You talk as if you were in love with him."

"Jealous even of a friend?"

"I want you, Jameel."

"But——"

"Yes?"

"I am in love with somebody else."

She applied the brake so impulsively that the car gave a loud shriek as it came to a violent stop.

"Who with? Somebody here?" Her voice rasped in her throat.

I did not answer. She started the car again.

"Tell me, please, tell me. Do I know her?"

"No," I said coldly.

"Does Sulafa by any chance—" she hesitated. "Does she love you?"

"Whoever put that thought into your head?"

She drove in silence. And I hated her, hated her like poison, because she was crying, and because, to my horror, she looked beautiful, because she had at last succeeded in stirring in me a foul desire for her flesh.

"Suppose we go back again?" I said.

151

"Where?" she moaned.

"To the house we've just left."

"We haven't much time."

"We have," I said, and placed my hand on her thigh.

At the next traffic island she turned round. When we entered the dark house again her face was still wet with tears. She took me to a bedroom with an unmade bed, and there spitefully, ferociously, I vented upon her the violence, the venom, the misery of a desperate lust. But in the dark, with my eyes shut in one kiss after another, I imagined the body of Sulafa writhing hotly against mine.

# 22

When at about midnight I went up to my room, there was nothing I could dread more than a telephone call from Sulafa. So I took up the receiver and left it off, as though I had thus put out of action a bomb which might otherwise have blown up in my face. I did not replace the receiver until the following morning.

At night Sulafa rang up.

"Jameel!" her voice pleaded.

"Yes, my love?"

"Can I see you tomorrow?"

"Could you? How?"

"It isn't easy."

"Don't do anything rash, Sulafa." Last night's feeling of guilt had not abandoned me.

"No. I shall only see you for two or three munutes in any case. Have you read my letter?"

"Yes, many times."

152

"Well, listen. At about four tomorrow afternoon I shall drop in at Matheel's Bookshop. Could you be there at that hour?" She sounded strange and upset.

"Of course," I said. "I'll be there before you."

"Do you love me?"

Matheel's Bookshop had a queer shape: like a long wedge, it was narrow at the entrance and wide at the far end. The entrance was choked with magazines, paper-bound books from England and America, and pamphlet-like books printed in Baghdad. The portly owner, ever-delighted, ever-loquacious, sat near the door at a desk piled up with more magazines and books some of which he seemed to read himself during the less busy hours.

"Hello, hello, hello, Professor Jameel!" he exclaimed. "I was hoping you'd come. I've just received the Oxford University Press Catalogue." He rummaged in the pile in front of him and produced it. "Would you mind taking it home to mark the books you think your students might want to read?"

"Certainly," I said. "I don't know what we would do without you, Mr. Matheel." I took the volume from him and walked down to the other end of the shop where the more solid books were placed. There was only one other customer, going over some magazines. I was praying to God that Matheel would not leave his desk to tell me about the last consignment of books he had received. Fortunately he opened an Arabic book—I watched him from the corner of my eye—and started to read.

About five minutes later a car stopped outside, and Sulafa came in. I looked intently at Matheel's face, as he looked up, to see if it betrayed any signs of recognition. I was not sure it did. At least Matheel did not fall over her neck as he seemed to do with the people he knew.

Sulafa and I enacted a little scene of happy surprise. We

153

even shook hands. God, how young she looked, I thought. Her eyes, like wild birds, flew this way and that: she, too, wanted to know whether she had been recognised. She held a small handbag. She wore a white sleeveless blouse which made her look darker, and perhaps cooler, than she actually was.

"What do you advise me to read?" she said, a little too loudly even for Matheel's benefit.

"Let's have a look here."

We turned our backs to the entrance as we looked at the book-lined bottom wall. Behind us was a long table arrayed with books and magazines.

Elated, I whispered over an open book, "Darling!"

She smiled. She opened her handbag and, before I realised what she was doing, produced a ten dinar note which she slipped into my hand.

"What is this?" I whispered.

"I want you to buy me a gun," she said in a soft but sure, unhesitant voice.

Dumbfounded, I looked at her fixedly. I did not even mind Matheel seeing us then.

"What for?" I said.

She took a heavy volume from a shelf and said aloud, "I want to read it."

I could not return the money without spoiling our act.

"What's the title?" I said.

"The Oxford Companion to English Literature," she answered. Then softly, "Please, bring it along at our next lesson on Monday. I need it, I need it badly."

I remembered all those cryptic remarks about 'determination' and 'crime' in her letter.

"Can't." I shook my head violently.

"Please." Her face, so often blank and impassive, was for a second intense and agonised. "I love you," she said

154

by soundlessly moving her lips. Then aloud, "Good-bye, Professor."

Leaving me behind, she took the volume for Matheel to look at. I watched her like an idiot, incapable of even accompanying her to the door. She paid for the book and went out. The car door banged. The ten-dinar note was crumpled into a ball in my closed fist. I shoved it into my pocket soliloquising as I pretended to examine more books on the shelves, "So with this I am to purchase somebody's death? My lover's death, perhaps, as well?"

# 23

The next two days were long, very long. Not even work could peacefully bridge the span between one hour and another. Every minute, every second, had to be experienced. Every minute, every second, tore its way through me. I realised how the sand slipped down in an hour glass, only the sand was made up of pulse, of blood, and the movement downward was not as smooth, as slipping. I did not buy the gun for Sulafa—I thought I had that much sense at least. But I had to wait for the lesson hour on Monday, when Sulafa might explain, when I could see her eyes wild and frightened again, and hear her voice. She did not ring me up. I stayed in both evenings. I sat up all night in bed waiting for the cold black messenger to ring. It did not. Two abysmal days yawning out their vacuum, which I had to fill up with the blood of my waiting.

Then it was Monday 5 o'clock, when the Nafawis' chauffeur was due to collect me. I had been looking down through the window on Rashid Street, sorting out the cars that passed in a steady stream, hoping to spot the black

155

seven-seater Humber up the street, so that I might rush downstairs to meet it. But I looked for a long time to no avail. It was 5.02, 5.05, 5.08, 5.10, 5.15. I was perspiring. The covers of two books seemed to melt in my hot fidgeting hands.

"Something has gone wrong," I said. "I must call."

I had not known Imad's number until then. I looked it up in the telephone directory, then dialled.

The burr-burr sound of the telephone went on and on, like an out-of-breath creature panting without rest. Finally a woman's voice shouted back at me.

"Who's speaking?" it shrieked.

"Jameel Farran."

"What do you want?"

"I want to speak to Imad Beg."

"He's not here."

"To Sulafa, if I may. I am her teacher."

"She's not here either."

"Who are you?" I said with irritation.

"Fatima, the cook."

"Is there no one at home?"

"No. They've gone to Baquba."

"Oh. Thank you." I hung up.

"Hell, hell. What are they up to?" I imagined Sulafa being taken by old Imad to Baquba's orange groves where, under one of those slender-branched sweet-smelling trees, he would make her lie on her back, saying, "I am sorry, my love, but I have promised to slay you for the glory of the God of my forefathers." There would be no ram in the trees, no angel to divert the knife from her virgin throat, and Imad would later come round in his Humber to tell me, "Professor Jameel, will you kindly write an elegy on the death of my daughter for publication in tomorrow's newspaper?"

156

# 24

My landlady knocked on the door then diffidently opened it enough for me to see her face.

"Come in," I said.

She came in and whispered, "There's a man in Arab costume at the door who wants to see you. Shall I let him in?"

"Oh, it must be Towfiq al-Khalaf. Yes, yes." I made for the door myself, when she stopped me to whisper again.

"Be careful of these sheikhs," she said. "They're always running after girls, bad girls."

But I hurried to the apartment's door and welcomed Towfiq whom I had not seen for some weeks.

"I am infuriated," he said as soon as we were back in my room.

"About Adnan?"

"Yes. For the last three days I have been running around, visiting notables and statesmen, ministers and ex-ministers, consuming in this heat large quantities of coffee and tea, in the attempt to get him released."

"Any luck?"

"None. Of course, if he insists on being a bum," he added, removing his diaphanous cloak and placing it on a chair, "he'll have it coming to him. Live like a bum and die like a bum, merely to have a bunch of idiots call you hero and martyr." He sat down.

"Well, if he doesn't get out soon enough, he'll get his heart's desire."

"I am sure the whole thing is considerably exaggerated."

"Or misunderstood."

"I hate city politics."

"How about some coffee?" I interrupted.

"No. Let's go down to the Shahrazad and have a glass of beer. It's nearly sunset." Towfiq was the only man I knew who *refused* to carry a watch.

"All right. But when we've had our coffee." I went out to tell the houseboy to make us some coffee, then returned and said, "So you hate city politics, do you? At least in the desert there are no prisons."

"There are no prisons, and values are sharply distinct. The city is the only place where your values are so mixed up that you cannot distinguish friend from foe, good from evil."

"I don't know why I should have to defend the city against your onslaughts, Towfiq. I hate it as much as you do. But, you see, once so many people are massed together, how can you avoid developing a complex social structure where values cease to be merely black and white, but have an infinite gradation of colour?"

"What's the use of developing a complex social structure when within the folds and interlockings of such a structure you lose your confidence, your peace of mind, your knowledge of right and wrong? Not one among all the people in authority I have visited could tell me anything precise about Adnan. Adnan the dreamer, the poet, the angel, the ne'er-do-well, who in my tribe would be left with a flock of goats to make up rhymes as he crushed his lice between the nails of his two thumbs—I ask you, such an Adnan is, in the city, a seditious character, a wild rebel whose every word and act is a threat to public security. Isn't it mad, I ask you, isn't it mad?"

"But Adnan is not the only one who is looked upon as a wild rebel. Even you and I might be considered rebels if every act and word of ours were known. Within your tribe rebellion would be unnecessary——"

"Rebellion within the tribe? Unimaginable. New ideas are heresies, and heresy is punished by death. Pure and simple."

"Well, we're not very far from tribal life then. Only in the cities, it seems, rebellion has its function. If the cities are to develop, that is."

"Damn development. It'll only mean women will gain even more power than they already possess. More power over men, more power for evil."

"But development also means better homes, healthier children, cleaner streets—a fuller life, you know."

"Nothing of that interests me. We develop from the masculine to the feminine, that's all, and in the process we lose our intrinsic freedom to institutions, to wives, to abstract thoughts. All feminine, all emasculated. And if that's what Adnan is rebelling for, God help him, he deserves what's coming to him."

The houseboy came in with two cups of Turkish coffee. "However," Towfiq resumed, holding the small cup in his large hand, "I love Adnan. He has a good core. Sooner or later I shall take him away, teach him to mount a horse, and keep him from slumming and rebelling and the rest of this adolescent stuff. You should have seen how two or three years ago he was shattered because he couldn't marry his cousin Sulafa. But later on——"

"You know about it?" I jumped from my seat. I was in agony to talk about Sulafa. Many days had passed without a word from her.

"Oh yes. Adnan at the time made no secret of it. He filled the local newspapers with love poems, and everybody knew who the 'wine-mouthed* prisoner by the Tigris' was.

* 'Sulafa' in Arabic means 'strong wine'

159

But he has learnt his lesson since: never subject your mind to a single woman. There's God's plenty of them everywhere. Similarly, he'll learn his political lesson now. Never subject your mind to a single idea."

"What a Machiavelli you are!"

"If you are not a wolf other wolves will eat you up."

I wanted to revert to Sulafa, but my friend was hardly the man I could trust with such a subject. Nor did I care to make her the theme of one of his diatribes.

"Shall we go to the Shahrazad?" Towfiq said after a while. "Or rather—". he stopped and gave me a quizzical look.

"Yes?" I said.

Towfiq's knife-pointed eyes narrowed, shifted, then relaxed. "Do you know the Rising Moon Hotel?" he asked at last.

"Very well indeed."

"Really?"

"I spent many weeks in it when I first came to this city. It was called City Hotel in those days."

"Would you like to come along and see an old friend of mine there?"

"Do I know him?"

"I think you do. Abdul Kader."

"What, Abdul Kader Yassin?"

"Yes."

"Why not give him a ring and ask him to come and join us at the Shahrazad?"

Towfiq uttered a short sarcastic laugh. "He can't come out."

"Why not?"

"He is wanted by the police ever since the day of the demonstrations. You see, he left his home and couldn't think of anything better than moving into a hotel—by way of escape. He has even assumed an alias: he is no longer Abdul Kader Yassin, but Abdul Kader Haj Hussein. That is how the proprietor knows him, and that is how his name is reported in the Lodgers' List which is examined by the authorities every other day."

"And you want us to call on him?"

"Yes. The poor fellow must be bored to death. He pretends he is sick and stays in bed all day long. Otherwise the servants will wonder why he never goes out."

"But has it occurred to you that the authorities may be aware of his identity but refrain from apprehending him?"

"Nonsense."

"So that they can find out who calls on him."

"What?"

"So that he'll act as a decoy."

Towfiq's mouth opened wide to release a loud hilarious laugh. His chest heaved and fell as he bellowed with laughter, his head tilted back, his teeth, with a few gold ones, bared.

"Jameel, Jameel! God help you. Foreign education has vitiated your mind. Do you honestly think it would ever occur to anyone here to do such a vicious thing? God help you! Come on, let's go. The place is no more than a brothel with a clean front. Abdul Kader couldn't be more safe."

"I wonder how sound your judgment is. But I think I'll go with you. Out of bravado, and no more. I couldn't care less for Abdul Kader."

Towfiq stood up and with a graceful flourish donned his cloak. He turned round, displeased with my remark.

"You must realise, my friend, that belief is one thing, friendship another. If my attachments were influenced by

161

beliefs I would turn my back on most of the people I know in Baghdad."

His long handsome face filled with a strange expression, half-suffering, half resignation. In spite of his garb his face reminded me of a Renaissance painting. I dared not tell him about it. "I don't know whether you're a saint or a fiend," I said. "Let's go."


# 25


At the Rising Moon we found Abdul Kader in pyjamas lying coverless in bed, reading. He was startled to see me enter with Towfiq, but trying to look composed he stretched out his arm for a handshake. The skull-face with the globular eyes was black with the stubble of several day's growth. A servant was called and Towfiq gave him some money. "Get us three bottles of beer from the shop below," he said. Abdul Kader protested, but Towfiq was gently blunt with him. "You haven't got money for tea, let alone beer."

"All right, you blood-sucking sheikh," Abdul Kader said. "How can a poor city lawyer compete with a lord of horses and cattle?"

"Never, of course," Towfiq said. "Be seated, Jameel. These degree-holders are the most envious lot under the sun. I beg your pardon! You're a degree-holder, too, aren't you? You're all plotting for power, I know, and when you have failed to get it, you will go underground and grow beards and subsist on hatred."

"The only thing that keeps me alive," I said, "is the thought of love. Love, not power."

"You must remember," Abdul Kader said to me, "that Towfiq himself is a college graduate. Four years—and no less—of law in Baghdad."

"Pooh!" Towfiq curled his lips in scorn. "Four years of listening to lecturers in whom I had as much faith as I have in a bunch of whores. It was students like you and Adnan who made that period tolerable. But you, all of you, are reaching out with your newly acquired intellectual equipment for power, because you've put all your trust in your equipment—and in nothing else. Look. Every country east of the Mediterranean is torn to bits by ever-competing jealous politicos coming to power by some kind of inheritance. I agree. But I can envisage the day when these countries will be even worse torn by degree-holders more self-interested and sycophantic than their predecessors, and far, far less charitable. If you think the sheikh grinds the faces of his tribesmen you should wait and see the Ph.D. grind the faces of all and sundry, without even a touch of the magnanimity we pride ourselves on. What the old sheikh may do in a slapdash way, the new Ph.D. will do with the thoroughness and ruthlessness of a chemical formula."

"In our class struggle science and knowledge have to be exploited to the full," Abdul Kader said. "We have to be thorough and ruthless. But don't let's talk about it. The problem is that whereas the semi-ignorant are easy to sway, it is the ignorant who are impossible to convince." For a second his large eyes shone in his head like two powerful bulbs, then dulled again.

The servant, without knocking, flung the door open and entered with three glasses and three bottles of beer on a tray. He opened them one by one, poured out the beer and handed it to us, when taking a good look at me he recognised me. "Ahlan wa sahlan, Professor," he said and beamed. "You haven't been here for months."

163

"No, I haven't. How are you?"

"Very well, sir. Let's see you more often," he said and went out.

"Well, well," Abdul Kader said with a suggestive smile. "So you used to come here?"

I explained. "My room was the one next to ·yours," I added.

"I don't know how much of that to believe. Cabaret artistes stay here every now and then, you know." He gave Towfiq a big-eyed look, meant to indicate his amusement though, to me, it was frightening. "Thanks to Anita," he resumed with a wink, "Towfiq found me here."

"Oh, shut up," Towfiq said, delighted. He gulped half his glass of beer, smacked his lips and said to me, "Do you know Anita?"

I drank some of my beer. "I'm afraid I don't," I said.

"Well, I'll take you along one evening to Cabaret Metropole to show you the best pair of legs in town. Imported stuff, of course." Happiness was all over his face.

"I thought you disapproved of this kind of imported stuff," I said.

"Let me be honest with you. There is still in me a tiny doubt, especially when what we get from Europe is a beautiful woman. Nevertheless, I know what it means to possess such a woman, though for only five minutes."

"I can imagine," I said.

"That's not what I mean. Women in bed are not all the same, as people claim. Each woman, if you know what you're about, does not only taste different from all other women, but gives you a different experience. And not only sexually. In Anita, for example, who is an intelligent girl, I find an epitome of Christian civilisation itself. It is an unhappy civilisation, a very sad one. Why? Because it is obsessed by sorrow and haunted by death. You can see it

164

in Anita. Tragedy, you must remember, is a Western art. We may write a sad poem or an elegy, but in the West the whole thing must be enacted on the stage, and death must be seen and apotheosized. So even Anita, who is Viennese, when she is all lust and abandon, suggests that obsession with sorrow or death, or whatever it is." He shook his head. "These people have no peace of mind: they are searching for something they cannot define."

Abdul Kader sat up in his bed with the beer glass in his hand. "It's just like you," he said, "to look for an argument for your thesis even in an ordinary third-rate cabaret dancer. You look at her well-shaped thighs and think, 'H'm, worth five dinars a night: a good example of the decay of civilised races, but worth five dinars a night', when all you want to say, perhaps, is that she is bourgeoise. All prostitution is bourgeois."

Towfiq drank up what had been left in his glass. "You will never understand me," he said calmly. "You see life through a foreign phraseology which makes you incapable of seeing anything the way others do." Although his phraseology was not at all foreign I wondered if Towfiq himself could see anything in the way others did.

"For you," he resumed in a rising voice, "although Moslem, are the outcome of Christian civilisation. You're a hybrid, a mongrel. Even you and you, Jameel—after all, you are Christian—are searching for things you cannot define. You're all obsessed, like the mother civilisation that gave you suck. You think you are engaged on a great quest of emancipation, whereas actually you're driven by a lust for self-destruction, disguised in your alien phraseology. You have lost your peace of mind. Look at Baghdad now. Gradually it is being contaminated with the same evil. We bedouins and tribesmen, however, have found what we want. We have had it for centuries."

165

With brows contracted, his narrow eyes were sharp and ruthless. "As I see the cities expand and brick structures spread, as I see in the streets more and more unveiled women, more and more cinemas, more and more motor cars, I become fully aware it is nothing but this obsessive, self-corroding search for the indefinable and I feel like stopping the traffic and yelling: 'O evil, O abomination. Stop it, stop it, stop it!' He poured out the beer left in the bottle. "In my way of life, if I can contend with an ungenerous soil and a few lean cows and goats, I know at least I am above it. Above it all, and only God, praised be His name, is above me."

Hot breeze blew in through the balcony door.

"Your creed is the undoing of all man's creative work," I said. "Based on one of those questionable religious principles that are not in harmony even with Islam."

Abdul Kader spoke slowly, ponderously. "All civilisations based on religion," he said, "are now doomed. We are the beginners of a new age. We are no Romantics, though," he continued. "We are not returning to Nature, to the Desert, to the Tribe, or whatever you want us to return to, Towfiq. We are beginning right here, in the heart of the city, and leaping forward. We love the city. But it is a sick being and we have to cure it. It has been sick for centuries."

There was a knock at the door, and old Dawood, with his slouch, his small round eyes, his long string of amber beads, came in and put an inconclusive end to the argument. Exuding warmth and perfume he shook hands with me and almost embraced me as though I had been a long lost brother. "The boy told me you were here and I said I must go and say 'welcome' to the professor." Turning round, he said, "How are you, Sheikh Towfiq? Is everything all right? I hope you're better today, Mr. Abdul Kader? Why don't

166

you let me call a doctor? I say, this room is hot. I must get you a fan. Summer is upon us, I am afraid. It always comes too soon."

Towfiq stood up and, with great suavity, took Dawood's arm and led him out to the balcony over Rashid Street for a private word.

"I think I know what he wants to tell him," Abdul Kader whispered.

"About Anita, I suppose."

"Yes. He wants Dawood to give him the room which is connected with Anita's by a door, although she is the 'epitome of Christian civilisation'. The rascal."

When Dawood came back he said to me, "You probably don't know we've expanded the hotel considerably since you were here."

"Doing well?"

"Not badly, Professor. Come, let me show you how we have connected this building with the one adjacent to it."

I went out with him. He flicked his beads as he took me down to the end of the corridor, where there was now a doorway leading to a shorter corridor with rooms on either side, ending with a staircase. Upstairs was another floor. The walls were painted in a depressing dark green, and everything I saw through an occasional open door was shoddy: beds, tables, chairs, and all.

"I always inquire after you," Dawood said as he proudly guided me through his establishment.

"Very kind of you," I said. "Who from?"

"From your English friend, Mr. Flint."

"Mr. Flint?" I stopped short. "Ah, I remember. He told me he comes here every now and then."

"Yes, he does. Quite a lot. A perfect gentleman. But," he lowered his voice, "he gets the queerest visitors. They say most Englishmen are like him. Is it true?"

167

"You'd better ask Mr. Flint about that."

"I don't ask unnecessary questions, Professor. I keep my eye on my business. Every man has his own way in this life of ours." One hand flicked the amber beads while the other went up to his cheeks, alternately, to wipe his sweat.

# 26

I had to wait, locked up in my silence, as the minutes of the heat and the fear passed with the intent tardiness of worms crawling on a corpse. All the houses of the city, throbbing with the sun they had imbibed in the day, now retched and disgorged their human contents into the streets. The beggars, blind, maimed, emaciated, sat cross-legged or lay recumbent under the arcaded sidewalks and stretched out long bony fingers, some of them chanting verses from the Koran about God's forgiveness and God's wrath. White-shirted young men, hand in hand, three-deep, four-deep, guffawed and swore and swaggered on their way to open-air cinemas, open-air cafés, open-air arak shops which preluded their short climax in furtive brothels. Small boxlike buses, with more men crouching on their tops than shut up inside them, rattled past with trumpets blaring, to the crashing of cymbals and drums, to celebrate a wedding or advertise a lottery. The shops blazed, the pedlars shouted their combs and socks and handkerchiefs, the movie posters screamed with the Egyptian sensuality of thigh and navel, the American sadism of dark lover and blond victim. And I forced my way through the thick and loud density of the crowd, hopelessly looking for Sulafa's face among the walkers, the criers, the drivers. In time, I said, I was sure to see her face, to hear her voice to know why, suddenly, inexplicably, she had wanted a gun and then left with her parents for Baquba. In time— and the minutes crawled on my hand like worms.

"Ask Salma about it," I kept telling myself. All I had to do was to telephone. But Salma was no longer a friend to whom I could turn in an hour of distress. All I had to do was to ask her when Sulafa was to come back, whether she was coming back at all, and possibly, why she had gone away. But Salma was already suspicious, might already consider herself a rival of Sulafa. I was certain, moreover, that no sooner had I got in touch with her than she would demand another meeting in that unoccupied house.

I had to wait, locked up in my silence, going through the human flux of Rashid Street, looking for the one face I knew I should never see against those painted columns, in that sea of lurid lights and sewer stench, in which arms and faces, turbans and abas, tossed about in laughter and torment, minute after minute, in the long airless night.

# 27

At the College the following morning I saw this item in my newspaper.

"At nine o'clock last night the Police, having received information from an undisclosed source, made a surprise attack at the Rising Moon Hotel and apprehended one Abdul Kader Yassin, who was found reading in bed. Readers will remember that Abdul Kader Yassin is a short-story writer and a regular contributor to the *Morning Telegraph*, whose licence has recently been revoked."

"Let us hope Towfiq is impressed," I thought.

Surrounding this paragraph in the Local News page were a dozen others with tremendously diverse titles: "He Knifed His Wife: Had Seen Her Talk to a Stranger"; "Young Woman's Body Found in an Irrigation Channel, Stabbed in Seventeen Places"; "Struck His Creditor on the Head with Club, Skull Broken." The reporting was simple and straight-forward, usually taken from police registers. There was nothing sensational about it. Clean forthright crimes with motives direct and uncomplicated.

I had folded up the newspaper when a sharp pain jabbed at the back of my neck. A horrible thought had come to me. I almost lost control over my trembling fingers as they tore open the newspaper again at the Local News page. I hadn't read one of the items carefully enough—"Young Woman's Body Found in an Irrigation Channel, Stabbed in Seventeen Places. . . . A young woman's body was found clogging an irrigation channel in the Village of Bani Hamad near Baquba. Her face had been so mutilated that identification was impossible. Neighbouring villagers claim that no girl known to them is missing. The police are investigating."

I rushed to the telephone in the Staff Common Room and called Salma's house.

But a calm masculine voice answered: "Ahmad Rubeidi."

"Oh, good morning, Ahmad Beg," I said. How much agitation he could detect in my voice, I could not tell. "Jameel Farran here."

"Good morning, Professor Farran."

"Could I speak to Mrs. Rubeidi?"

"I'm afraid she's out at the moment. Any message for her?"

"Well . . . I wanted to ask her if she knew when Sulafa would be back. You know, I am giving her private lessons."

"Yes, yes, I know. I'll tell Salma to call you, if you like. Did she get in touch with you yesterday?"

Oh, the fool.

"I'm afraid not."

"We would like you to come to dinner next Saturday."

"That's very kind of you," I said. "Very kind of you. Er . . ." I nearly put my horrific question about Sulafa to him, then said instead, "What time, please?"

"Eight-thirty on Saturday."

"Thank you very much. Goodbye."

"Goodbye."

I went back to the newspaper. "Stabbed in seventeen places. . . . Her face—" (it was a face cut in marble) ". . . mutilated—" Leila came back to me, her hand resting on a stone dripping with blood, her face flattened under a ton of rubble and metal. No, it couldn't happen again, it couldn't. ". . . clogging an irrigation channel." The channel ran with Sulafa's blood through the orange groves, and the oranges were red.

A student came to me and said, "Aren't you coming to class, sir? We're waiting."

"Class? Oh yes, of course. But wouldn't you rather have this hour off?"

"With Finals beginning next week—we'd love it!" He hurried out.

A little later Salma was on the telephone, as I had expected.

"Ahmad told me. Listen," she said.

"Yes?"

Her voice descended to its soft, almost inaudible, conspiratorial tone. "Can you be at the . . . American apartment . . . in about three hours—around twelve-thirty?" So that was what she called the unoccupied house.

"Yes, if I can find it."

"You can't mistake it. The front is painted blue. You'll come, won't you?"

"Yes. But—about Sulafa. Is she coming back soon?"

"I'll tell you about her when I see you."

How I could curb my tongue from telling her I loathed her, I did not know.

Three hours later a taxi dropped me at the gate of a house with a blue front. I pushed the gate open, walked up the short concrete path, pushed the entrance door, and, right behind it, Salma's arms received me and her lips, cold and soft, were against mine. In the sitting room a ceiling fan was going at full blast, and Salma's arms were round my neck.

"You must be very hot," she said. "I've got some iced beer for you in the refrigerator."

"I'm terribly upset," I said.

"What's the matter?"

"Read this."

I cleared myself from the embrace and flicked the newspaper I had brought with me on to the right page.

She took the paper and I pointed to the short news item. She read it, looked up at me, and said, "Why should this upset you?"

"Couldn't the girl mentioned be Sulafa?"

She was taken aback, her eyes round with sudden terror. "Sulafa?" she said. Then her face relaxed. "You're a fool. I never realised you were such a fool." She laughed and threw the paper away. "That sort of thing happens sometimes. But why on earth should it happen to Sulafa?"

"Isn't she in serious trouble with her father?"

"I knew you loved her—but her father knows nothing about it, so don't worry."

"You haven't answered my question, Salma."

"Oh, you're a fool." She put her sleeveless arms round my neck again, and I saw the roots of hair in her armpits. "I'll get you some beer, darling. Sulafa is perfectly safe.

Her father is crazy about her. He is not the man to kill his daughter and dump her in a water channel."

I held her arms with both hands and pushed them firmly away from me.

"I hope you're right."

In spite of the smile on her lips, her eyes were pained. She tried to conceal her uneasiness, but it was only too visible. When she went out to get the beer, she had lost her self-assurance and her walk was unsteady. I heard the refrigerator's door slam to in the kitchen, but she did not come back. A minute later I went to the kitchen myself. She had collapsed on a chair with the bottle still in her hand, crying silently.

"I wish you wouldn't," I said.

The bottle slipped from her hand and crashed on the floor in pieces. The frothy liquid spread in a puddle giving off a faint alcoholic smell.

"Come to the sitting room. It's too hot in here." I took her hand and she followed meekly, her head fallen on her chest.

Huddled in an armchair she burst into violent sobbing, biting her knuckles in an attempt to muffle her gasps.

"I was hoping we'd have lunch together alone," she said at last, wiping her cheeks.

"I'm afraid I could only think of Sulafa."

As if she had not heard me, she continued.

"Ahmad was having lunch out today, so when he told me you'd called, I thought at last we could be alone for an hour or two. I had been waiting for just such an opportunity. You don't know what's happening to me. Having to be with people every day—people I despise. Having to entertain or be entertained every night. Having to say the same silly things over and over again. Having to spend one sleepless night after another. The ever-widening hell, the ever-deepening abyss."

173

"It's either that, or Sulafa's kind of horror," I said. "And not one of you has the guts to do anything about it."

"Most of the women don't complain. They have their own parties, they gorge themselves with food, they gamble most of the day——"

"That's really what you should be doing too, Salma. Only you went to college. And now you don't know what to do with the things you learned there."

"Oh, you're cruel. I cannot even read two pages on end. Whenever I do, a monster breathes down my neck."

She looked up at me with red swollen eyes. It was the look of utter loss and utter shame. "I think of you," she continued, softly, miserably, "of your hands ravaging me while I know, though I try to forget it, how little you want me. I'm becoming dust, dirt. Why don't you go away and leave me alone?"

"That's just what I'm going to do. In a couple of weeks the academic year will be over and I intend to get away from all this hell."

"I wish I could get away with you too."

"From one hell to another? Back home, while you worry about your soul falling down the abyss, which is a luxury, a million people around you in dirty refugee camps will be worrying about a crust of bread to eat, a drop of water to drink."

"That's not where we should go. To Rome, perhaps——"

"You keep evading the issue, Salma. What's happened to Sulafa?" I sat in an armchair next to hers.

"Nothing, absolutely nothing. She's gone away for a few days' holiday in the country with Imad, and he didn't have to get your approval before deciding on it, did he?"

"You know it isn't as simple as that."

"Has she told you anything?"

"Unfortunately not. But——"

174

She sat up in the chair, agog to hear what I wanted to say. "I know you're very fond of your niece," I said. "So I might as well tell you. One day she gave me ten dinars to buy her a revolver. The following day the whole family, unexpectedly, moved to Baquba. Does it look natural to you?"

"And did you buy the revolver?" she asked eagerly.

"No, I did not."

"Well, I don't know what to think. Whom would she want to kill?"

"There must have been a quarrel, Salma. I'm sure you're not telling me all that you know."

She got on her feet and, squarely facing me, looked at me in strange thoughtful silence, her eyes large and static.

"Well?" I said.

"It's useless, Jameel. You should know that by this time. She might have had an argument with a member of her family—why should it concern you? If you don't want a knife in your back, forget all about her. She is young and beautiful, but she'll never be yours. And stop romanticising your affair. Sulafa is like me. We both carry the seed of our own destruction. But don't romanticise your affair with her too much. She is safe and sound."

I said nothing. She gave me her hand and I took it, first reluctantly then, as though reconciled, I pulled her hand, and down she came on her knees in front of me.

"I look awful just now," she said.

"You're beautiful, and you're mad." I held her face between my hands, as she shoved her torso between my parted knees, and I took her hot sweet lips between mine. My hands ran through her silken black hair, feeling the perspiration round her neck.

"It's hot as hell," I said.

"Take off your shirt," she whispered. Above our heads the fan sang as it rotated furiously, like a mighty propeller.

175

I felt numb and tired and disgusted. I had hit another wall, and had to turn back and look for another way through.

I undressed Salma and lay down with her on the hard, uncarpeted floor. Hers was a body that could not age: white and smooth and resilient. Hot and cold in turn, hard and soft, yielding and perverse. Cold drops of sweat trickled down my spine.

"Do you love me?" she demanded, her eyes shrieking with lust.

Within my head Sulafa kept lifting a wide-eyed face that receded and advanced in a rhythm of its own. "Do you love me?" Salma pleaded. I could only respond with a silence as grim as the silence of the wide hungry eyes that faded in and out in close-up on a large screen in my head. Salma's thighs, rounded, firm, rested on the bare tiles like some object of great beauty left by mistake in the midst of the furniture, a fragment of a statue in a deserted room. Yet sometimes, when she moved her arms, and her breasts stretched or sagged, and her knees bent to the sound of her voice (the young face with the terror-stricken eyes and mouth kept flashing at the back of my eyes) she looked like some enormous insect intent upon devouring me. In defiance, I fell savagely upon her smooth thighs, and my hands tore at her white breasts. "If you talk about love again, I'll kill you," I said.

"Darling, darling," she murmured, her eyes shut, her fingers stiff.

She was taut and motionless for a few minutes, then she gradually relaxed. She wound her arms round me, and never stopped talking love and stupidities, until I realised it was nearly seven o'clock.

"What?" she exclaimed, springing to her feet.

"Yes, and I'm famished," I said.

"I must rush. Don't let's go out together, though."

176

She started dressing quickly while I watched her.

"Shall we come here again?" She asked.

"Of course," I said.

"I'll give you a ring. Don't turn on any lights before you leave. Here's the front door key. Please don't forget to lock the door when you go out. And don't take a cab from anywhere too near the house."

"I know. Too many eyes around. Isn't it a wonderful life? I come to ask you about Sulafa, and instead I make love to you."

"Darling!" she whispered and kissed me good night.


# 28


After Salma's departure, I was too restless to linger alone in the strange house. At the risk of indiscretion, I went out, darted a look around to see if there were any people in the sparsely built-up street, locked the door with confidence. I put the key in my pocket thinking, 'Even if a suspicious eye were to fall on me now, I might be taken for a new tenant.' Fortunately, with the exception of a couple of black-clad peasant women standing near their mud hut almost a hundred yards away, the street was deserted. No one took any notice of mud hut dwellers, of course. They were faceless and anonymous, like animals which nobody claimed.

On the main road I took the first taxi that passed by to the river promenade. When I emerged from the car, the Tigris was heavy with the reflections of a bloody sun sinking behind the palm trees. Behind improvised stalls along the bank, the fishermen and their boys had already begun their evening work. Live fish wallowed and shook in the water of their troughs. Every now and then a man would wade kneedeep in the river to a boat moored offshore to come back with one or two large fish, jerking wildly and hanging by hooks in their mouths, from a stock of live fish in a net submerged in water and tied to the gently rocking boat. He would place them in the trough, and when a customer came, he would lift them up one by one to his gaze shouting, "It still jerks!" When a fish was finally chosen by the customer and the usual haggling about the price was over, a wiry boy whose long *dishdasheh* revealed a dark rib-marked chest, would hit the jumping creature on the head with a hammer, then cut its body open, gut it and transfix it with wooden spikes arranged in a circle round a small fire.

Five or six large fish would be placed head to tail, with the open inside up against a fire fed with thin tamarisk branches by a stoker. All along the bank, between one café and another, the *masgouf*-fish circular fires blazed and smoked, casting ever-shifting reds and blacks on the faces and bodies of the determined little satans around them, and permeated the air with icthotic smell. When a fish was thus cooked it was spiced and served together with onions and tomatoes on a copper platter to the customer who waited in one of the many cafés nearby. I stopped at the next stall and ordered one.

Salma's white breasts and opulent thighs, which I recoiled from and lusted after each time they were offered to me, were inextricably mixed up with the vision of Sulafa's dark body. The carcasses of the fish, white and brown and brilliant, impersonated the two women lying alternately head to tail round an ever-fed fire. Salma, Sulafa, Salma, Sulafa . . . I wanted to sit down in the midst of the café crowds and uproot both bodies from my head: I wished to God, as I sat at a table by the river, I could dangle my legs

178

into the water and, like a child, dream of things that pertained to no woman.

Life was coming back to the city, as though the miracle of resurrection was to happen every evening. Sunset was a time of restlessness: when life came back to them after the terrible siesta hours, men and women did not know what exactly to do with it. If flowers shut at the approach of night, here it was only at the approach of night that body and mind would open up. But they would open up on a renewed aridity, a repetitive purposelessness. The men piled up in coffee shops (in which, to cope with the large numbers, benches were mostly used instead of chairs) and the women—oh, I'd seen them in multitudes overflow their slums and sit in black abas on the earth and the dung by the Tigris. The Sulafas perhaps gathered in one another's gardens and listened to the radio, even played records of South American tangos and *paso dobles*. The Salmas entertained or played cards. Tens of thousands filled the cinemas. The professional clubs filled with gamblers. The two halves of humanity went their separate ways, equally arid, equally purposeless.

A little later, I was to voice my thoughts in detail and revulsion, to Towfiq. Whenever he came to town, Towfiq was ubiquitous—although it was easy to tell that if at a certain hour one walked down Rashid Street and River Promenade there were very few friends that one was unlikely to meet. He had spotted me with his sharp bedouin eye and came straight to me, just when the *masgouf* fish was brought up on a platter by a small boy with a sooty face. It was big enough for two at least, and I was happy to have a dinner companion. Towfiq munched away silently and listened to me while I, almost in his manner, held forth without interruption. "You see," I said in conclusion, "the problem, as Abdul Kader would have said if he hadn't been arrested

179

last night, is time. Time here is vast and relentless."

He wiped his fingers with a piece of left-over pancake bread. "Poor Abdul Kader, another lost soul," he said. "I was shocked when on coming back from the Metropole I was told he'd been arrested. Time, did you say? Another Western misconception."

"Oh, for God's sake, Towfiq, don't overdo this bedouin stuff. It's all so false. And if you're going to tell me about prayer in the middle of a boundless horizon, I'll scream. Even prayer takes only a small portion of the day's twenty-four hours in a succession of sterile days. Nor will you tell me about horse-back riding, when all the once cavalier sheikhs have taken to Cadillac driving."

"That doesn't change our basic attitude to time. Time, the way you think of it, doesn't exist for us. We don't worry about the hours of the day."

"I'll say you don't! There's precious little for you to do in a day, so why worry about the hour?"

He looked at the palm trees far away silhouetted against a copper-red sky. "What's to be done will be done," he said, "as long as the sun rises and the moon peeps over the horizon. Haste is the devil's work."

"No doubt—especially when there's nothing to be done between one sunrise and another. But that's just the problem. There is nothing to do all through the eternity between one hour and another."

"I know what worries you, Jameel. You've seen too many church steeples in your time."

"I'm afraid I have, with all the clocks in them striking not only the hours, but the quarters and the halves and the three quarters——"

"Ah, but look at our minarets: they flaunt no clocks with black figures over the heads of men. Nothing but floral patterns, if that. We are part of the endless, the eternal, the

180

immeasurable. We ignore time's accurate measures because they're a foolish attempt at dividing the indivisible. Does anyone here, born more than thirty years ago, know when exactly he was born? Nobody except the pedants bothered in those days to record the hour of birth, so that everyone's life was like a stream whose beginnings were in remote unexplorable springs. It's all the same attitude. It's sufficient for a man's life to be divided into childhood, youth and age, and what marks them off is not the number of years he has gone through, but the experience and maturity he has achieved. The day is divided by the sun's moving position— for the sake of prayer, and nothing else. When there's little to do no one is worried about 'missing' anything, therefore no one is afraid of time. I could almost say no one is aware of time. But you carry the germ of a Western disease: the fear of the clock. The West is afraid of time because it is enslaved to it: so it has had to devise a method of conquering it. And what do you get? 'Time is money'. God save us! And consequently, the hideous stress on work, production, acquisition. And the end of it all? Getting even more obsessed with time and the money which the hours are supposed to stuff into our mouths." He paused, but before I could answer, he added, his fist banging the end of the table to the rhythm of his words, "By intensifying man's sense of time the West has precipitated man's prosperity and man's disaster at once. We shall not buy prosperity at that price. We don't want it." His complacency was maddening.

"I am not worried about prosperity and disaster," I said petulantly. "I am worried about this vacuum—the vacuum in the midst of which people like you can feel contented when people like me are harrowed. You may think it's an honourable desert tradition—all right; but here, in the middle of a city, desert ways are an anomaly and a curse. You

181

pretend that yours is not a tormented soul, because you seek no prosperity at the price of possible disaster, whereas the truth of the matter is, you possess no soul to be tormented. That's it. Such a philosophy as yours is based on the absence of a soul."

His eyes glittered at me in silence and in anger. But presently he leaned over the fishbones and the mess on the iron table between us and said, almost with a smile, "So you think all our rebellious youngsters in town and country are now conscious of a soul? And are therefore tormented?"

"Yes," I answered.

Suddenly he held my arm with a hand decked with two simple silver rings: it was an affectionate gesture to which my response was a sudden feeling of hate.

"Are you in love?" he asked.

"I am," I said, sullenly.

He leaned back, hit the table with the flat of his hand, and chuckled. "Poor fellow! You've done the most terrible thing a man can ever do. I see now why time is so heavy on your hands. Love is the crystallizer of time, that greatest of all illusions."

"The destroyer of time, you mean."

"If you're lucky. More likely your time illusion crystallizes into terror. What lover in the Moslem world can get away with love? Our literature is full of it, I agree. People cry over love stories like idiots, too. But when you come to reality, it is an entirely different affair. What in stories is so clean and pathetic is in real life simply a dirty thing—which has a way of inflaming the imagination—and you know what human imagination is. They can only imagine the worst and the foulest. Right away they are enraged and want to see the lover destroyed. Love is adultery, and hell-fire is its only reward: that's our belief. So be

182

careful, Jameel. No father, unless already infected with the new sickness from the West, will allow his daughter to marry a man known to be in love with her, for such a marriage would reek of shame. Love is a disgrace. You may ascribe it to your neighbour, but who will not be outraged if it is ascribed to a member of his family, let alone himself? After all, look at our famous lovers, Majnoun and Leila: what was the cause of their tragedy? Leila's father would not allow Majnoun, though her cousin, to marry her because he had declared his love for her in his poems, and that the old gentleman considered the height of shame! No more, no less. One may regret, even lament, lovers' fates, but they are a warning and not an example. Besides, how could you 'love' a woman before marriage—or after marriage, for that matter? You love a singer, a dancer, a boy—all our poetry is a testimony to that. But where an honourable woman is concerned, you either marry her or you don't. However, if you have to commit the shameful and dangerous folly of loving such a woman, you have to keep it a jealously guarded secret, it must gnaw at your vitals while you smile, until some poet or songster expresses your unfortunate, God-abandoned passion for you, when you may safely shed bucketfuls of tears over the doom of all lovers and your own. But tell me, is the girl you love very beautiful? Christian, of course?"

"You're a horror, Towfiq."

"Oh, I just wondered. There are so many lovely girls around, and they can't all be Christian, you know. But if the girl you love is not Christian——" He stopped.

"Well?"

"Oh, nothing. The sickness is spreading far and wide. But look out in the dark, my dear friend. Look out in the dark. Incidentally, how about coming to Cabaret Metropole tonight?"

"To see the most voluptuous pair of legs in town? No, thank you."

"All right—go back to your room and count the hours of the night."

As the hot damp air vibrated with electric song and human converse, the little fires of the *masgouf* fish blazed along the bank, and a thousand lights were reflected in the river like a thousand dancing flames. I looked round and called for the waiter to come and clear the table and fetch us two cups of tea.

"If ever I need a gun," I said afterwards as tentatively as possible, "could you get me one?"

"A gun?" He was more amused than surprised.

"Yes, a gun. I'd pay you for it, of course. Mind you, I may never need it, but just. . . ."

"Why not have a gun, whether you need it or not? When do you want it?"

"Oh, I don't know."

"Tomorrow?"

"No, no. Not so soon."

Towfiq laughed. "You see? You can't even define your need. What did I tell you? You're the product of Christian civilisation, which is haunted by death, but haunted even more by doubt. Never mind. Depend on me. You shall have your gun, and may you use it well!"

# 29

Things sometimes happen in a funny way. So funny that you want to cry. It is as bad as the affliction that makes you want to laugh, which the Arabs say is the worst of all afflictions.

I was coming out of the bathroom in my dressing gown when the landlady, looking upset, faced me squarely to stop me from going to my room. "Good morning," she said, almost resentfully, and added, "there's a young lady in your room."

"A young lady?" I said incredulously.

"You know I don't like girls calling here. And so early in the morning, too. It gives the place a bad name. But," she continued with the faintest touch of emotion, "she seemed very worried, and she said she had to see you——"

"Excuse me," I said and pushing her aside dashed into my room. Sulafa was sitting in a chair. She stood up and fell in my arms.

Dizzy with joy, I stopped the exclamation in her throat with kisses. I kissed her mouth, her cheeks, her eyes, and they were wet. I could not think what had happened, but there she was, alive and real and supple as a green branch and in my arms.

"I've just arrived from Baquba," she said in between kisses. "By train. It's such an early train." It was some time before the words registered.

"And your parents?" I asked anxiously.

"I suppose they'll be missing me at about this time."

"So you ran away?" I looked in her face. She was haggard. Her eyelids were swollen, her lips dry under their smudge of rouge.

"What else could I do?" she said.

"I'm completely mystified, Sulafa. Ever since you asked me to get you a gun I haven't had a moment's rest."

"Have you got me a gun?"

"What would you want a gun for?"

"I'll tell you. I hope you won't think I am mad."

"Has it got anything to do with your father?"

185

"With everybody," she said angrily. "Oh, it's a hideous thing. I'll tell you later."

I took her in my arms and brushed her black hair away from her pale cheeks with a trembling hand. "You must have suffered very much, my love," I said. And I wished I had got the gun. I thought I must go to Towfiq and beg him to get me one as soon as he could, no matter what Sulafa wanted it for.

There was a gentle tap on the door at which Sulafa sprang guiltily away from me. When I opened the door the landlady's small eyes met me with an uncomfortable look. "Please, Mr. Farran," she muttered and beckoned me to come out. I did and shut the door behind me.

"Please," she said again very softly, "don't be angry. But are you going to keep that young lady in there?"

I was exasperated. "She's come a very long way to see me. You don't expect me to throw her out in the street, do you?"

"That's all right. She looks like a girl from a good family."

"She is, she is."

To my utter surprise her eyes beamed, and with a wicked smile she said, "And pretty, too."

"I'm glad you like her. Can I ask her to wait in the hall while I get dressed?"

"Certainly, Mr. Farran. And, er . . . would you like me to prepare breakfast for both of you?"

"You're a wonderful girl!" I said. Her eyes fluttered with delight.

Back in my room Sulafa asked, "What is the matter?"

"The landlady suggested breakfast for two."

"I couldn't eat a thing," she said. Her eyes, which never lost their hunted look, travelled round the room. "I've always wanted to see this room. I had dreams of it, but it

186

looked different in my dreams. It always looked out on the sea, which for some reason frightened me."

"You are a brave girl." I held her shoulders in my hands. She was dark and thin and smooth and helpless.

"But you won't be alone any more. If you wait out in the hall for a couple of minutes, I'll get dressed."

When she went out and I was getting dressed, I found among the various objects and coins on the table which I put back in my pockets a strange key. I had already made up my plan.

"Come, let's go out," I said to Sulafa.

"Into the street?"

"You say it as though we were going out naked."

She laughed. I took her hand and led her out to the landing. "Do you know you are the loveliest woman in Baghdad?" I said. "Incidentally, will Abed be waiting downstairs for us with a dagger tucked in his belt?"

"Abed?" she said, and her lovely wide eyes were wider than ever. "He is dead."

When we stepped out of the taxicab Sulafa was stunned. "This is Salma's house, where the Americans live," she said.

"They've left," I said.

"Have you rented it?"

"Not yet. But I've got the key to it right here." I unlocked the door. "My landlady wouldn't have left us alone in my room." Had Sulafa asked me why I had that key I should have told her a lie. I loved her too much at that moment to talk about her aunt.

Behind the door, where Salma only the day before had received me with eager adulterous lips, I held between the palms of my hands Sulafa's innocent face, a record of suffering and rebellion and fear, pale and hot, marble and flesh.

"Here we shall be alone. For an hour or two," I said.

187

The morning was hot already, so I turned on the ceiling fan. In an atmosphere of false security Sulafa, now in my arms, now yards away from me, told me the story of the last few days. I retell her story here uninterrupted as it was with the innumerable exclamations and comments I then made which, to the uninvolved gods, merely emphasisèd the cruel irony that they loved.

# 30

My father said, "Sulafa, don't be difficult. You will have to marry Towfiq al-Khalaf. His father, Sheikh Abdulla al-Khalaf, is an old friend of mine and a dear one. He has a following of two thousand armed tribesmen. His word is law among them. Al-Khalaf tribe, in case you don't know, is an ancient one, whose forebears fought for the Prophet and finally settled, as conquerors, in this country. Their lands are extensive. Their camels, their sheep and cattle, are countless. I cannot possibly disappoint Sheikh Abdulla. He wants you for his son Towfiq, and I find the boy very pleasant. A bit talkative, even in his father's presence, but very pleasant nevertheless. He is certain to become as powerful as his father when the right time comes."

The Khalafs had come for the third or fourth time and my father seemed to promise them well. For the hundredth time I refused to listen, and each time my father brought up the subject, my resistance stiffened further. "You claim you love me so much, and yet you throw me away like a worthless object to a bedouin," I said.

Uncle Ahmad Rubeidi was there, Aunt Salma was there, my mother was there. They were all there in force.

"A bedouin indeed!" shouted Rubeidi. "He's one of the richest men in the country."

"I don't care," I said. "I just can't think of myself as the wife of a sheikh in a cloak, headkerchief and *agal*."

"But his son—after all, you're marrying his son—is a college graduate," my father said. "He went to the Law College. What more do you want? Salma," he turned to my aunt. "I wish you would persuade her. This is the third or fourth time Sheikh Abdulla has come with the notables of his tribe. It is getting embarrassing. I've more or less committed myself. They'll say Imad Nafawi cannot rule a twenty-year-old daughter. And you know the state of my heart. You know that, Sulafa, don't you. You don't want my anger to be roused, my daughter, do you? You must realise the importance of this match to me. Please, Salma, convince her. Come along, Ahmad, let's leave the ladies alone." And they left us alone.

But mother and Salma were both against the match. They were against it ever since the subject was broached by Ahmad Rubeidi, about four months ago.

Towfiq's father had gone first to Rubeidi, with whom he sat in the Senate. The two senators have interests in common. Although Ahmad is a townsman, he relies on the vast revenue from his barley fields in the south. His farmers' security, and hence his own, depend very much on the good will of the neighbouring Khalaf tribe, who can, if they wish, make things very difficult for them. Three years ago a savage feud broke out between the two sides in which the Khalafs, more numerous and powerful, were victorious, and as a result most of Rubeidi's farmers were fleeing to unknown places with their families. Finally, somebody intervened and Ahmad and Abdulla al-Khalaf were brought together and reconciled. My uncle had to slaughter many sheep for the benefit of his enemy, and a large sum of money, I cannot

189

tell how much, went to the Sheikh before he would call a halt to the blood feud. Yet, mysteriously, in a way I could never understand, a friendship gradually replaced the deadly hostility between them, and to seal it, Rubeidi thought, there was nothing like a marriage between the two families. It was for Rubeidi's benefit that I should marry the Sheikh's son, whom I had never seen!

I could therefore see very clearly why my uncle was such an ardent advocate of the match. He kept telling my father of lands to be annexed, of handsome gifts in money. My father has been worried for some time about the large investment he made in two housing estate projects mostly run by Jews, which have now come to grief because of the Palestine war. To my horror he was persuaded that this so-called alliance between our family and the Khalafs would put an end to his financial decline. My father, of course, never referred to such matters with me. Although he stressed the importance of the marriage, he would in no way suggest that I was to be given away for such crude material gain.

But I kept saying, who is this Towfiq? If he studied at the Law College, he must be an educated man. Why does he then use his father's influence in this ugly way? I've heard he is Adnan's friend. But I have also heard he is the useless idle type who comes to Baghdad every now and then only to drink in cabarets and visit the whores. You know, women hear all kinds of talk. I have even heard that two or three years ago he killed one of Rubeidi's farmers, but no charge could be brought against him, out of respect for his powerful father's name. All this, however, meant nothing to me. A year ago I might have married him, merely to get out of my father's house—though I don't think I should have cared very much for a bedouin's house. But I have changed, changed, changed, completely changed, in the last few months. What choice had I ever made in life until now, I asked myself, over and over again. What choice had I ever made? And I wondered what the choice should be. My father's love imposed a frightening burden on me. A selfish, obdurate love, which obliterated me completely. Did he keep me like a nun, away from all evil, as he supposed, only to satisfy his pride? And did he now throw me away to his dear friend, the Sheikh, only to destroy that very pride? What choice had I ever been allowed? I asked myself. Well, here was the chance. "No, I will not marry him," I said to father. "I shall marry a man I love."

"Silly answer," was my father's contemptuous comment.

As the days went by, he became more and more insistent. I never knew whether Towfiq was told of my refusal to marry him. But my mind was set on opposition. I was determined to take my life into my own hands, even if it meant running away from home. I had fallen in love with you, and it gave me a strange sort of courage. It was like a hand in the dark, giving me now a push, now a pull. I wanted to tell you, but I did not dare. Because just as I was the wrong person for you—didn't you say I was incommunicable and a prisoner?—you were the wrong person for me. Christian, foreigner, refugee, moneyless—oh, everything. Yet, I loved you more and more, and it gave me more and more courage. I was determined to marry you. And I started writing that journal-letter to you.

The very evening I gave it to you, as though by sheer spite from God, my father returned to the subject of marriage and Towfiq. Only two hours earlier I had been in your arms—how could he bring up the loathsome subject? But this time he was different: he was conclusive. He said he had spoken to Towfiq, who had just arrived in town, and liked him tremendously. He had fixed the date of our marriage. "In a week from today," he said. I was furious. I shook all over and screamed, "Never, never, never, never." Abed,

191

the servant, was standing by, and I suspected that he smiled. I flew at him in my rage and slapped him. He cowered and whimpered, and my father got hold of my arm and pulled me away so violently that, reeling back, I slumped against the wall. "You left me no self-respect," I shouted as I rose to my feet. "Why should I have a dirty servant in my room during my lessons? I shall never allow him to come into my room again when the teacher is there." "You'll have no more lessons," my father said grimly. "You'll be married next week. And if you don't give your consent, you'll have to go with your husband without it. He'll know how to break that obstinate will of yours."

"I'll kill him!" I screamed. The secret wish had become articulate. But my father seemed not to hear. He glowered at me with such terrible eyes I thought he was going to strike me. He didn't. He told Abed to get out, and left me alone. That night I could not go to sleep.

In the morning Ahmad and Salma came. The same subject was discussed again, but I stuck to my room. I could hear their voices, especially Ahmad's, going on and on and on, while I was thinking how I could obtain a revolver. It was imperative, I thought. I should hide the revolver until the wedding day. I should look sweet and docile. And at night I'd kill Towfiq. If necessary I should blow my brains out too—but only if necessary. Salma came to my room and, to my unspeakable surprise, she had changed her attitude completely. She was all for my marriage to Towfiq! She praised him. Praised him lavishly, although I was sure she had never set eyes on him. Then she said suggestively, "Last night I saw Jameel."

I don't know whether my face betrayed me. I said, "Well?"

"I think you love him."

As calmly as I could, I said, "And what if I do?"

192

"Darling Sulafa, it's useless."

"It is not useless."

"He loves somebody else," she said.

I looked at her squarely and said, "Liar!"

That was the day I telephoned to ask you to see me at Matheel's Bookshop. When I left the bookshop, a wonderful sense of peace had come to me. My will had taken a definite course, and I was at rest. I was sure in two days you would turn up to our last English session with a revolver in a paper bag or something. I did not know there was yet another horror in store for me that very night.

My father was out. Mother had been collected by friends and taken to a women's card party. Fatima, the cook, had gone to spend the night with her married son. Of our two servants there was only Abed moving about the house. Not having had much sleep for the previous couple of nights, I turned in early. It was very hot, but we hadn't yet started to sleep up on the roof. I placed a fan on a table near the bed and turned it on. I fell asleep immediately, but was troubled by one confused dream after another. With a start I'd wake up in a sweat under the single sheet, push it away, then pull it up and go to sleep again.

A light fell on the wall and I woke up. Somebody came in. "Mother?" I said. There was no answer. I turned my face to the wall away from the light and muttered, "Please mother, shut the door." The door was shut. The person shuffled forward and grabbed my sheet. I sat up in bed and in the dim light coming through the window saw Abed's face, his hideous mouth wide open. He was panting like an exhausted dog. "Sulafa" he managed with difficulty—then fell on top of me trying to hold me in his arms. I struggled to keep him off and get out of bed, but he placed his body's weight on me and pushed me back with his sweaty face on my chest, drooling all over me. Screaming, I planted my

193

fingers in his face. I wanted to gouge his eyes with my fingernails. He jerked in pain and in the scuffle hit the fan, which turned over and crashed down on his foot. He sprang back to the wall whimpering. I kept screaming, "Father! Mother!" but the house was dead. I jumped off the bed, making for the door, but he pounced on me like a mangy beast gone rabid and grabbed my shoulders. "You little bitch," he hissed foully against my face, "I know what you and that Christian fellow talk about all the time in English, you bitch, you." When I wrenched myself free my nightgown was ripped right down my back with his claws. I don't know how I managed to open the door and run down the corridor. Panting and gasping, he followed me. My knees seemed unwilling to carry me as I staggered to the front door, and in my blindness I just could not find the latch. From behind he had me in his arms, and I thought I was collapsing, when I heard a car pull up outside the house. I screamed, though not much sound came from my choked throat. Suddenly, he let me go and ran away in the direction of the kitchen, and I flopped against the door. A key turned in the lock, and my father entered. And I blacked out.

When I revived enough to tell him what had happened, my father went mad. Blue with wrath he bellowed, "I must kill that dog!" and rushed through the various rooms, the kitchen, the servant's quarters looking for Abed, thundering in horrible fury, but found no one. He telephoned to the nearby police station and demanded that Abed be hunted immediately in the neighbourhood.

My nightgown was in tatters, and ugly bruises were all over my body. I looked at myself in horror. I had been dirtied, befouled. Who was responsible but my father? When my mother turned up, he wreaked his fury on her head. Did she have to gamble every night? He yelled, and did what I had never seen him do before: he gave her a

194

resounding blow on the face. Finally, in utter futility, he flopped on my bed and his wrath turned into tearful sobbing. "Oh, the disgrace, the terrible disgrace," he repeated. I was full of hate. I loathed him. And I pitied him.

Early next morning Abed's body was found in the Tigris by the Old Bridge. It seems he tried to escape by jumping from the garden into the river, but could not swim all the way across it. Somebody recognised the body and my father was telephoned by the police to go and identify it. He sent our chauffeur instead.

It was decided I must be taken away at once for a long rest. Until further arrangements could be made we were all to go to our country house, before the incident became a subject of gossip all over Baghdad. Our friends were to be told I was very sick and had to go away. In our Humber, lest the chauffeur should overhear, we did not even refer to the subject all the way to Baquba. It was not difficult to guess, however, that father was now more intent than ever on marrying me off to Towfiq—and as soon as possible. But first I had to recover: many days had passed before my headache eased and I could eat anything without throwing it up. In the meantime I was planning my escape back to Baghdad, back to you.

# 31

I then told Sulafa all I knew about Towfiq. It was not much, I found, as of all the people I had met in Baghdad he was the most elusive and, in spite of his powerful argumentativeness, the most impersonal. Perhaps in trying to be the voice of the tribe, he was concealing a good part of his own identity with the skill of a ventriloquist.

195

"Towfiq is in town at this moment," I said.

"Perhaps still waiting for my consent?" she said.

Hesitantly, gallantly, I asked, "Would you like to meet him?"

"Certainly not!" She was alarmed, as if I had made a terrible suggestion.

I loved her grimness, her obstinacy. However, if Towfiq was at the centre of the agony, perhaps I could deal with him myself, though I was not sure. "I am going to try and save you," I said. Her large black eyes, tired for lack of sleep, looked at me, unseeing. With all my involvement and all my love, her weary distracted look made me feel I was an utter stranger in a strange house with a girl no more familiar than a ghost. Suddenly I saw us in fearful detachment. 'What have I to do with this painful melodrama?' I thought. It was nightmarish and sordid. And who exactly was the villain of the piece? Perhaps it had too many villains, not least of them myself, the unfaithful lover, and all of us strangers, unreal, irreconcilable. But the ceiling fan, humming furiously, stressed the reality. So did my perspiration. So did Sulafa's small pouting breasts as she looked at me, dark, lovely, and unseeing. I had to act the saviour, whatever the plight, the unreality.

"I am not afraid of death," I heard her say,

"Of what?"

"Of death," she repeated.

"No, no, my love," I said. I took her in my arms and kissed her lips. "It is life one shouldn't be afraid of, even when it is so foul."

"Ask me to do anything, anything . . . Darling, will there be an end to this horror?"

"Not easily. Why didn't you tell me about it before?"

"I didn't think people could sustain their cruelty for so

196

long, or events develop so abominably. But I am not afraid any more. Ask me to do anything——"

I laughed. "What, for instance?"

"Oh, I don't know."

"Look. Your father, no doubt, will be driving to Baghdad right now."

"Well, he must have spoken to Salma on the phone by this time."

"If I know your aunt she'll be looking for you at my place. Meanwhile, Towfiq will have got me a gun."

"What?" She shouted in utter surprise.

"Yes. Of all people, I've asked Towfiq to get me a gun for you to murder him. Isn't it fascinating?"

Sulafa leapt and screamed with joy in my arms.

"But you won't have to do that now," I said. "I intend to contact Salma and Towfiq. We shall meet here and discuss the whole mad business openly, like civilised people."

"No, no. You don't realise what it'll mean to——"

"I realise everything. Your father will consider his name disgraced. Rubeidi will smoke in fury. Even Salma will not like it. As for Towfiq—well, he'll think Arab virtue has gone to the dogs. But we shall set about the whole thing without your father or Rubeidi."

"Father won't like it, I tell you. Nor will Uncle Ahmad."

"Hire killers to get rid of me?"

"Not father. But Ahmad—he can be very spiteful."

"Oh, come, come, Sulafa. Let us first call your aunt. Would you like to speak to her yourself?"

I pushed her up towards the telephone, but she balked. "No, I couldn't. I simply don't know where to begin."

I took up the receiver and dialled. For me to see the two women face to face and declare my choice unequivocally would put an end to the sordid situation. For a moment I wondered how Sulafa would react if she knew that only the

197

day before I had slept with her aunt right on the spot where she was standing now. But I relied on Salma's good sense. The telephone burred on. Then there was an answer: Salma was in, a servant said.

When she came to the telephone, she sounded as if she had expected my call.

"Can you come to your apartment?" I said. Sulafa watched with evident anxiety.

"Now?" Salma's voice thrilled, but apparently she was careful not to give away the drift of the conversation to any possible bystander.

"Yes," I said.

"Ahmad Beg is out, and I am going to see the Nafawis. I am afraid you can't come here now."

"It seems you have company. But this is very important. I am in the apartment right now."

"You can telephone later. About twelve, say? My husband will be back then."

"With me, here, is Sulafa."

There was a pause. She had to collect herself before answering very briefly, "Very well, very well, thank you. Goodbye." And she hung up.

The next thing to do was to arrange for Towfiq to appear at the apartment, which was a much more delicate business. He should know beforehand whom he was to meet and why: Sulafa insisted that she was not to be sprung on him as a surprise. He might even want an explanation of the apartment which, though Rubeidi's property, might · seem to belong to none of the interested parties in a respectable sense. So we decided I should go and collect him and, on the way, do the preparatory explanations.

"We must finish the whole business before your father arrives," I said.

"I can't believe it, I can't believe it," Sulafa kept saying.

198

"By the time I've collected Towfiq, Salma is sure to be here."

"And I shall be left alone until one of you turns up?"

"I shan't be long," I said, and kissed her.

Towfiq was not at the Rising Moon. I left him a note that he should come to my place as soon as he received the message, and stated that it was very urgent and very important.

Dawood, the Proprietor, observing my agitation, took the note, folded it, and pressed a button. "I shall send it with one of the boys right now," he said.

"Do you know where he is?"

"No. But the boy can go and look for him in the coffee-shops. He is sure to find him."

I hurried back to my place where the landlady met me, breathless with curiosity.

"Mr. Jameel," she said as soon as I set foot in the hall. "Is everything all right?"

As placidly as possible, I answered. "Yes. Why?"

"You left with that young lady rather hastily, and without breakfast."

"It's nothing, Margaret."

"Then your friend the Sheikh called."

"Did he say anything?" My excitement was too apparent.

"No. But he left you something in your room which he wouldn't hand over to me."

In my room I found a small bundle on the bed. It was a *keffiya* wrapped round an object not difficult to guess. I locked the door and unfurled the large headcloth, to find a revolver, already loaded. Very quickly I wrapped it up again. The landlady, I was certain, had done the same thing before me.

I rang up Sulafa at her hiding place and informed her about the gun.

"I am restless," she said. "Salma hasn't come."

"In an hour, everything will be all right," I said.

"Please, hurry up."

I did not have to wait long. Towfiq came in, out of breath, having run up the three-storey staircase.

"Are you all right?" he exclaimed. "Your urgent message gave me a fright. I thought you had mishandled the gun or shot the wrong person. Are you all right?"

"Yes, Towfiq, thank you," I said. I felt embarrassed, even a trifle ashamed. In spite of everything, in spite of the inexplicable hatred I had felt for him the night before, and the hatred I should have felt for him that morning, I liked him. I saw myself putting a bullet through his head, then bending over and kissing him.

"What is the matter then? Why do you look so feverish?"

"Oh, it's the heat. I am not used to so much heat."

"You'd feel much hotter if over that open-necked shirt of yours you had to put on a cloak as well."

"Yes, yes, of course."

"Where is that gun?" He looked round.

"I've put it away—under lock and key."

"I'm afraid it is not quite new, but it works. You know, you look sick."

"Well, look, Towfiq. I've got something very important to tell you."

He had not sat down yet. Giving me a fixed look, he waited for me to talk.

"It's about Sulafa," I said.

"Oh?"

"Will you please take off your cloak and sit down?"

His eyes narrowed, and cruelty seemed to seize the few lines in his face. "What have you to tell me about Sulafa?"

"You know she was away in Baquba?"

"Well?"

"She is back in Baghdad today and I have suggested that she should see you and talk to you."

"Shame, Jameel! That's a woman's job." The cruelty in his countenance had disappeared.

"I am not acting as a match-maker. I am doing the exact opposite." Before he could interrupt, I continued: "I have been teaching Sulafa for the last few months. So I've come to know her. Not that she is easy to know. I had no idea you wanted to marry her. Until this morning. She never gave me a clue. I suppose the whole thing was part of a very complex scheme of things to which I was a complete outsider, so there was no point in bringing in another confusing factor. But things came to a head, and Sulafa, harried by her parents, by Ahmad Rubeidi——"

"That sly fox," Towfiq hissed from between clamped lips. His reddening face betrayed the incipient eruption which he struggled to hold back. "But what have you to do with all this?"

Ignoring the question I said, "Sulafa must be getting very desperate to have to run away from home. Have you ever met her?"

"I have seen her two or three times, but I have never spoken to her."

"Pity you haven't. Perhaps you wouldn't have approved. But at least there would have been no need for all this."

"Ahmad Rubeidi told me it had all been arranged. I assure you I'm not entirely crazy about marrying a Nafawi, and against her will at that. But it seemed a sensible arrangement, and Sulafa is an attractive woman. Has she run away from home on account of me?"

I told him how she had come that morning by train from Baquba. To my surprise he let out a vicious bark-like laugh.

The furious all-destroying explosion I had been careful not to touch off was replaced by an anti-climax of horrid silly laughter.

"Old Imad must be crazy," he said through his guttural cough-like laughter. "Crazy to think he should torment the poor girl to please me, crazy to make what I took so lightly look so grim. There are at least half a dozen girls in Baghdad I could marry this very day, without having to resort to their fathers' coercive measures. Of course most of them want love, love. And you know what I think of this Western disease. Later on they will demand your time and your soul. Well, you may go and tell Sulafa Towfiq is an honest fellow. For a wife, he wants a round-faced, round-bottomed slut with no fancy ideas about love. Tell her, if you like, I want something comparable to Anita of the Metropole. Provided, of course, she is a virgin." He paused. "You may also tell her," he added with unexpected vehemence, "I am sick of families like her own, families that pride themselves on possessions acquired nobody knows how. Families with as much muscle as jelly, with minds as clean as a Rashid Street gutter. Families that turn with cunning every law in the country to their own advantage." His tone of voice had no traces of laughter in it any more. He had already moved towards the door. "Tell her," he continued, "I shall live to see them all blasted, to see their sapped gutless race removed from the face of the earth when only those who live by virtue of their honest flesh and bone can survive. To be honest with you, Jameel, if Sulafa were a relative of mine, I should feel it my duty to put a knife in her belly for what she's done."

"Then I am glad she is not. Do you know why I asked you to get me that gun?" I said, and he stopped at the door.

"To give it to her?"

"She was determined to kill you if you insisted on marrying her."

He swivelled round and raised his arms in a wild gesture. Swooping forth in his cloak, which flew about him like great brown wings, he took me in his arms and kissed my cheek. "Tell her I love, I love her! A girl who could think of killing me must be the greatest prize in the land! Renounce your faith, Jameel, and marry her."

"I must admit you surprise me."

"Hurry back to the girl. Cling to her. But keep that gun handy. Somebody is sure to give you hell."

"You know, you have the makings of a great man," I said, overwhelmed.

"Magnanimity is the desert man's greatest virtue, Jameel."

# 32

Like a successful peace negotiator, I drove back to the apartment, happy with my achievement, proud of my tact and skill. Everything in the taxicab was scorching to touch, the sun bearing down upon the city, vicious and all-consuming, but my exultation made me even more restless, more incapable of sitting still, than the hot seat and the fiery emanation from the car's one ton of metal. When I swung back the creaky iron gate of the house, I pricked up my ears for any voices inside. I heard nothing. I turned the key and the lock snapped back, and yet no sound issued from within. To make my entrance as audible as possible, I flung the door open then slammed it to, but heard nothing save the persistent hum of the ceiling fan. The house was deserted. It even smelt abandoned, as though the rot had mysteriously set in immediately before my arrival. I went round and round the house, opening every door, looking in every corner. I felt I had been duped. The bathroom floor, in the parts nearest to the tub over which hung the shower pipe, was splashed with water. A few drops still glistened on the tub's enamel. Sulafa must have had a shower a little while ago, I thought. That was the only indication that somebody had been there. Otherwise, the whole thing might have been a dream, a creation of an oppressed mind. My exultation turned into anger, then into disgust.

How could Sulafa be persuaded to leave the house when I was supposed to come back with Towfiq for his final renunciation? Had her father arrived in the meantime and carried her off to the rose-smothered house on the Tigris to read her another lesson in filial duty and obedience? Perspiring all over, I prostrated myself on the settee by the wall, receiving in my throat a whiff of dust shaken off the long-neglected upholstery. 'You're so bloody innocent,' I said to myself. 'Innocent to the point of stupidity. You thought you were organising one of those dramatic last scenes, in which all the characters are brought together to effect a happy dénouement, a resolution of conflict to suit your purpose. First Towfiq lets you down. He gives in almost before the battle begins, and gives you a parting kiss. Then Salma turns up with the outraged Imad and kidnaps your heroine. Meanwhile Adnan languishes in another world, and you are left alone in a house that is not even yours. If you touch that telephone again you'll be the silliest man alive. Swallow the dust, mop your sweat, flush your love down the drain, have intercourse with a forty-year old woman whenever she feels like it, and see if you are not thus better off, dead among the dead.'

# 33

When I heard a car pull up at the gate, I knew it was Salma.
I unlatched the door and she rushed in, her face white and
badly made up. A thread of perspiration went round her
neck and down between her breasts.

"At last!" I said. "Where is Sulafa?"

"What are you trying to do?" She shouted in a hoarse
voice. Her nostrils were sore, her eyes lustreless. "Kill that
old man?"

"What have you done with Sulafa?"

"I've taken her home."

"So easily?"

"Her father is having a crisis."

"I'm sorry to hear that," I said, unmoved.

"Soon after your call, her mother telephoned from Baquba.
They'd just discovered Sulafa had run away, and Imad
seemed to collapse. I assured her that Sulafa was with me
in the house and advised her to keep Imad where he was.
But his voice immediately came over the phone. It was
cracked and unrecognisable. He said they were driving back
to town immediately. I said, please, relax, go to bed. But
he wouldn't listen to me. So I came here in a tremendous
hurry and found Sulafa alone."

"And of course her heart melted when you told her."

She gave me an angry look. "You are bad. Evil. Cruel.
As bad as all the others. How could Sulafa refuse to go with
me when her father might be dying?"

"So they came and found their daughter in your house."

"Yes."

"And nobly you did not tell them that she had gone first to me."

"They're all now back at home. We've called Dr. Zeid al-Kamari to look after Imad."

"No fights, no quarrels?"

"Well, look, I'm not staying here a minute longer. Good-bye."

"Just a moment, Salma. Here is the house key, the symbol of my shame, as you might say. I am damned if I know how to explain it to Sulafa in the future. You may tell her in private that Towfiq al-Khalaf sends her his kindest regards. He will be looking for a wife elsewhere."

She took the key and looked up at me, her lips firmly shut. She went out. I followed.

"A lift?" she said.

"No, thank you." I said.


# 34

TWO EXCERPTS FROM ADNAN TALIB'S

AUTOBIOGRAPHICAL JOURNAL

I

27th March, 1949

Hurry, hurry, hurry—or you'll miss it. Love, freedom, agony. Hurry, hurry. You're missing it. You're missing it, I tell you. You walk up and down the street, through the garbage and the fumes, through the pillars and the lopsided squares, through the big-eyed men and the soft-skinned women, you walk up and down the street, idly, sluggishly, your back in a hump, your hand hanging from a dangling arm, flicking drowsy beads. Oh for God's sake, hurry, you're missing it, I know, and I am angry to see you always crawl in a slimy marshland. One day you will go down, right into the bog, and leave not a bubble behind.

Hurry, I keep saying, because I know how much there is to be had, how much has already been missed. And I have to make up for what my father and mother and their fathers and mothers missed, too. Missing life, the flow of it, the running of it, has been my ancestors' sin now visited, Hebrew fashion, upon me. But I refuse to give way. So I keep saying, hurry, hurry, hurry! Rush through the crowds that are your lovers and enemies, throw around your kisses for anyone who cares to pick them up, then climb up the rotting brick, hang on to the ledges with the skin of your teeth and see if Gargantua was not right in flooding the city with his urine. *Par ris! Par* not missing it.

My belly has often hit my back through an empty stomach, but I have also loved Sulafa al-Nafawi, Butheina Ammar, Amina Sadi and a dozen other girls, all enjoyable in various degrees, all hovering in space between reality and dream. I have participated in street brawls and I was once stabbed in the arm—I was seventeen then—and had a terrible job trying to conceal the fact from my evil-tempered father. Husain and I have often slept on the pavement on hot moonlit nights to hear the earth throb and gasp against our sides. I have seen middle-aged large-bellied shop-keepers corrupt the youngsters that come to buy cheap cigarettes for their mothers, even respectable old Imad Nafawi I saw once emerge from his respectable old Humber to nose his way through filth for a private little perversion. On coming out he realised I saw him and never forgave me—he did not

207

know how little I cared, how much I laughed. O hurry, hurry. Through filth, through grime, through neatly cut lawns, before you go head first into the inevitable pit. Let Imad enjoy his brand of pleasure, but I wish he would not pretend to so much saintliness. Pride, pride. The ugliest sin in the eyes of the gods. Let him enjoy his pride too, only let him give his daughter a chance to step out a few yards into our world, however vermin-ridden, that she may inhale our street air and guess at our sweat, our sewage, our lust. O Sulafa, what can you be doing back there in your room over the Tigris, listening to lesbian chatter and women's dirty jokes and reading English poetry? If Jameel has not already seduced you, he is no friend of mine. But Sulafa is the last girl to hurry. Once she does, God help her and that dear old father of hers. Her mother must be counting the days. If ever the old man dies she will turn his assets into cash, rig up her daughter like a courtesan, and leave for brighter cities beyond this desert of ours. I shall stay behind, having hurried through a dozen kinds of love, a dozen kinds of futility, having gone through possession, beggary, rebellion, prison, flogging, after which I can say I have not stayed still, I have not stagnated, no grass has grown under my feet, no bird has mistaken me for a tree and deposited its droppings on my head.

II

20th July, 1949

The other evening, down Rashid Street, I ran into Abdul Kader. Abdul Kader is tall, athletically built and obviously very strong. But on his face, in spite of an emphatic moustache, you can easily perceive the impression of fear, a disabling cowardice generated in him by some vicious

208

intimidation. He is the loneliest man on earth. I often see him at such hours loafing about, eager at the slightest encouragement to air his views on things. Having, as usual, no definite aim, he walked along with me and in one long monotone reeled off his repetitive monologues. "You and I," he said, "are not doing very well, you know. No fun, you know, Not much to do. Eat, drink, defecate, and sleep. When I can afford it I drink, which is not often. No women, either. Hell, what's one to do? Look at a woman twice and ten stories are fabricated and ten reputations ruined. I am sick of it. In other countries you could do any damn thing you liked, no bastard would notice you existed. This place is just no good, Adnan. It's all very well for foreigners, who live off the fat of our land unbothered by our problems, to say it's a wonderful place. A boom town—for them. But for you and me, what good is it? I am getting away. I've been waiting for something to happen, you know, and I am fed up with waiting. Nothing happens. Riots? Oh, they're not enough, they don't last long enough. And they bring about no real upheaval. And when you're not making money, and people gossip about you, and you want to do a bit of honest work, you know, and can't find any, why, it's just hell. Just hell. No place for me, this, or for you either. To top it all, the police are on my track wherever I go. You'd think I was a homicidal maniac. You remember the story I wrote some months ago in the *Morning Telegraph*? Well, somebody somewhere didn't like it, and the police have put their tabs on me ever since. They had me twenty days in a lock-up, isn't that enough? I say, I hope we're not being overheard. We've had enough trouble, hey, enough trouble. What's the use of reading books, of learning anything, in a place like this? I am going to a country where, you know, no one will notice I exist at all."

I had muttered a few yes's and no's, but at last I laughed.

209

"Why don't you throw yourself in the river?" I asked. But Abdul Kader thought I was joking. His moustache stretched out as his upper lip lifted and expanded in a hopeless laugh.

He, however, will never commit suicide, or even think of it as a possible cure. It takes a man like Husain to see the futility and the wisdom of such a death, and to accompany me to the river for the final dark saving plunge. Oh hurry, hurry, through the flood of death and the shadow of the vast arching unintelligible bridge. Oh get it over with, then after your death swim back to where the crowds wait in the cafés for the newspapers that will report your jump into the arms of the ancient god that cleaves the desert in two and decks it with ribbons of green.

That day Husain and I had come out of jail. We sat together in our casino by the Tigris and wrote our valedictory poem, our joint message to the world, on which we had ruminated all through the infinite hours of our incarceration.

> "When you have found us planted in the slime,
> Green and decayed——"

(and I thought of us green and decayed and wondered if worms ate drowned corpses, but Husain said no they didn't)

> "When you have found us planted in the slime
> Green and decayed,
> It is not because we sought to grow
> Into fruitful palms
> But rather to make you smell
> The stench that our corpses will give
> In return for the stench
> We have received from yours.
>
> But if you fail to find us,
> We shall have settled in the mud
> To generate green poison there for you
> Each time you drink a glass of water
> To drink your death."

210

We wanted no delay, and decided to do it that same night.

"Do you want to write to anybody in particular?" I asked.

"No one whatsoever," Husain said. After a pause he added, "I would like to write a note to Brian, though—an Englishman, of all people! I am sure he'll be very sad when he hears the news."

"Don't worry. He'll manage without you."

"I know he will. But I've liked him in a sort of Platonic way."

"You've made love to so many whores and yet you can't give up your adolescent perversions."

"All right, all right."

"I'd like to write to Jameel," I said.

"So that he'll tell Sulafa. I know."

"So that he'll tell Salma. But it's stupid. We're writing to no one."

"However, we must make sure that our poem is seen and published. I am damned if I am going to end my life without letting the whole city know about it. Knowing the police, I am sure they'll do their best to suppress the poem. Isn't it ghastly? They wouldn't give you credit even for your suicide."

"Let us go to my room. We'll write the farewell message on a large sheet of paper and stick it on the wall. Sooner or later someone will discover it."

I was at peace with myself and the whole world. Looking at the people around me I felt at last I had no quarrel with anyone, since I was killing myself out of my own frustration and futility, out of my own inability to impress my life upon the city I loved. My death would be no protest, but a statement of futility.

The open casino was as usual full of men, hot, weary, impatient for the midnight that would bring about a little cool air. We threw forty fils in the cashier's plate and walked out into the street. Along the river long strings of coloured lights shook gently over the crowded cafés whose tables and chairs spilled over the embankment down to the dry parts of the river bed. Our metaphorical poison, I thought, was not enough for them all to drink their death, but they would at least learn that Adnan Talib and Husain Abdul Amir in their search for life and freedom saw it fit to die hoping thereby others also would look for their death before they were tempted into a similar search.

"The water is pretty low," I said.

"I know some parts where it is still many feet deep," Husain said.

"The best thing is to jump off the centre of the bridge. We're sure to hit a deep spot there."

"What, and attract attention? The meddlesome police would in no time fish us out, bring us back to life—back to the beds of the Lily of Dawn."

"It's all over, Husain, all over. No more vermin, no more lice."

"No more poetry either. I only wish I had sent my poems to the press."

"They will not perish."

Husain let out a sound halfway between laughing and sobbing. In his drawn face and long unkempt hair and soiled blue shirt I saw my own reflection. I remembered how often we had reeled down the colonnades of Rashid Street as we alternately recited what Husain called our Baudelairean poems.

"To no purpose," Husain said. "We blinded ourselves to evil and cruelty."

"We didn't, Husain. But it's all over now."

My room was like an oven. As I got out a couple of fool-scap sheets my perspiration streamed down my cheeks. I copied out our poem hurriedly, then wrote in large letters

212

at the top of it: "To those we leave behind". In the meantime Husain had written on another sheet:

*Go, my poems, for ever nourished*
*By the blood of my short life.*

*Adnan*

and stuck it on the wall.

"It's your name you should write there, not mine," I said.

"I am not all that stupid," he said. "Your poems, not mine, deserve such an invocation. For God's sake hurry up!"

"Hurry, hurry, hurry, down to hell through water and mud! Poor Salma—she will have to claim all these books before they go to somebody else. God! who will inherit me?"

"Oh, who cares!"

I stuck the Message on the wall over my bed with some drawing pins. I did not lock my door on going out. We walked down stairs to the narrow smelly alley which vibrated with heat. The half blind grocer, with whom I ran up a bill for my eggs and sugar and tea and cigarettes, was sitting on the doorstep of his small shop, while a small discoloured fan creaked and whiffed as it turned in a semicircle on his counter. His naked electric bulb had a million mosquitoes flying around it as it bestowed upon his tawdry fly-specked wares an unmerited brilliance.

"Welcome, Adnan, welcome to the rose, to the jasmine . . ." he exclaimed as soon as he saw me.

"How are you, Abu Ali?" I said shaking hands with him.

"Full of longing, my dear. Welcome to the rose."

"I am terribly ashamed of you," I said.

"Why, my dear?"

"I still owe you a bill," I said.

"It's you I worried about, by God, not the bill. I hope it wasn't very nasty in your jail?"

"How much was it, Abu Ali?"

213

"This is no time to pay bills. How about some tea, hey?"

"No, no, we're in a hurry."

."Come on, surely you have time for an istikan of tea. How are you, Husain, my dear?"

"Still alive," Husain said.

"Yes, we're still alive," I said. "How much was the bill?"

"You're paying no bills tonight."

"I shan't be here tomorrow, you see."

"So what? The day after. Next week. What does it matter? Welcome to the rose!"

When we left him I mused aloud: "For his kindness he'll be poorer by one or two dinars, while I shall be no richer at all."

"If kindness doesn't cost you anything," Husain said, "it's worthless. At least he will never forget you. I can just imagine the story he'll be telling everyone he knows with a lot of emotion—and with some pride, too, perhaps."

"Perhaps." I heard the word echo in the hot airless alley. The lights were so far from one another that they were completely overpowered by the darkness. "At least there is one who may tell our story with pride," I said.

"Pride doesn't interest me any more. Look here, Adnan," Husain said with sudden enthusiasm. "How do you feel?"

"What?"

"I mean, you know, walking towards your doom, with no dawn to break upon your night?"

"Rather defeated, I am afraid."

"Myself, I feel like having a woman. A big voluptuous woman with fat thighs and heavy buttocks. All my life I have dreamt of sleeping with a wispy slender-waisted college girl, who as I kissed the hell out of her would discourse on love in classical figurative language. But just now, now that is bounded by no hereafter, I should like to plant myself in the flesh of a sensual fat-thighed woman who might as I

214

make love to her fart right and left for all I care."

"Well, there's Badia in the next alley."

"Do you mind if we go there?"

There was a long slit of a passage leading to the alley in which was Badia's house. The passage smelled of fæces right through, and when a man coming in the opposite direction slunk past us he looked like a murderer.

Round a bend in the alley a short cul-de-sac ended with an arched entrance with a massive door which had been left slightly ajar. When we pushed the door a little, a corpulent bare-headed man emerged and peered in our faces to ascertain whether we were bona fide customers. "Is Badia in?" Husain asked.

"Please come in," he said.

We stumbled across a short open space into a poorly lit room. There was the usual hard-bottomed settee. An overhead fan was creaking away.

"I am stifled," I said.

"It's so bloody hot," Husain said.

I had no lust, no desire.

"Please hurry up," I said.

An inner door opened and Badia came in, large, bosomy, big-eyed. "Well, well, my two young singers!" she exclaimed happily.

"Poets, you bitch!" Husain said.

"What's the difference? How are you, my love?" she said to Husain, then to me, "He has the loveliest pair of eyes in Baghdad."

"Come on, come on." Husain was pleased. He gave her thigh three or four successive smacks as if she were a horse.

"Come on in," she said.

They went in together. I stood right under the fan to get the full benefit of its blast. A moment later a small mousy fellow was ushered in, and he looked at me with suspicious,

215

rather frightened eyes. I could see he was drunk. When he settled on the settee it creaked, even under him.

Presently Husain was out. "Have you got a dinar?" he said.

"But——" He couldn't have slept with the whore. Nevertheless I gave him a dinar which he took to her and came back.

"You've had your last wish?" I said.

"I couldn't do it. Why don't you go in?"

"I've no such desire. Let's push off."

"May the dream of sleeping with slim college girls ever haunt the minds of men after us! It's so much cleaner."

The man at the door demanded a tip. I threw him a couple of silver pieces.

"College girls?" I said as we limped out. "You've reminded me of Amina Sadi."

I remembered how as a school-girl she used to come to us at home and I would corner her under the staircase that led to the roof and kiss her. When two years later she became a college student she often had the courage to sneak into my present drab room, disguised in her black aba. She would come white with fear, her ears prickèd up for any noise behind the door. O white arms of Amina, O tigress eyes of Amina.

"We're heading for the river—for the last time," I said. Husain had shrivelled up, his head seemed to be mechanically attached to his shoulders.

"Who is sorry, anyway?" he said. "In Najaf we used to see the dead brought in from India and Persia in sacks for burial in holy ground. In sacks. They'd bulge in queer embryonic shapes, those hempen coffins. Dozens of them came in every day. The stench of death never left us. I lived out my early youth in funerals. Who is afraid of death? I've never so much as touched a clean honest woman. And my knees ache like hell."

216

The bridge was not very far. When we arrived there we could hear the song and throaty tormented sighs of female singers coming from the loudspeakers of cabarets on both sides of the river. "We shall not die unbemoaned," I said.

But the bridge was not entirely deserted. It was nearly midnight when people went out for a stroll after a long breathless day.

"I still think we shouldn't jump in from this place," Husain said. "They won't let us alone."

We leaned over the massive parapet. The water shimmered with a thousand lights. It was alive: soft, alluring, decked out like a woman.

"We'll wait," I said, "until the coast is clear. It'll only take us a second to hop over. Can you swim?"

"No."

"Good."

We stood there in silence. My mind was numb and blank. I just wanted to die, to cease, to end.

For a moment there was no one around.

"Come on," he said.

We clambered up the parapet and dropped together feet down into the Tigris. It was a short rapid fall, sharp with the lights of both banks flying up like shrapnel against my eyes and skin. The water heaved to meet me, a dark mirror that opened up to receive me among its reflections. I thought I hit the mud of the bottom but I buoyed up and on my way to the surface swallowed some water. "When you have found us planted in the slime green and decayed green and decayed green and decayed . . ." the words spun in my head as an overpowering impulse urged me to move my arms and get into a horizontal position and keep afloat. But a hoarse gurgle that sounded "Adnan!" pierced my brain. The gurgle sounded again and I looked in the direction it came

217

from and saw an arm struggling, splashing the water as it drifted past me, and a head bobbed up almost within my reach. "Oh no, no, no," I heard myself scream, and I hit the current with desperate arms, which moved with an involuntary upsurge of life, and Husain's body was at once against mine, taut, wooden, giving nervous uncontrollable jerks. I held his neck in the crook of my left arm and swam with the other arm along with the current, then off towards the shallow bank, until we foundered in black mud. Husain fell down in a heap and I had to stand up, knee deep in mud, and drag him by the armpits towards the bank. Music from a cabaret a few yards above us pulsated like madness against my head.

"Oh why did you, why did you. . . ." Husain moaned.

"Shut up!" I yelled. I was exhausted and my legs were plastered with mud. Carefully I stepped back towards the water and splashed about with my feet to get the mud off them, then bent over and cleaned my legs and trousers.

"O horror, horror!" Husain shrieked. His body convulsed and he retched violently and spewed some water. When the cabaret singer started a new number—it was a gay one this time—my friend gasped and broke into tears that got mixed up with the drops glistening all over his face and body. He wept bitterly, as I stood dripping with water, and my eyes welled up with hot large tears. I felt them glide off my cheeks and bore holes into the earth.

"Let's go," I said.

"Leave me alone," he said. "Go away."

"Go back to my room, I'll meet you there," I said and climbed up the dry bank. Each time I moved a foot it squelched in the shoe. My soggy shirt and trousers, I thought, would dry in an hour or so. They were cool, and in spite of the mud smearing them in places, felt clean. But

218

I wanted desperately to sit down. In an automatic gesture my hand reached to my hip pocket, and I was reassured: my wallet was still there.

I walked along the cabaret's wall, parallel with the bank, then near the foot of the bridge turned round and made for the entrance. The two men at the cash desk, unshaven, with faces bearing the ravages of smallpox, looked up at me with indignant scorn. "I look pretty wet, don't I?" I said, and took out a drenched note from my wallet.

"What, did you slip off the bridge?" one of them said, and both of them laughed.

"Yes," I said.

"Hundred and fifty fils," they said. They took the wet dinar and gave me some dirty change together with a yellow ticket.

My eyes felt hot and swollen. The open-air cabaret was vast and dim except for the flood-lit stage where the members of the band sat and the artistes performed. Green and herbaceous, it was a garden without flowers, unless one cared to call flowers those jaded dancers and singers with their flat painted faces, their eyes calling out for customers. All the tables seemed to be occupied, and everybody talked at once, volubly and loud. To the accompaniment of the *oud* a female in the limelight was going through her belly-wiggling and breast-shaking. A couple of men at my right craned their necks over the drink-and-food-laden table and loudly expressed their admiration of the dancer's figure. Along the walls were secluded boxes, partitioned by creepers and neatly cut shrubs and occasional vinetrees—veritable bowers where the artistes could be invited for a private though expensive tête-á-tête over a few drinks. I walked past the boxes which were occupied until I found a free one. As soon as I sat, my clothes walloping uncomfortably against my chest and thighs, a waiter slunk in and, taking a good look at me, was taken aback. "What do you want?" he shouted in my face.

"Quiet!" I said firmly. "Get me a whisky, and when that dancer is through, call her in."

"Sorry, she's engaged," he said arrogantly.

"I don't care." I gave him the change which the two cashiers had returned. "See that she comes straight here, see?"

He softened. "Yes, sir," he said humbly and hurried out. I took off my shoes and shook them, when out of the inferno and the mud and the horror of my mind the image of Imad Nafawi rose like a long, black snake to stare me in the eye. I shook my shoes again one by one, their soaked leather giving a faint smell. But Imad filled my head. I put on my shoes again in time for the waiter to come back with my drink. I gulped it down at once and said. "Another. Two others. And forget about the dancer. Hurry up!"

The waiter seemed to be ages before he came back again. I wanted to see Imad. I wanted to see him immediately. I couldn't wait. I had to see him. He was in my head, in my blood, in my bowels, all over me. I looked at my wrist watch: it had stopped at twelve-twenty.

"What time is it?" I asked the waiter when he returned.

"A quarter to one," he said.

"Good. It isn't too late. Wait."

I gulped the two whiskies in succession and, taking out another soaked note, paid him.

I went out. My clothes were beginning to get dry, my hair did not drip, and my feet had stopped squelching in my shoes. Back in Rashid Street the colonnades were still emitting their stored up heat. One column after another cast its shadow upon me as Imad lured me on to his house in Jafar Street.

"To the Gate! to the Gate!" shouted the urchins hanging

220

out of the small box-like buses which plied up and down the street after midnight. They'd slow down as they approached me, a boy would shout, "To the Gate!" and getting no response from me they'd shoot away with a terrifying rattle. But I preferred to walk to my uncle's house: walking was more in keeping with the urgency of my impulse. The meeting with the old man had to be given the significance of a pilgrimage, a hard-won grace. Besides, my clothes would be drier by the time I arrived.

I was soon at North Gate: a wide lonely square with a central double light. The oldest cars in the world made an endless racket in the attempt to whisk away would-be passengers to their destinations. I, however, had left my destination behind me in the shadow of the bridge. I was not sure I was alive still. I only wanted to see Imad, a kind of posthumous unaccountable wish, a visit from the world of the dead to the world of the dying. And the wish was like a skewer driven through my intestines.

Then I was there. A brass plate in the dim light was luminous enough to spell out his name. I pushed the gate and it opened. Suddenly I feared he might have gone to sleep on the roof. But there was light in one of the windows. Behind the curtains of that window I was certain Imad waited for me. I walked straight ahead on the tiled path, then turning away from the entrance I went to the window and said softly, "Imad!" No answer. Again I whispered, shooting my voice off like an arrow through the shuttered window and the drawn curtains, "Imad!" An answer came from within, "Who is it?"

"Me, Adnan," I shot off again.

"Adnan?" It was Imad's voice coming like a sigh from beyond the wastes of the desert.

"Yes. I want to see you."

"This is no time for a visit," the feeble voice answered.

'Does he suspect I am the angel of death?' I said to myself.

"Open the door, Uncle."

"Just a minute."

Would he call his servants? His slippers shuffled on to the front door, the latch snapped and the door opened. Imad stood silhouetted in the door-way, tall but bowed, in a *dishdasheh*.

"Is that you, Adnan?" he asked. "What brings you here at this hour? You know I am a sick man. Everybody in the house is on the roof asleep and I don't like to be disturbed when I am alone."

"Would you let me in?" I said.

"All right. Come in."

I walked in. He shut the door, and led me to his library. Cool air blew in my face when I entered the room: it had an air-conditioning unit.

"You look like a resurrected corpse," he said.

"I am a resurrected corpse," I said.

"You could at least comb your hair."

"It's too clotted."

"Well, really. . . ."

"My hair needn't worry you."

"When did you come out of jail?"

"This morning, at sunrise."

Imad relaxed. He sat down in an armchair and I did the same. "So that's why you've come to see me? Very nice of you. But you should have rung me up as soon as you got out." He took out a string of beads from his pocket.

"That's not what I came here for. You never cared what happened to me."

"That's not true, Adnan. After all, you're my nephew, you know."

"A very unfortunate accident."

222

His colour changed, though very slightly. I looked him straight in the eyes. I wanted to see him writhe as my look went through him. "Now look here, Adnan. I am a sick man——"

"I know you're sick. Even at your best you were sick."

He shot upright and the beads dropped on the floor. "Have you come to insult me?"

"I should have done this a long time ago. But I am not going to insult you now. I am going to kill you."

His jaw fell, and his eyes jutted out. With a violent thud he crashed into his seat, and his cramped twisted fingers dug into its armrests until they sank into their upholstery. I think he had wanted to shout but all that came out of his throat was a short arrested sound, and his Adam's apple seemed on the verge of bursting with an unreleased terrified groan.

"You've always been sick," I said as I stood up and approached him. I bent over his petrified face. "But you've never been weak. For all your sickness you've been too strong. You're the other half of my life with which I have always grappled. You're the evil one, the power that ever says No, the mud, the filth, the dung of the ages kept in silken clothes behind impregnable brick walls, amidst sickly roses. You are the darkness and the disease, the blight and the curse of our lives."

There was a gasp in his throat. His lower jaw trembled but his lips seemed incapable of meeting. What wide repulsive eyes he had which would not bat or close! His Adam's apple bulged like an oversize egg in a leather purse. I grasped his neck with ten fingers hard as nails. But I had no need to press too long. The eyes registered a glassy immovable terror, and I found that I was laughing. The old fiend looked pathetic in that terror-struck attitude leaning back in his brocade-covered armchair amidst his ancient books.

It was a large corpse in a long silk nightshirt, befitting his fortune and his standing.

The air-conditioner emitted its coolness. My hair (and I ran my fingers through it) was all over my face, rough and clotted. I looked around me for a comb, then remembering I might find one in the bathroom, nearly walked down the corridor to it, but changed my mind. I walked to the front door, pulled the latch to open it and went out, shutting the door behind me. It was still very hot outside. A vast star-filled sky was like a lid on a simmering pot, while the frogs croaked unwearily in their mud behind the big house. On my way to the gate I noticed the rows of zinnias lifting their proud heads to the stars, and stepping two paces from the tiled path towards them I plucked a large one which happened to be white. I opened the gate then shut it behind me. When at North Gate I got on a rickety angular cube of a bus and my chin nearly hit my knees as I sat on the low narrow seat, among four or five others who smelled strongly of alcohol and vomit, the white zinnia looked uncomfortable in my hand, and I flung it out of the window.

"Your money, please," the urchin said, hanging by the half-open door of the bus, on the look out, simultaneously, for customers. In my posture, getting a coin out of my pocket was extremely difficult. But the boy was patient and very polite.

# 35

This was Adnan's story as written by himself some time after Imad's great funeral. The newspapers, however, said Nafawi had died peacefully in an armchair in his study of heart failure. There was not the least suspicion of foul play, and yet Adnan's story, which he then told me in confidence and later incorporated in his autobiographical journal was not implausible.

The old man's death proved the extent of his influence and prestige. Thousands of people, from ministers to scavengers, joined in the funeral. And it was at the cemetery that I saw Adnan among the mourners. With difficulty we forced our way through the crowd towards each other.

"Are you impressed?" he said.

"God rest his soul," I said. "When did you come out of jail?"

"Two days ago. I am free again. Very free." His voice was joyless.

"Let us get out of here," I said.

"How is Sulafa?"

"I don't know. I haven't seen her for a long time." Although our telephone conversation was a daily ritual, I had seen her only twice since her return from Baquba.

"The Shadow has passed on. I shan't worry about her any more. You are in love with her, aren't you?"

"I am, Adnan. It's no good denying it. Are you angry?"

"Angry, Jameel? But you'll have to take her away—" he paused. "If you can," he added.

"I shall take her well away from here—to the refugee camps back at home."

"And a good thing too. Let her get out of that—you know—" and he struck his forehead with his fist, "that mental misery of hers and get to learn about the physical misery of others."

During the next few days, while I waited for the first mourning period of the Nafawis to be over, I saw a great deal of Adnan and Husain again. Husain was going back to his poetry with renewed passion, but Adnan was dazed, im-

225

patient, obsessed. "My uncle's death is an event," he would say. "It is the end of a whole period. Imagine. I have helped put an end to a long period of—" and he would seem so overpowered by the significance of his act that words failed him. "It may not have ended quite," he would add dubiously. "But I know a new life is bursting out, as if all of a sudden the desert went green. Green with grass and red with flowers. And you know, I am not sorry for what I did. There are at least a dozen others I'd like to give similar treatment."

Brian Flint, in the meantime, becoming proficient in Arabic was learning to play the *mutbidge*, that very Arab twincane instrument. It was a comic and sometimes rather uncanny sight to see the fair-haired blue-eyed Oxford graduate bulge his cheeks lustily and blow away at the silly thing like a bedouin at a wedding. Almost every night we made a group and took Brian in a boat down the Tigris. Then on one of the numerous little islands that the river reveals in its bed every summer, we drank beer and cooked *masgouf* fish. Brian would play the *mutbidge* and say, "Extraordinary how like a Highlander's bagpipe, isn't it?" Towfiq, however, had disappeared, and had it not been too hot, we should have gone south for a few days with his tribe.

When at last it was possible for me to see Sulafa at home, I was shocked at her thinness and pallor. She was in mourning and was supposed to remain in black for a whole year. But she had wasted away. Without make-up, her lips, ever so slightly red, were full but suggestive of sickness.

Her mother, to whom I was introduced for the first time, looked remarkably like her sister Salma, only her face was ravaged by merciless lines which seemed intent on multiplying. Our meeting was ceremonious and short. She left us alone and sent me by a servant I had not seen before a cup of Turkish coffee.

"Mother can't get over the shock," Sulafa said.

"I don't suppose you have told her about us yet?"

"No. But I shall very soon. In fact, she suspects it already. She wouldn't have left us alone otherwise."

When I kissed her cheek very mildly she burst into tears. "I love you so much," she said, sobbing. It exasperated me. I did not know whether it was her father's death or our love that made her cry so easily.

"I am taking you away," I said firmly.

"As soon as I am out of mourning."

"Oh no, I shan't keep you waiting another year. I'd go mad."

"So would I. But my mother has to agree first."

"And Salma? I have not seen her for weeks."

"She went to Lebanon a fortnight ago. But Uncle Ahmad is in Baghdad. He's been taking care of us."

"You must love that!"

"Out of spite, sheer spite, I am going to tell him all about us the next time he calls on us."

# 36

The heat came on every day, a diurnal fever, inexorable as fate. But I waited. I waited through the heat, the merciless unrelieved monotony of a wake that went on day after day.

And then there was relief. A letter was delivered at my pension by Rubeidi's chauffeur. It was short and polite. "*I should be honoured,*" it ran, "*if you could free yourself tomorrow for an hour or two and come and have a drink with me. I shall be at home at 7 p.m. Yours sincerely, Ahmad Rubeidi.*" The old man was wearing his mask for my benefit now.

When I went on the following evening, he received me at the door himself. Over the first drink he told me about Salma and how she had found the heat unbearable and had to go to Lebanon for a month or two. But she was already feeling lonely, and he would soon be joining her. On the way he intended to pay a visit to what was left of Palestine in Arab hands. He was very distressed about the condition of the refugees. "They are our new problem," he said. "We must find a way of repatriating them."

He was coming round to the point with great care.

"You yourself," he said suddenly handing me a second drink, "wouldn't find it very pleasant if you went back and had no employment there, like a million other people, would you?"

"I suppose not," I said. "But I've gone through so much that a little more wouldn't frighten me."

"But you have a family to support, surely?" In his voice a nasty tone of threat was beginning to be audible.

"You don't have to worry about my family, Ahmad Beg."

"I don't know. Both Salma and I have liked you. I don't want you to do anything that might spoil your chances of employment here."

Tired of his oblique manner in broaching the main theme, I said, "Obviously you want to tell me about Sulafa?"

"Yes. You must stop interfering in her life," he said suavely, the imperative *stop* sounding more like an invitation than a threat.

"I am sorry. I intend to marry her."

"You can't. Sulafa is not twenty-one yet. The law is on her mother's side."

"In that case, though I hate it, I shall wait another year."

"But I could have your contract at the college terminated in two days."

"All right, go ahead," I said calmly and put my glass

228

down. I had no intention of accepting his hospitality any further.

"Will you please tell me what connection you had with a girl called Azima last October?" His question fell like a blow in the dark at the back of my head.

"Azima? What Azima?" No name could have been more meaningless to me. He might have said Salma, and I might have attempted an answer. But Azima?

"It isn't such a long time, you know. You couldn't have forgotten so quickly."

"I don't know what you're talking about."

"She was killed at City Hotel by her brother. Because of an affair you had with her. Killed in your room at the hotel."

The thing was so monstrous that I shook with wrath and almost choked on my words. "Wherever did you get that story from? A poor girl I had never seen was knifed by her beastly brother on my doorstep. In accordance with a savage practice not one of you in power moves a finger to stop. What have I to do with it?" I stood up.

"Calm down," he said with the equanimity of a disinterested magistrate. "It is your interest I am trying to protect. There always comes a time when a person is called upon to account for his deeds. I've seen this story in your personal file. It can cause you much harm. You will be thrown out as an undesirable. You are a very unreliable man, after all."

"For God's sake, why don't you learn a little tolerance? A little love?" I said trying desperately to stop my voice from vibrating abominably. "You've driven Sulafa mad with your persistence. You've involved Towfiq al-Khalaf against his will. You're a rich man, you are a senator, and you have a lot of land. Can't you afford a little tolerance? I am in love with Sulafa. All right. Give the girl some liberty and we'll both probably fall out of love. I am Christian, so what? For an Arab it is pure accident. Do you have to pick on the story of a poor girl's murder and twist it into a mean dishonest threat? But then, I know, it's all part of the same thing. You're slipping and the times are catching up with you, and it frightens you."

"Thank you for the sermon."

"Didn't Salma ever sermonise you into a little charity? Why don't you for once stop interfering in Sulafa's life?"

I was trembling furiously when I turned towards the door, but Rubeidi had turned blue, and with an awkward move he knocked over his glass on the small shiny side table, and it crashed into pieces on the bare floor.

"Pimp, bastard!" he shouted in agony from his chair.


# 37


There it was. Rubeidi was slipping. A whole order of things was slipping. He probably even knew that his wife was unfaithful to him. The thing for him to do was to cling on hard, to resort to every trick, to every pretence, to every possible lie. He still had power, but the crack in it was wide, however much he deluded himself about it.

Against the distant background of my people's homelessness, his threat to dislodge me was not only despicable, but funny. When I left his house my fury gradually dissolved into laughter, terrible laughter. I laughed aloud in the dark road. I laughed like a madman. The madman and the cuckold—it was the funniest thing in the world!

I went straight to the Nafawis. Sulafa, who was in the garden with some friends of hers, rushed to me, her hands fluttering, not knowing in her surprise what to do. She introduced me to the girls who twittered in shyness and embarrassment, then led me to her father's study and turned on the air-conditioner. I shut the door myself and asked her to draw the curtains. She did.

"Sulafa," I said, "I am the most unreliable man in the world."

"Please, don't say that," she said.

"A most faithless lover. I must tell you that right now."

"What is the matter with you, darling?" She threw herself at me, but I pushed her gently away.

"Your uncle Ahmad invited me tonight to his house to tell me he would throw me out of the country if I did not stop interfering in your life. I must tell you, I am a most faithless lover."

"I don't care, I don't care."

"Don't you want to hear about my faithlessness?"

"No. I don't want to! I love you—whatever you may have done. In fact I should be disappointed if I knew you'd had no love affairs before we met."

"I am not talking about affairs before we met. I am talking about affairs I have had since we met. I am talking about my faithlessness."

"No, no, no. I won't hear of it. I don't care, I tell you."

"Do you still want me?"

"Like no woman you've ever known," she said and wound her arms round my neck. "But," she pleaded, "will you be faithful to me for another year of agony?"

I kissed her mouth. I kissed her hard and long, her flesh supple and resilient and wicked against my arms. Though inside me the terrible laughter still rose shrill and mad, Leila's hand, so long forgotten, seemed suddenly to fall over my eyes, large, twisted, dead. But I kissed Sulafa again and again before we had to go out to the garden to talk to her waiting friends.

231

In the long months that followed, while we waited, while
the Adnans and the Husains and the Towfiqs impaled themselves on rows of political and social swords, the crows and
the kites in squawking formations flew over the palm groves
of a slowly refurbished land.

ROCKVILLE BANK
CONNECTICUT'S BEST COMMUNITY BANK

(860) 291-3600
www.sbr.com